CW00506713

THE CUSTARD TART CAFÉ BY THE SEA

ISABELLA MAY

"God always has another custard pie up His sleeve."

Lynn Redgrave

For Mum and Nan: thank you for introducing me to
Ambrosia Devon Custard and Bird's Original Custard...

CHAPTER ONE

MY NAME IS Willow Schofield, I'm five foot nothing – which jars a bit with my parents' calling me after a tall, elegant tree – and I'm a custard tart addict.

There's no known cure for my affliction, not in a pharmacy nor on a psychologist's couch. And I intend to spread it over Somerset and beyond, like the cheeky little enchantress that I am; ensnaring adults, teens, and children in my gastronomic web. I know this makes me sound like the Wicked Witch of the (south) West (of England), but once you've tasted a *real* custard tart, you have a duty to share that joy far and wide. Too many secrets are selfishly stockpiled for the enjoyment of the select few. In the history books and in our fast-paced modern society. Here, in my little dot on the map, I'm just doing my bit to help humanity.

I stand back to admire the cornucopia of golden pastries twinkling their glossy middles in front of me. I peer closer to the counter to consider each sweet stack of heaven in turn with my heterochromic eyes – one green and one blue. I've created a veritable feast for all five of the senses, if I do say so myself. Yes, even for the eardrums. It's a pudding aficionado fact that patisserie speaks a crispy-layered language all of its own. I smile triumphantly, despite my nerves at the momentous occasion which is about to unfold this morning.

I can still recall the very first time my teeth sank into the flaky pastry and the deep, eggy vanilla promise of a Portuguese custard tart. Fourteen years old. August. The Algarve. Vilamoura, to be precise. I can even remember my all-important hairstyle that day; a pair of neatly coiled space buns sitting on top of my head, before they'd been given their name. Oh, all right, Princess Leia's giant and impressive earmuffs may have officially coined the term, but having experimented at length with that iconic Star Wars look, I always felt like I was wearing headphones. I preferred my dinky mounds instead.

I'd just enjoyed (survived) the thrills and spills of the nearby waterpark, super proud of myself for acing it on the wiggly, partially vertical, kamikaze slide after Lauren's dare, sporting the bruises on my back to prove it. The package holiday bus had dropped me, my parents and my two sisters off a couple of stops too early on the way back. Caitlyn (then eight), and Lauren (then sixteen), had whinged incessantly at walking less than a kilometre to the hotel in the late afternoon heat. But I was a happy-go-lucky soul in my early teens, always effortlessly focusing on the brighter side of life. Within moments of beginning our leisurely stroll, a pretty, blue-tiled bakery had reeled me inside its sloping doorway, and from that moment onward my destiny was written in the stars.

Azulejos, the Portuguese call their gorgeously elaborate glazed tiles, which come in every hue of blue. The *padaria's* exterior was encrusted in them, so that seeking out its treasures deep within felt a bit like opening a jewellery box and stepping inside.

That reminds me, the late twenties version of Willow

really needs to chase up the courier company. They're a couple of days overdue with my own delivery of authentic Portuguese tiles from the ceramicist in Porto. My ribbon-blonde balayage cornrow-braided side-bun updo (yeah, try saying that after you've had a glass of the aforementioned city's famous Port) bobs up and down as I make a literal note to chivvy the order along, circling the telephone number of the courier company and double-tapping my pen on the notepad, as if sending a sign to the logistical goddesses above. I'd planned to have the tiles in place ready for opening day, but thankfully they are to be but a small feature on one of the walls, giving a respectful nod to the seed of inspiration that grew into my café and its products. I may be young but I'm a stickler for honouring tradition, even if I do love to fuse it with my slightly divergent ideas.

Back to my memories of refreshingly authentic Vilamoura…

I don't think I'll ever forget the heady scent of cinnamon, sugar, and freshly baked bread as I walked inside that bakery with my purse gripped tightly in my hand, my poor wilting sisters forgotten. There were only a few varieties of cake on offer but they were displayed irresistibly on the shelves, and it took me ages to evaluate the likely taste sensations from each of the works of art commanding my attention. Most fourteen-year-olds would have opted for something neon-light obvious, like the dominant chocolate pyramid-shaped creation, which I later learned was constructed of recycled cake trimmings – undeniably ingenious! – but I had never been most teens, most kids, or most *anything*. Carving my own path in every activity since the day I arrived on planet Earth, be it bottom-shuffling instead of crawling; turning a colouring book upside down and filling in its boring black and white illustrations with psychedelic pastels, watercolours and acrylic paint (often all at once); crooning along to Prince and his funky purple rock pop as opposed to more on-trend mainstream chart 'delights'; learning the complexities of double-Dutch skipping before attempting to jump with a single rope; fishtail-braiding my hair before it became a social media craze; or sewing sequins and ribbon on my jeans, I simply love to buck the trend.

Perhaps I could have allowed the *queijada* to whisper sweet nothings in my ear – whilst other holidaymaking kids would have undoubtedly recoiled at the fusion of eggs, sheep's cheese, milk and sugar, I somehow knew it would prove surprisingly gratifying. And I might have been tempted by the pastry pillow *travesseiro* with its rich almond and egg yolk centre. But I only had eyes (one green, one blue) for the simplicity of the buttercup-yellow, ever-so-slightly charred custard tart that piqued my curiosity.

Love at first sight.

There was never a sweeter contender for my affections. Now or then. Even before that Portuguese holiday, the highlight of my school dinners had been the 'unhealthy' pudding choices that came drowned in giant pools of standard, chocolate, strawberry – or if you were really lucky – mint custard.

And so I, Miss Willow Schofield, fell head over heels with the art of patisserie. Many who've trodden the same culinary path have been inspired by French *mille-feuilles, profiteroles* or *éclairs*. Those tried, tested, and trusted elegant stalwarts of the dessert industry. Walk into any Parisian establishment selling dessert, and defy their culinary collections to be anything but airbrushed production-line symmetry featuring that trio.

* But I like my cake the way I like my people. Full of surprise, full of character. Uniquely shaped, uniquely weathered. No two custard tarts are the same and therein lies the beauty. I have remained helplessly and hopelessly spellbound by the rustic *pastel de nata* (*pastéis de nata* if you're talking of more than one of them): the humble Portuguese custard tart.

My passion and commitment have burned brighter every day. Determined to introduce the delicacy to the British seaside town where I live, I practiced my art by supplying a handful of local bakeries with a daily delivery of my specialty, until, once perfected to my exacting requirements, the time came to tap into my savings and go for gold, opening a custard tart café in Weston-super-Mare.

That's it, that's *all* that my shop sells: glorious custard tarts.

I can sense your eye roll as you process these words, and I can maybe even hear the distant tinkling of your giggling fit. But never judge a cute little café by the sea by its cover.

My establishment is so much more than a mere bakery with tables and chairs. In fact, I still can't hide the grin that's permanently plastered itself to my lips since I've lucked out. I've only been and secured myself a unit with dream-like porthole windows, that make you feel as if you're at the helm of a cruise ship. And it's only in prime position at the back of the pavilion on Weston-super-Mare's magnificent Edwardian seaside pier!

Never mind that infamous movie pose struck by Rose and

Jack on the Titanic. Romance on the Seven Seas is nice, as you gaze at the horizon, wondering what the future holds, but have you eaten a custard tart and stood (okay, sat) in the virtual bow of a ship?

Oh, God. Now I sound like one of those 'Yeah, sex is cool but have you ever tried (and fill in the blanks with chocolate/garlic bread/had a hairdresser accidentally scratch your itch while getting your haircut)' memes.

You know what I mean. And if you don't know yet, you soon will.

Welcome to The Custard Tart Café…

CHAPTER TWO

ALAS, AS WITH all matters in life, swooning over success accounts for one percent of the journey. I've got my work cut out over the next few days and I can't rest on my laurels... or my Lauren. My older sister, now thirty to my twenty-eight, is supposed to be lending a helping hand in the early days of set-up and exposure. But Lauren (was Schofield, now Masters) has forever been distracted by better offers and, knowing this is par for the course, I've resorted to making a sketchy plan B, comprising leaflets, loudspeakers, and crossing my fingers for luck. Well, there are sure to be a gaggle of summer students willing to parade sandwich boards along the pier and the seafront in return for holiday money and free custard tarts, if my sister doesn't come up with the goods.

I'm not going to kid myself as to the reason for my sister's sudden benevolence. The swish Bristol-based marketing company, where Lauren has zippily worked her way from assistant to account manager to director, is experiencing a very rare lull in incoming projects. Then again, I can hardly complain. Optimum local coverage at one third of the going rate is a pretty sweet deal.

Pulling out my checklist, I run through every item on my agenda again, ticking methodically with the green of my BIC four-colour pen as I go:

- Chase the courier company for my missing tiles (for the third time)
- Make sure Caitlyn, Reggie, and Tim are happy with the monthly rota (kind of too bad if they're not, now it's written)
- Put out an ad for additional part-timers (subject to inaugural week's success)
- Double-check positioning of today's half up, half down hair-do, prior to pics and interview
- Order flowers for liberal dotting about (pretty pastel peonies are not for the sole benefit of brides, features in *Good Housekeeping* magazine and/or Elton John's house)
- Triple-check that the tarts are nicely tipped to show their fillings, and that the calligraphy cards under each type is legible at a reasonable distance
- Final, *final* wipe-over of seats and tables, sweeping of floors, buffing of windows...

I am just about to add another couple of bullet points to the list, ref. ingredient deliveries and a final-final-FINAL last minute trip to the nearest Ikea for more plates and some cute napkin rings (okay, and a side of their delicious meatballs plus a Daim bar for dessert) when Lauren barrels in with her laptop and a ridiculously young male photographer. It's hard to say which of them is clutched closest to her breast.

"You're half an hour early!" I greet them with a jump. "I mean, better than late, of course, but I'm not quite ready... I still need to—"

Keen to impress his boss, Lauren's skinny, overdressed sidekick immediately begins snapping away at the interior of the café. His blinding white shirt, one-size-too-small charcoal suit and his forward-swept, feathered tufts of hair only make me want to scream all the more. He's not so much as offered a handshake or a name, let alone checked in with my requirements.

But Lauren is looking me up and down. "Christ, could you look any more like that Eloise bird from *Bridgerton* today, sis?"

I scrunch up my features and pat at my floral headband in confusion. I'm actually a big fan of the Netflix series, despite watching little TV – but I am no clone of anybody, thank you very much.

"What do you mean? I got this in Ibiza, not Bath."

"It's the regency mullet shag-fad, isn't it?" Lauren sticks a finger in the air as if it – and her word – are magic wands. Her own poker straight, *ghd*-ed to the max, platinum-blonde sheet of salon perfect hair, which hasn't been updated since the noughties, nods reverently in agreement as she continues to assess today's hairstyle through eyes ringed and winged in piercing blue eyeliner. "All that's missing is the short fringe curled inward, like a pair of insect pincers."

"I think you're muddling Eloise up with her *impossible-to-live-up-to-in-the-competition-stakes older sister*, Daphne, but thanks for the compliment… I think."

That soon shuts Lauren up. Although, I suppose there are worse things to say about my appearance. Truth be told, I do rate Claudia Jessie, the unassuming 'middle-child' actress, who plays Eloise Bridgerton, as the most beautiful of all the ladies in the show. And, like yours truly, she certainly has an independent streak.

Reluctantly, I stash my list away behind the counter, resigning myself to the fact that launch day has started already. I step out into full view on the café floor. Now Lauren finally remembers her charge, directing the young whipper-snapper to capture the custard tarts in all their glory, before shoving him out the door into the sea-breezy spring air.

"I think a few external pics of the premises would be good," she tells him. "It's key to capitalise on the blue, yellow and white of the café's signage and interior décor. Match it up with whatever natural and man-made elements you can find out there. I know you're not dressed for it, but maybe hunt out some pretty shells, rocks, and bits of seaweed on the sand." Two words spring to mind there: 'needle' and 'haystack'. "Ooh, and before you do that, a shot of the pier, looking back toward the beach, is a must. And a few contrasting pics of the amusement arcade. Here you go." Lauren extracts a note from the roll in her giant designer purse and hands it to the lad. "Treat yourself to a full English brekkie while you're at it, and I'll meet you at the Jag at 10 o'clock, ready for today's biggie."

So much for the kid's apparent enthusiasm for *my* foodie offerings. Custard tarts are worshipped in a certain country two and a bit hours' flight south of us, at this particular time of day. And so much for my mugshot appearing in any of the promo. If I'd known he'd zip around the premises with the speed of a bullet train, I wouldn't have bothered trowelling on this amount of mascara and blusher.

Lauren finally puts her laptop and handbag down, dumping them with a mammoth huff on one of my spotlessly clean tables. I cannot help but wince.

"Well?" She raises her manicured hands into the air. "I've just come off the motorway, where I've had to endure the joys of that oversized kid intermittently – very loudly, I may add – chewing gum and rapping Cardi B songs over the soulful mezzo-soprano lyrics of my Adele CD. Are you going to offer me a coffee to settle my frayed nerves, or do I have to pour it myself?" she says with a pout.

"Oh, right, erm, yes." I get back behind the counter and fling myself at the coffee machine, cursing myself under my breath. I'm not employed by my sister, for goodness sake (and thank the career goddesses for that). Lauren's all right really and her heart truly is in the right place. It's just, well, she's a tad bossy. Always has been. It's as if the midwife sent her home with a decree the day she was born: 'thou shalt be mother hen to your little chick sisters the second they join you.'

"Are you sure he'll be all right out there – whatever his name is? Has he been to the pier before?

And what about his suit? He'll get it wrecked on the beach after all the rain we had last night. It's like a mud bath out there. Those shoes looked expensive, too." I call back over the counter as I press the magic buttons that transform bean to elixir. "Shouldn't you be supervising?"

"Perk of the job. I point, he moves."

"I see." I wrinkle my nose at the wall so Lauren can't see me.

"I certainly had to do my share of skivvying when I started out in the industry. Fair's fair." Lauren adds self-righteously. "I've also warned him before about the pitfalls of dressing above one's station."

I know I should be used to that acid tongue by now but I'm actually a little speechless. I could never imagine taking any of my staff for granted, not even our little sister who will be joining me imminently during her uni holidays, not even if I end up running a fleet of custard tart cafés, doing what *Dunkin* has done to *Donuts*. I will be rolling my sleeves up and mucking in with every aspect of the business. Treat the janitor with the same respect as the MD, that's my ethos. But knowing Lauren, she sees her method as tough love.

I'm not as convinced by all things alternative as my good friend Kelly, whose current obsession is numerology, but I am a firm believer in reincarnation. Who knows how and when we will meet the people from this lifetime all over again in one of our future lives? That's my mantra as a business owner and it was my mantra throughout school and catering college. It's my mantra pretty much everywhere I go. Just recently my friends and I somehow managed to acquire an entire movie screen all to ourselves on a girls' night out at the local Odeon. Kelly and Radhika had gone a little haywire having a popcorn fight, and I'd painstakingly scrambled around every single seat and row during the less dramatic parts of *In The Heights* to locate the errant kernels, dispose of them in the bin, and pen an apologetic note to the cleaners. None of which is to say I'm a pushover. It just pays to be smart about these things, and manners are an investment.

"Talking of perks, my goodness, this new role comes with visual benefits." Lauren stares dreamily into space. "The new guy working with me is an absolute hottie."

I try my darndest to control the tremble of my hand as Lauren's shop talk jolts me from my own daydreams. It's ridiculous, when I'm about to serve real customers day in, day out, but this is how it has always been with my older sister. Sometimes Lauren's demeanour makes it hard to relax. I set a steaming cup of black coffee in front of her, returning briskly to the counter with my trusty tongs to seize what she will hopefully consider the most acceptable custard tart to accompany it. I've barely laid the pastry on a plate when Lauren is off again.

"Heck, no, Bonsai!" We'll get to where that moniker came from in a bit. I can assure you my sister will use it more than once before this morning's through. "What are you like? I can't take liberties in *my* line of business. Put that back immediately."

"But you'll walk off the calories on your way back down the pier," I dare to bargain, hovering between counter and table. "And this is the perfect breakfast custard tart: cherry and berry; the sheer amount of fruit in it eradicates every gramme of fat. It's Mum and Dad's favourite, and Caitlyn's pretty partial to it too. I'm sure she'll be breakfasting on it soon enough when she's back from uni."

I wish Lauren would make a concession, just this once. Surely a taste test is an integral part of efficient marketing, only helping Lauren describe the flavours more accurately? Besides which, it's not every day that a family member opens a café in such a special location. But Lauren bats the idea away as if it were a seaside wasp.

"Mum and Dad are both sliding into their mid-fifties a little too languidly for my liking, and Caitie really needs to keep an eye on her pot belly." She takes a sip of her coffee. "Of course I'm no stranger to the gym, but this promotion and all the extra responsibility it entails comes with extra desk time... and not just in my own office." Three, two, one: big sis is back to buzzing about *her* career again. "I'll have you know a marketing account director's role goes above and beyond mere, erm, directing in front of prospective clients. I'm in constant demand around the building and in the meeting rooms, ensuring I engage in a healthy mix of phone, email, Zoom, and face to face conversation."

Ha, the latter I can well imagine. I'm all too familiar with the way Lauren impressed her boss, Jamie Masters, so very quickly that she is now married to him – and his eye-watering wealth, oodles of cars, Bristol harbour-side penthouse, and megalith of a Salcombe estuary villa. Which isn't to demean anybody who has followed a similar path to management and just so happened to fall in love with a tycoon. The difference is, they've probably done so in a longer timeframe. Lauren's career was turbo-charged; the jumps in title AND her wedding day happening within a year of her joining Muse Masters, her most recent promotion coming six months after that.

"Oh, my days, Bonsai..." she says.

I grit my teeth. There it is again. Told you so. I hate it when she calls me that, of course I do. But I've long given up on trying to correct her. It started in our teens, when it was pretty clear that I was never going to mirror the grace and stature of my namesake tree. Don't get me wrong, bonsais are cute in their own right, but that's hardly the point.

"...The guy is exquisite," she carries on, completely unaware of my annoyance. "Worthy of wall space in the Tate *and* the Louvre. Think of a young Antonio Banderas. Not as scruffy, mind you, nicely groomed, and a wearer of the understated but crisp CK One Shock fragrance."

"Who, *what*?" I'm genuinely confused. On a selfish note, I really don't need all this waffle-style gossip permeating my frazzled brain when I have a business to launch this morning.

"Get with the programme, sweetheart. I was telling you about the plus points of directorship, *remember*?"

Oh, so now we have moved on to the subject of the eye candy perks of my sister's career. What a surprise. It hasn't taken Lauren long to tire of my bro-in-law. I almost feel sorry for Jamie. Except he and Lauren are peas in a pod, truly deserving of one another's antics. That may seem harsh, but Jamie gives as good as he gets and no less than three other women from the company have either graced his arm in the past or sported a Jamie-gifted rock, to rival anything in Weston-super-Mare's seafront sweet shops. According to Lauren, anyway. None of which seems to phase her a bit. I can't help but shrug. At least both of them know the level of fickle they're getting into.

Why does everyone have to be compared to a celeb nowadays, though? Nothing irks me more than people being categorised at face value. Ironically, I know the refreshingly down-to-earth Antonio Banderas would probably feel the same. But that's Lauren all over. Branding and ROI equals everything.

"Last time I checked, you were married," I state, matter-of-fact.

"There's nothing wrong with a little harmless window

shopping. Keeps Jamie on his toes." Lauren winks.

For a split second, my own ego gets the better of me and I can't help but wonder if this is where I've been going wrong. Particularly with Callum, my last boyfriend in the long list of males who, once the novelty of lust and magnetism has worn off, invariably either try to change my quirky ways, or hide from them. Maybe I really do need to take a leaf out of Lauren's marketing book and fling myself across desks (and glass meeting tables), making it abundantly clear I'm available.

Thanks, but no thanks, says my heart. The right guy hasn't come along yet, that's all. And if he never does, well, then I would rather not compromise. If I hadn't walked away from Callum, once it was clear the jesting over my café plans had become a permanent fixture in our relationship, I wouldn't be standing here now, re-aligning my delicious (although unappreciated by Lauren) breakfast pastries back into their previously perfect positions, would I?

Waste not want not. I carefully clamp the unwanted fruit tart between my tongs once again and pop it back on the plate for myself, giving it the attention it deserves.

Lauren quirks an immaculately arched brow, as if to insinuate the pastry won't help me indulging in any window shopping of my own. But I don't care for drooling over my colleagues and I definitely don't care for calorie counting; **#eatwhatyouwant #eatwhatyoulove** are my hashtags… something I can't wait to announce to my sister once we go through the brand plans.

"So then. Down to biz," Lauren announces as if reading my mind. "I'm going to come up with something whizbang for you. Normally, as you know, I wouldn't get so hands-on at grassroots level but you are my sister, after all, and it's important that I oversee every aspect of the campaign."

I feel a pang of remorse over my earlier thoughts. See, Lauren really can be a gem when she wants to.

I let out a meek "thanks," depositing my own full fat coffee and beloved breakfast tart on the table. I take the cinnamon shaker and dust the tart liberally. Truthfully, I could eat at least three (and that's just for brekkie), but I'd best restrain myself in front of my present company. I take a tentative nibble, and, predictably, flaky pastry crumbs and copper dust coat my mouth in a way guaranteed to make my sister scowl. On the other hand, Lauren doesn't know what she is missing and there's no danger of her cameraman capturing this moment. The burst of sharp berries, mingling with and balancing the sweetness of the custard, is extraordinarily good; the spice warming everything up with a delicious kick.

"You've just met Todd," Lauren continues, speaking of the little devil. So that's his name.

"Well, yeah, kinda," I mumble uncouthly between mouthfuls.

"He might be straight out of art and design college, but he's incredibly switched on for his age and learning really fast. I briefed him back in the office too so he could maximise his time today and capture as many wow factor images as possible. I'll cast my eye over them later and then we'll use them in a variety of ways. He's also out there with the drone camera." At this unexpected announcement I baulk. Those hideously intrusive things remind me of pterodactyls going in for the kill. Images of small dogs and wobbly grannies being

17

knocked off the pier and cast into the sea flash before my eyes. "Relax, it's fine. We procured all the necessary permissions from the pier's management last week. Nothing to worry about."

"Surely there's no need to take things to those extremes? Not the permission. I mean the overhead shots."

Lauren tuts. "Drone videography is big business nowadays." I shudder inwardly at the V word and the play button it threatens to press on a bunch of hideous teenage memories from days that are thankfully long gone. She doesn't twig and ploughs on. "Not only can we produce some amazing footage for your website, but the effect is mesmerising on Instagram and the like. We'll knock up some professional trailers for you, adding sound effects and copy. The pier will look a million dollars at four-hundred feet above; the sea a bit bluer, the mud... I mean beach... a little blonder. All of which ties in fabulously with the café's colour scheme. You'll have visitors bookmarking you and turning up from all over the place, just you wait and see. I might not be a fan of stodge but this specialty of yours has the potential to become something epic. Other than a few capital cities around the world, and totally overlooking Portugal, of course, I don't see anybody else going for broke with such a unique spin as you on these *natas*. I hope you're prepared because you're going to set tongues wagging!"

Hopefully Lauren means that in a good way. I desperately want things to be a success and try to ignore the loose cannon vibes surrounding Lauren's ideas, nodding at my sister's expertise instead, trying in vain to get a word in edgeways with my beloved hashtags, which until now have only festooned my amateur attempts at showcasing The Custard Tart Café on Instagram and Facebook. Alas, it isn't to be, and now my sister is grilling me over my non-existent Google Maps listing and my paltry social media advertising budget.

"Clearly you haven't done anything about either," Lauren chastises, taking her second sip of coffee before adding both facets of marketing to a spreadsheet whose entries are growing by the minute.

"Give me a chance," I mutter, pulling a beast of a frown, "I've not even started trading yet... On that note," I look up to register the clock showing it's a quarter to ten already. "Hadn't you better get a wriggle on? Didn't you tell Todd that you were meeting him on the hour? I've no idea where you left your car but even the closest car park is a brisk twenty minute walk away."

"Shit!" Lauren flips down her laptop cover, allows herself another miniscule sip of caffeine and jumps to her feet. "I got more carried away than I realised with this little baby of yours, and we haven't even covered the subject of influencers yet. Grr... why couldn't you base yourself on *terra firma,* rather than halfway out in the muddy Bristol Channel?"

Admittedly, the coffee-hued waves are nowhere near as aesthetically pleasing as the sea surrounding Cornwall, much less the Caribbean, but the silt in the murky waters of North Somerset has long created a haven for birds and other wildlife in the nearby Severn Estuary, and I like to think that anybody brave enough to take a dip at our beach (at any time of the year) is rewarded hippo-style with a nutrient-packed mud bath. Weston-super-Mare even has the second highest tidal range in the world! All of this whilst somehow magically retaining its quaint village feel. Surely my kooky location, slap bang at the very end of Weston's Grand Pier, is every marketer's dream?

Lauren leaves me air kisses and flies out the door without a backward glance. Just as well I had planned to open up at ten-thirty on my first official day in business. May's predictable smorgasbord of weather has gone awry already, throwing a brief but highly inconvenient freak hailstorm at the town and its pier. It's impossible to hold back a laugh now that I'm alone. Lauren must be pegging it back to the car park in her heels, trying in vain to avoid the cracks in the pier's wooden flooring, to return to her young tog. He is no doubt already soaked to the skin with a cast of crabs biting at his skinny ankles.

IN HINDSIGHT – as I epitomise the height of rock n roll, cradling my mug of Ovaltine, tucked up in bed in my Winnie the Pooh onesie in my tiny top floor apartment – it has been a decent enough first day. Both Tim, my second-in-command pastry chef, and Reggie, my head server, who is on a never-ending gap year before heading to uni for his English Lit degree, were in high spirits all day. Both arrived in style on the aptly custard-yellow pier train, waving The Custard Tart Café banners and blowing party streamers at the scant groups and lone walkers with their umbrellas and hoods, scattered along the three-hundred-and-sixty-six metres of boardwalk.

Reggie is an old school friend who's postponed higher education for ever and a day… until he's had quite enough of propping up the counters in Weston's knick-knack shops, penny arcades, and fish and chip joints. At six foot two, the contrast between our vital statistics has always been a talking point, especially since Reggie always has his mass of dreadlocks tied up and balancing on his crown at work (making him six foot four). His summer stint at The Custard Tart Café will be his *absolute final brush* with the tourist industry before Shakespeare calls. God love him, he's even gifted me the most hilarious gold-framed quotations for the café's bathrooms. They range from the Hyman Rickover quote saying that running an effective government is akin to sewing a button on a custard pie (the mind boggles), to the footballer, Ronaldo missing his post-training apple crumble and custard like mad when he left Manchester United. Recently, he had the good sense to return to the club, and I can't say I blame him. Even the King of Bling needs his custard fix.

As for Tim, although we haven't worked together before, his CV is as silken as the custard you'd expect to find simmering on Nigella's kitchen stove. And that's good enough for me. Tim has worked his way up from porter to *commis pâtissier* in two of the South West's swishest hotels as well. I'm lucky to have him.

Caitlyn is a question mark on the rota for now, which is frustrating given I've just finalised it, but she's promised to fill me in on her term's end date as soon as possible. It's dependent on her passing her exams, otherwise she'll need to hang around for resits.

So what if there was only a trickle of custom today – most of it coming from my extended family (who were after cheeky freebies – I made them pay), catering contacts and former clients? That was to be expected. Low tourist season has only just started and the nip in the spring air would have deterred most from setting foot on the pier.

Word of mouth will soon do its thing. Oh, and hopefully Lauren's fancy marketing will kick in. I'm glad we never got onto the subject of Gen Z influencers though. I can't be dealing with all that pouting and posing on my premises. I've got the eateries at the pier's entrance to take into account too. Once somebody has plied themselves with candyfloss and hotdogs, there's little room left for custard tarts. But all of that will change quickly; the best culinary seaside experience coming to those who wait.

With or without Lauren's help, it's always felt like this was what I was born to do. Folk might fear the unknown initially but individual, fresh Portuguese-style custard tarts have become a staple in English supermarket bakeries already. The (Weston-super-Mare) tide is definitely turning. And my first genuine customer reflected this back to me. He, unlike the rest, absolutely did warrant a freebie – as I had always decided my first shopper would. Frank (we'd soon got on first name terms) removed his flat cap as if it were a top hat, revealing a shiny bald head and cobalt-blue eyes, tossed his walking stick aside as if it were a cane, and danced a mini but merry Sinatra-style jig at his discovery at the end of the pier.

"I've not wandered down here in years, love." His broadly-accented Somerset voice warbled with what sounded like genuine emotion for times gone by, and I panicked that I'd not added Kleenex tissues to my ever-growing checklist. "Reckon you might have changed all that. Oh, be gosh... look at this lovely lot!" His sparkly but glassy blue eyes could hardly believe their luck. "How's a man to make a custard tart decision?"

"Why not eat one here and take the rest home in a doggy bag? Well, doggy box," I said, pointing at the various-sized recycled cardboard boxes at the end of the counter where our separate takeout queue would eventually, hopefully, be lining up come the summer. "We recognised this would be a dilemma for many customers when we opened," I explained. "That's why we came up with a range of takeaway options. Not to mention our eat-in-or-out afternoon tea treat."

I pulled a pretty three-tiered cake stand out from beneath the counter as if I were a magician. I hadn't expected to do this so quickly. Afternoon teas were something I assumed would be taken up by groups celebrating birthdays, or the winter crowd looking to do some serious carb refuelling after battling the elements to make it to the café.

"You're on," said Frank decisively, retrieving the accessories he'd flung far and wide. "But there's no way I'm going to play cheapskate and let you give me that lovely lot for free. Knock off the price of a single tart and I'll gladly take you up on the afternoon tea offer – well, breakfast offer – and pay for the rest."

"Seriously? You're that hungry?"

"Happens I am," Frank winked. "It's a momentous day f-for you *a-and me*." He tripped over his words and they lingered on the air. I couldn't help but wonder if he'd received some life-changing news upon waking this morning. "And here's a good tip, my dear. The customer's always right. Don't you be giving them get out clauses and questioning their appetite. Now load that stand before I can change my mind."

He nodded, taking the best seat in the house, next to the largest porthole window that offered the ultimate view over the sea, her current mood, the distant plasticine blob of Lundy island, and the wheeling gulls.

I proceeded to run through the tarts on offer as Frank appreciated the fragrance of the watermelon-red peonies in their striped blue and white vase in the middle of his table.

"So, I've got original custard, molten chocolate orange volcano, banana split, espresso kickstart, spiced apple and brown butter, cherry and ber—"

"Stop!"

Frank's reaction – and his walking stick tapping the floor *à la* Dick Van Dyke – had me in stitches. When I'd imagined my first customer in my head, they'd definitely not been this animated.

"I'm a huge believer in the *Countdown* number game methodology when it comes to decision making. Give me two of the same from the top, a different from the middle, and three the same from the bottom," he pointed an arthritic finger at the counter.

"Okaaaay," I replied, scrunching my face up, trying in earnest to remember how the glamorous Rachel Riley might attend to that instruction on the brainbox Channel Four TV programme. The Custard Tart Café's shelving kind of mirrored the game show's… at a push… Fortunately, Reggie's hands gripped my shoulders and gently deposited me to one side.

"That's two banana splits, an original custard, and three espresso kickstarts," he said without hesitation, his finely twisted dreadlocks swinging lightly from his high ponytail as he displayed each tart neatly on the stand, holding it aloft, and giving it a little spin for Frank's approval. Reggie has also grown one of those neat 'mid fades' recently, transitioning his hair into his closely clipped beard. It suits him. Somehow it makes him look ready for uni life at last.

"But you need to choose another six tarts to fill the stand up!" I said.

"No I don't. I'll pay them forward," Frank insisted. "Recent, and not so recent, world events have given me a new perspective on life. Not everyone's as lucky as I am. And that'll be the way it goes every time I set foot in here – so long as you give me your word that you'll respect my wishes and use your discernment to give the tarts the best homes."

Could there exist a more perfect first customer?

"Aw, you're the best, Sir!" Reggie bowed at Frank before depositing the mouthwatering display of treats in front of him.

"That is just lovely," I added, my heart swelling at the gesture. "You hear of this kindness with a single cup of coffee… but six custard tarts is taking things to a whole new level." And it was. My tarts sold at one pound fifty a piece, and paying forward nine pounds worth of delectable food each time he visited was positively angelic of him. "Bless, you Frank."

Something told me we'd be seeing a lot more of this character and it definitely warmed the cockles.

Within minutes, Frank's presence at the front table had become magnetic, and a young family trundled in with a tricycle, pushchair, buckets and spades, discarded raincoats (now the sun had finally won over the clouds) and wriggly-eel toddlers. Behind them were a couple of giggling teens who looked suspiciously like they were bunking off school, and even two of the pavilion workers popped their heads in to see what all the foodie fuss was about. It may not have represented much to most, but to me this was the diversity I was looking for; the chance for the tarts to be discovered by every age group and taste bud. I didn't want to get ahead of myself, but nor could I hide the giant beam on my face.

Typically I'd only ticked off half the things on my to-do list before Emma Hawkes, the glam local radio presenter, showed up for the opening day's live interview. Emma was a popular DJ who'd been a couple of years above me at school and had done very well for herself. She was famous for cleverly grilling her guests, Oprah Winfrey-style, to squeeze the juiciest of answers out of them, so I could only pray she didn't have any tricks up her sleeve today. Hopefully one of the aforementioned takeout boxes of freshly-baked custard tarts with a mixture of fillings would put paid to that, and Emma wouldn't somehow try to steer me off at serious tangents and onto the subject of past *relationships*... or past *relay races*... or past *really bad stage management.* Gulp!

Yes, I know I'm being mysterious with those latter two Rs, but I can't revisit emotional teenage turmoil just yet.

Frank had strung his 'afternoon breakfast' out for a couple of hours by the time Emma and her crew arrived. He continued to gaze nostalgically out the window in a world of his own as the team set up their recording paraphernalia, and whilst my heart knew he was helping us – because how could any passerby not be entranced by the magnificent cake stand and pot of tea gracing the floral table before him? – my head worried that his slow pace of dining might lead to him thinking he could spend the whole day here. Which would be fine if I was running a New York skyscraper of a café, with hundreds of seats on multiple levels, but wasn't so appealing when I aiming for a quick turnaround operation that captured the essence of the iconic *Pastéis de Belém* in Lisbon; arguably the most famous custard tart café in the world, where the queue for a table snaked down the street, and then some. Give him his due, though, Frank had worked through two-thirds of the tarts already. It was anybody's guess just where the twig of a man put them all.

I couldn't believe Emma didn't recognise me from school. I seem to be one of those complete oddballs who can recall every student's name, birth month, eye colour, catalogue of love interests, best friends and enemies, favourite crisp and can of pop flavour, preferred make of trainers, *and* their school house. All with the click of my fingers. Then again, I suppose Emma's had so many guests on her show over the years that her head must be swimming with names and faces. It slightly helped to ease my paranoia. All of this was flipping Reggie's doing in any case. There's no way I'd have dared get in touch with Emma's show, to see if she wanted to do a feature on us. She would have been in Lauren's year in upper sixth when calamity struck. *Twice.* I could only hope that my current hairdo wouldn't ring any school bells, taking her back to either of those catastrophic events. It shouldn't. I mean, today's Ethiopian style of braiding required heaps of patience and practice, and would have been way too detailed for sixteen-year-old me to aspire to back then.

"Are we all ready, set, go?" Emma asked. Those last three

words made me break out in a cold sweat, bringing back the smell of freshly-cut grass at the school playing fields, as a distant crowd roared in anticipation.

I nodded with as much enthusiasm as I could muster, hoping not to make a fool of myself in front of invisible viewers, and slightly more visible ones. A curious huddle had gathered at the door to catch a glimpse of Emma in action. See, I told you she was famous in these parts.

"And lights, camera, action!" declared one of Emma's crew. Okay, now I really was paranoid that this was some kind of practical joke being played on me in loving memory of my school days, and that all and sundry in Emma's crew were privy to the events of my chequered teenage years. My eyes darted left and right, seeking out an errant giggle from one of the radio team, but either they were brilliant actors or the recent dialogue was an overwhelming coincidence.

She started off with some standard questions, like 'where did you get your inspiration from to open a café selling just custard tarts?', 'how do you think you'll fare with the ever popular and slightly more traditional seaside outlets that don't put all of their eggs in one basket?' and 'can me and the guys do a little taste test live on air?' At this point we quickly rigged up a super-fun blindfold test that had everyone in hysterics at some of the guesses ref. the tarts' fillings. After that, Emma's questions became much more book-based, and I felt my shoulders sag in glorious relaxation. I may not have tuned in to her show every week but it was a well-known fact that she was a fiction addict.

"Are you sure you got out the right side of the bed this morning, Missy?" Frank interrupted loudly, making us all jump. Talk about embarrassing. Reggie palmed his forehead, and even Tim peeped his head through the kitchen serving hatch, sporting the strangest of lopsided facial expressions, which I don't wish to be party to again. "Only our Willow's opened a *custard tart café*, not a blinking bookshop."

Our Willow? Heck. It really did sound like Frank intended to become part of the furniture, and evidently he had never tuned in to Emma's show himself.

"Oh, that's quite all right," I countered, panicking that this was no dress rehearsal and we were live on air. "I love the idea of blending café and bookshop culture, as many places already do. The two subjects go hand in hand. I'm planning on getting a couple of those gorgeous duck egg-blue book trolleys in here." *Was I?* Oh, well. I was now, so hopefully somewhere had them in stock. Thanks, Frank, for making me waffle, adding those extra items to my extraordinarily long list! "They're all the rage in the homes of bookworms," I nodded my head fervently as if to convince the listeners, who wouldn't be able to see my body language anyway. "And it's about time we brought that concept to eateries. Basically, customers will be able to bring books to The Custard Tart Café to add to the trolley – which will circulate the tables and the queue – and they'll be able to take books home with them too. A bit like a library, but it'll be trust based. Or they can just read a chapter of a previously undiscovered author here to see if they like their style, then head to a real bookshop to buy their own copy. Who knows, maybe we'll get local authors in for readings in time."

Okay, now I was getting carried away.

"Are you serious?" Emma whooped. "You do realise I will

be packing up my things tonight and moving in! Hey listeners, on that note, I'll be putting up a little online poll, so head over to Twitter later to cast your votes. It just so happens that I'm looking for unique venues to present my summer shows from. Let's give the traditional Radio 1 Weston-super-Mare beach party a bit of competition and base ourselves here at Willow's café for a morning, shall we? Willow, what do you say?"

"Well, erm, yes, okay, Sounds fantastic!" I spluttered.

And just like that, completely overlooking the vast scale of tarts we'd need to conjure up to feed the masses; completely overlooking Tim's startled expression as he popped his head out the kitchen again, I'd made my own bit of marketing luck. Or rather Frank had. I was grinning just thinking about it.

Ding!

I stir with a start. My mug is still in my hands and Ovaltine stains are flecked across my beautiful pastel quilt. Damn, I must have dozed off. This is not the start of a great new routine. I fling the covers back and pick up my phone from the bedside table, squinting at the screen to see who's contacting me. It's almost midnight. Not good! I have to be up at the crack of dawn to help Tim.

I flick on the table lamp. Hmm, it's Lauren, telling me to check my email. She's working uncharacteristically late to be messaging me at this hour. Or perhaps Jamie is 'out out,' and she's trying to distract herself from what that might mean.

I open the email to see the blank message with a Zip file attached. I shouldn't be shaking, but I can't help it. It feels as if I've rolled the roulette wheel and put my whole destiny in my sister's hands. Everything downloads unbearably slowly (another entry for the to-do list: upgrade my mobile phone) but eventually I am treated to some sneak peek footage of the drone's inaugural flight along the pier. I'm not so sure that Muse Masters has legally obtained the rights to play The Lighthouse Family's *Ocean Drive* song in the background, but that's for Lauren to fret about. I turn my attention instead to a cluster of dreamy photos that scream 'come here, eat here, take an Instagram-worthy picture here, and show the world you live THE quintessentially cosmopolitan life here!'.

There's no denying how fabulous everything looks. Todd really does know his stuff, credit where it's due. And yet all I can do is worry. Because what if Lauren's strategy makes me look as if I'm getting too big for my boots?

Sure, I want to be successful. What self-respecting, avant-garde café owner wouldn't? But incrementally. Manageably. Enjoyably. No matter the complexity of their fillings, these are custard tarts we are talking about. Not vintage wine, caviar, or edible gold.

Ding, ding, ding! Now a flurry of WhatsApp messages comes at me like the tide, completely negating all the malty goodness of my evening brew. The anxiety flows out of my fingertips every time I scroll down the phone to read a new update. I hold my breath.

Forget what I said about influencers, we need to brainstorm celeb chefs who'd be willing to pay TCTC a visit. Who's kind of local to W-S-M? Securing Nigella Lawson would be the apex, obvs! Just imagine her sashaying down the pier in one of her iconic black outfits. How marvelously seaside chic she'd look from above. Oh, my God, give the damned drone obsession a rest, Lauren – and I'm sure Nigella has better ways of spending her leisure time. *Needless to say, a low profile, G-list presenter from Somerset's Radio Gert Lush looking to get a leg up the career ladder with a bit of social media exposure would be more realistic.* What a cheek. Radio Gert Lush was Emma's radio station! *Marco Pierre White has a place in Bath but he's too much of a patisserie purist for rough and ready custard tarts.* Why, thanks. *Hugh Fearnley-Whittingstall would only be enticed if the pier had a flock of free range hens whose eggs embellished your custard – or an allotment from which you were growing and incorporating organic thyme or mint in your fillings... Ooh, I've just had a Eureka moment: we could get in touch with José Mourinho! I know he's head coach for Roma now but he's exactly the Portuguese icon and brand ambassador we're looking for. Football fans LOVE their pies, don't they? All they're subconsciously looking for, to swap the savoury meat and two veg pie for the sweet custard variety, is the thumbs-up from José... they just don't know it yet.*

My eyes are like saucers. I blink hard and read that proposal again. I can only imagine Lauren is halfway through her second bottle of wine at this point. I'm about to bat back a reply on the lines of, 'the videos are great! Let's just give them chance to do their thing... and I hate to point out the obvious, big sis, but I'm not fancy enough for any of this. OK, Nigella does always reply to my tweets on Twitter but she replies to virtually everyone, ray of sunshine that she is. It's early days, José is not exactly a chef, and WSM doesn't quite offer the level of sun, sand, and seaside opulence he'd be looking for.' But WhatsApp number two (a voice note this time!) beats me to it:

"Okay, scrap that. I was getting carried away." Thank goodness she's come to her senses. *"But we do need this to go global. Like Hollywood style."* Nooooooooo! We really don't, Lauren. Stop it! *"It's a long shot but if we could get hold of the agents or publicists for any megastars who are popping over to London to promote their films... and somehow entice them across to North Somerset... well! Can you imagine what that flicker of exposure would do for your little café? I'm thinking Jennifer Aniston ditching the diet, because custard tarts are too fricking irresistible to give a shit about her waist-line. And then how could we not invite David Schwimmer along for the ride now that they've had their little* **Friends** *reunion?"*

Is she for real? If my eyes were saucers five minutes ago, now they are dinner plates on stalks. What kind of budget does Lauren think I have at my disposal? My sister's own willpower was watertight enough this morning when I offered her a bite of a tart. I'm pretty sure Jennifer Aniston has guru-level discipline. And having put the rumours of their romance to bed (terrible quip, I know), I'm pretty sure that the last thing that Jennifer and David need is Punch and Judy audiences on a British seaside pier raking said rumours up again.

But here comes message number three, which is back in text form:

I'm sure the local council will see the plus points and dig deep into its coffers to help us achieve it. Jen and Dave feeding one another romantic custardy bites at TCTC, Jen and Dave fooling around at the crazy golf, Jen and Dave making sandcastles on the beach – headline: 'All David wanted to do was go for a Schwimm'. Alternatively, we could plump for Will Smith on the Weston-super-Mare Ferris wheel: 'Will wheely likes to be beside the seaside!' You've got a real vehicle for success here, by the way. Sauce defines pasta and your custard-fused fillings define pastry.

Okay, now Lauren really has lost the plot, she clearly hasn't been keeping up with the gossip magazines and the latest on Hollywood's dating scene, and I'm wondering how she ever got a foot in the door at Muse Masters, let alone into the boss's bed.

PS. Dreamboat has moved into my office as part of the departmental reshuffle. I know! I can hardly contain myself...

Okay, now I really don't understand what's going on in my sister's head, but at the same time I'm surprised she hasn't thought of roping in this Antonio Banderas lookalike to further embellish the merits of my *natas*. Lauren is six months married... six months married and ready to embark on an affair. How is this obsession with the new guy 'a spot of window shopping'?

My thoughts circle like my seaside town's Ferris wheel; the one that seasonally tries in vain to emulate the London Eye and something I can't imagine Jen, Dave, Will, the real Antonio B or even the publicity-hungry Hoff choosing to rotate on at their leisure. And I wonder if I'm also biting off more than I can chew.

CHAPTER THREE

"AW, LOOK. HOW cute is that?"

I'm not sure if Reggie is referring to the baseball-capped guy who has just walked through the door, and is now busily casing the joint, his eyes drawn to the decorative blue, white, and gold tiles that have finally arrived, or the pooch in his arms. Reggie is straight, as far as I know, so I assume he's referring to the licorice-black curly poodle with its sweet shiny coal eyes and bright red jacket, although it would make a refreshing change to hear straight males appraise their own sex. I'd be hard pressed to deny it, the dog's owner *is* pretty lush. The stud of a customer has also been rendered pretty awestruck by the azulejos. Maybe he's been to Porto and my decorative tiles have transported him back to some long-lost city memories. The thought is quite beautiful.

"Our first doggie customer, hooray!" I find myself replying uber-enthusiastically as I set to it with my next order, juggling cappuccino prep with custard tart assemblage.

Not that I want us to be inundated with canines, like some kind of dog version of the cat cafés that you find in the big cities. Indeed, it's most unusual for the town's pier to have waived the humans-only rule for the season – from Royal Sands to the Grand Pier this is normally a dog-free zone between May and September. But the council has agreed to trial the change this summer season, in the hope that everybody's furry friends will be on their best behaviour; that is to say, in the hope that everybody will pick up their pets' poop. It's a lovely gesture – thoughts of doggy business to one side – so people who perhaps live alone with their animals won't feel alienated and can benefit from the mental health boost of a gust of fresh Bristol Channel air as they stretch their limbs and exercise their charges.

The stranger who has drifted in on the salty air really is hypnotically blessed in the looks department. I avert my gaze before I flush. Although the fire-engine red UWE Bristol cap might hint that he's aware of his charm, and this is what he wears whenever he steps out to dampen down the effect, I can somehow tell that he's one of those jammy so-and-sos who doesn't know how lucky he is. I have only glimpsed a fleeting treat of his smouldering brown eyes and matching hair (that's to say it's brown too, not on the brink of combustion) but the sharp cheekbones are something else. I busy myself once more with table five's order. These afternoon tea packages are going down a storm and, unlike Frank, this group of customers has opted for a proper selection of one of each tart, ranging from the fruity apricot jam and the rich treacle and cornflake through to the light-as-a-feather baked pear and the nutty and boozy amaretto.

As I'm swooning, the guy starts to speak, loudly and abruptly. He turns to make sure everyone within the four walls of my workplace, every seagull circling out to sea, and every speck of a vessel on the horizon is giving him their undivided attention. "When I learned of a café..." he growls.

My tummy somersaults. I already know this is going to go

ISABELLA MAY

one of two ways, but there's no time to process potential disasters.

He carries on. "A café gutsy enough to put its own special spin on the Portuguese *pastel de nata*... a café ignorant enough to insult my country and my heritage, I just had to come and see it for myself," he continues in an undeniably Iberian accent.

I blink rapidly, hoping somebody will pinch me and wake me up from this utter nightmare, but Reggie is equally stunned and Tim, as ever, is in the kitchen, baking fresh batches of the tarts this stranger has burst in here to slate.

After the initial 'oohs' and 'ohs', an uncomfortable silence falls upon the room. Tarts and cups are poised mid-air. My customers resemble an arty still-life tableau from one of the impressive carnival floats that parade Weston-super-Mare's streets every November. I'd call the masterpiece, 'They really didn't see that coming'.

"Sure enough, this is something straight out of a horror movie." The man picks up the threads of his spiel, throwing in a comic-book laugh. "I suppose I should be thankful that this excuse for a business is hidden away at the end of a tired and tacky seaside pier, but now I'm here, now I'm taking in the full magnitude of this... this *freak show*, all I want to do is fire up a chainsaw, chop off the entire pavilion and throw it in the sea. That said, I doubt even the fish would come near it."

Another collective gasp fills the room. My pulse skitters and I decide it's best to carefully lay down the custard tart in my tongs before I accidentally squash it and spatter my face with gooey custard. His words have now frozen all of us into our places like a fairytale villain's curse. The man's back is

38

ramrod straight, perhaps interpreting our lack of reaction as victory. His dog whimpers. The high-pitched sound pierces the air like nails down a blackboard.

I feel utterly helpless. I always prepare for life's random events, armed with plans A, B, and C. Heck, I can even mastermind a plan Z if need be. But when I find myself in a pickle like this without warning, I am wading in an ocean of toffee. It's impossible. I try to speak but the words catch in my throat. As they are all expletives anyway, it's probably for the best if I want to retain not only my dignity, but any future customers.

"This is sacrilege." Now he sweeps his free hand out wide, as if he's in an opera. And oh, apparently he hasn't finished yet. He sniffs at the air, as if even its molecules displease him. Weirdo. The heady vanilla-infused perfume is the very thing that draws people inside my café!

"I heard the rumours about this place and I've seen the pictures and videos doing the rounds on social media, but I couldn't believe anyone would have the *audacity* to ruin the Portuguese national treasure like this. It had to be a very bad joke. Turns out such heathens do exist!" He narrows his eyes. "And what is it with the tiles?" He tilts his head toward the wall on his right, now. "Where in God's name did you get those sacred specimens, and why do you think you're the next São Bento railway station? And don't get me started on all the poncy bunches of flowers." He points them out unnecessarily with a finger that could be a loaded gun. "A proper *pasteleria* doesn't need any of this crap on its tables. The *pastéis* speak for themselves. It's all about the genuine Portuguese ingredients, baking methods, and history. *Nada mais!*"

So much for him admiring my pretty little collage then. I can't believe what I am hearing, and neither can my rocketing blood pressure. I desperately need to take lessons in spontaneous quipping from Radhika who, with her dry sense of humour, would no doubt have calmly boomeranged back a hilarious tile comeback at this infuriated male by now. Either that, or she'd have removed a real tile and smashed it over his head instead. But my brain is empty and my mouth is sandpaper. Actually, make that the contents of Weston-super-Mare's beach.

"I… w…would you repeat that again, please?" I finally manage a lame response. "On second thoughts, no, don't bother." I hold up a hand, as if that could possibly stop any further negative remarks being bandied my way.

Good grief. What am I like? Why am I gracing this idiot with Ps and Qs? He has just lambasted all of our hard work!

"And what makes you qualified," I put my hands on my hips. "To come in here and r… rip our creations apart?" I quickly raise my voice before he spouts off again.

He smiles at me. But it's not sincere. His eyes are as cold as the waves that pound several metres beneath our feet. It's a shame because the dimples that bracket his mouth are really rather cute, all things considered.

What am I like?

"Well, you see, it goes a little something like this," he replies, as if explaining the situation to a child. "My grandparents own one of the oldest *pastel de nata* bakeries on the Algarve."

There is no hesitation in his delivery. He is sure of his every word and his right to stand here and insult me. I grimace, but his ugly words fail to dilute his outer allure. "A bakery that has made millions of real, authentic *pastéis de nata* over the centuries; the kind of true, traditional recipe *that does not need to be mucked about with.*" His cheeks are hinting they'll soon be matching the colour of his cap. Ha, I've put a chink in his armour at last.

"It would wipe the floor with the nonsense you're flogging in this place," he continues after several beats, as if he can read my mind. He strides proprietorially across the floor until he reaches the counter, where he narrows his eyes once more – this time to peer closely at the custard tarts' labels.

"Lemon and thyme with Pernod, topped with sea salt? What fresh hell is this?"

He pans the counter's shelves forward and back, brain seemingly unable to process the sight of our beautiful and diverse pastries.

"Banana split and espresso kickstart? We wouldn't eat any of this rubbish in Portugal. What are you doing to my country?"

The poodle puts its nose in the air, wiggles it appreciatively, and clearly begs to differ.

"No, wait! It gets better, Cristiano." *Oh, surely not? Don't tell me the guy named his dog after the football player, Ronaldo!* I can see the colours of the poodle's jacket properly now, and besides the red, there are, indeed, splashes of a white and gold trim. I may not be a football fan but I'm clued up enough about the beautiful game to know my instinct is right. Today's outfit is paying homage to Manchester United. How naff. It's one thing witnessing holidaymaker parents kitting out their offspring in their beloved team's strips (each to their own and all that and presumably most kids are thrilled at the prospect), but footie canine couture is surely a criminal offence. "Matcha custard tart flavoured with vanilla and honey, drizzled lightly with dark chocolate ganache and garnished with a dark chocolate, blood orange and almond bark. How can anyone possibly taste the custard element of that? You've annihilated it!" He lets out a guffaw, bringing me back to the current scenario with an almighty bang.

On cue, Cristiano lets out a meek yap as if he agrees that this might be pushing the culinary boundaries a little too far. Meanwhile, Reggie, now rooted to my side, has suddenly developed a most impressive inflated chest.

"Are you going to put in an order, like everyone else?" His voice is laced with warning. "Or are you going to leave the premises before I give you a helping hand?"

"Do you honestly think I would choose to taint myself, for longer than is necessary, ever again, with any of this poison?"

What a wicked word to use. Thanks for completely screwing up the customers' perception of my wares – and my life's ambition!

"I can guarantee that somebody, or rather *something* will be making its way here, though. Unless you take my visit today as a friendly warning and stop jazzing up sacred recipes, meddling with things you don't understand."

Wow. I could never have predicted any of this. What did I do wrong in a past life? Evidently I've not yet repaid enough of some old karmic debt.

My own cheeks are burning now. I know this shade of fuchsia pink too well. And it's as if their flush has set off a chain of events because, the next thing I know, Reggie has dropped his tray on the floor in some kind of delayed reaction. Custard tarts splatter everywhere. Viewed from above, the effect must look quite arty, like one of Jamie Oliver's tray meals. But on the grassroots level of the café floor, during our first fortnight of trading, in front of customers we desperately need to impress, it is one big, inglorious mess. I can only thank my lucky stars that Emma hasn't decided to descend upon us today with her radio roadshow. Hopefully we will somehow have recovered from this by the time she is here again with her crew and an entourage of fans.

"Now look at what you've done!" I gesture fruitlessly at the destruction. "Don't worry, mate," I add to Reggie, who looks set to hit boiling point. I throw a pleading 'he's-not-worth-it-leave-it-to-me-I've-got-this' look his way, hoping it will suffice. "I don't see any of our clients complaining," I state calmly, my eyes burning into the intruder's before I look around at our diners in semi-desperation, unable to believe that even Frank hasn't sprung to my defence. Then again, though age is just a number, in this instance it's probably not such a good idea for a seventy-something to raise their blood pressure or propose a sword fight with their walking stick. "So I suggest you take yourself – and that admittedly cute pooch – out of my café. And don't come back... unless you want to spend a night in the cells!"

He can't be so bad if he owns a pet, he must have a heart in there somewhere, my own heart tells me as I watch the stranger weighing up my words (after throwing us the mother of all eye rolls). But still, what a complete prat storming onto

43

the premises like this and attempting to put the customers off.

At my words, the prat takes a mini-leap over the mess on the floor. He looks like he's taking part in an agility competition at the Crufts dog show. But I swallow the dangerously nervous giggle that has floated up my throat like an air bubble: nothing about this is remotely hilarious, because it is happening at my expense.

"Actually, no." I have a sudden brainwave and I shout at his retreating back. "Stay right there and don't you dare move a millimetre."

Unfathomably, he does as he is told. Despite the wide eyes of all of my customers, I press on with my harebrained idea, taking little steps back toward the counter in case any sudden movement has him fleeing the scene of carnage, or worse still, spinning on his heel to watch what I am up to. I work fast. I grab a takeout box and fill it with an assortment of pastries – making certain the offending lemon-thyme-Pernod, matcha, banana and espresso varieties are sitting in pride of place – before returning to him and his pet.

"Here. I'm giving you six tarts on the house. And don't even think about refusing them," I say, with the twinkle of challenge in my eyes. I'll be hard pushed to get him to accept it.

"It's your lucky day, mate!" I'm not sure which of the group of fluorescent hi-vis jacketed construction workers shouts this, as they collectively snicker over their mugs of tea. I shove the box of tarts towards the grumpy idiot's free hand which is about to dive into the pocket of his body warmer. He grabs the box reflexively, revealing a wrist sporting a snazzy frog-green Swatch watch that clashes terribly with the red cap, this side of Christmas. And now let's take a moment to return to the irksome body warmer: *what the actual heck?* It's June! I get that the irritatingly and devastatingly good-looking male standing in front of me, with the poodle tucked under his arm like a package, comes from sunnier climes. Somehow it feels he is wearing a body warmer to my café, at the edge of the Bristol Channel, just to prove how chilly and English the place is. And me, too, by extension. Boy has it served to get my back up.

"I suggest you take the tarts home and savour them slowly, one at a time." Oh, why did I have to say it like that? Now I'd set the flipping workmen off again. "And I suggest you think about the passion and hard work that has gone into their creation before you act on your threat."

I wait for the 'it's not a threat, it's a promise' retort, but surprisingly, it never comes.

Man and dog are statues. Evidently, this part of the show was missing from their pre-rehearsed script and they haven't bargained on departing with a present. Either that or they're looking for a bin before they resort to hurling the gift back at me.

"Wait. What the heck?"

Chair legs scrape across the floor and I don't need to look to know that Frank has risen from his table, unsteady on his legs until he reaches for his cane. In the background, Reggie doesn't know which way to turn, energy split three ways between protecting me, clearing up the tarts, and pre-empting what Frank is about to do next. The customers are still mainly quiet but pockets of subdued muttering are sparking up like little fires.

"Not on my watch!" Our most loyal customer beats Reggie to any kind of action. "There's no way my charity extends to giving freebies away to that prize-winning plonker. He didn't even remove his cap when he set foot in here. This is a traditional English seaside pier establishment, I'll have you know."

"If it's traditional, then why is *she* ripping off the Portuguese?" says the pantomime baddie, magically coming back to life at Frank's words.

"She? *She?* Wash your mouth out, young man and refrain from the use of pronouns in this café. The lady has a name. The lady is called Ms Schofield, for your information."

I am told that I have cute, pixie-like looks, a slightly upturned nose, naturally full brows, my own set of dimples, and a rosebud mouth – besides my penchant for extraordinary hair-dos and my mismatched eyes, which we've already covered. Just for a fleeting moment, before the blithering idiot turns to leave the café, I can feel the chaos of the scene melting away all around us as he drinks in every one of my features. Like I say, the sensation washes over me so quickly that I can't be sure I haven't imagined it, but it is enough to make me want to scream for doing the exact same thing myself, and gawping at him, too. This isn't some enemies-to-lovers movie scene, no matter how undeniably gorgeous the grump in my sights might be. This is real life. My life. And this is a real jerk, made of flesh and blood, who has stormed his way into my pride and joy of a café and sought to full-on, no-holds-barred destroy it.

Frank's words have not had the desired effect, and they buoy the guy up to scurry off with his prize, mumbling under his breath. I have no doubt that the tarts will be dumped in the nearest bin on the pier's walkway. At least the seagulls will be happy.

I stagger backwards and take several deep breaths to compose myself. Although I can hear the café coming back to life, my spatial awareness can't seem to move from the door and the older man standing next to me. Meanwhile my blood is roaring in my ears.

"I'm sorry, Frank." I say as I turn to him. "I... I just thought that maybe if he sampled a little of what we're doing here, the things our customers love... maybe we could persuade him to change his mind. A short, sharp shock. A good shock." I sigh in defeat. "I tried not to show it, but I'm deeply concerned about any tricks he may have up his sleeve. He had no qualms about causing a scene in front of a café full of customers. Who knows what he'll stop at? I was desperate. I had to do something."

Frank is silent and now I fear I have already lost my very best customer.

A trio of twenty-somethings meanders over to give me a sympathetic pat on the back.

"That was delicious! Check out TripAdvisor later," they tell me with a wink, and what I hope I can interpret as a medley of belly-satisfied grins.

I wilt onto a seat, watching them walk out of the door. Reggie instructs me to stay put while he fixes me a coffee, whilst Tim cleans up the floor. In a funny kind of way, we all have each other's backs.

"I've upset you good and proper, haven't I, Frank?" I can hardly stand to look at the disappointment etched on his face.

"I can only reiterate how sorry I am. You did make it clear that whoever the tarts were gifted to needed to be a worthy candidate. My gut instinct was way off the mark there."

"Don't be daft, lovie," Frank finally replies with a shake of his head. He pulls up the seat opposite me and sits down. "It was just one of those things. You handled it better than my Millie would have, that's for sure." Frank lets out a wistful chuckle. "Whenever our boys used to pilfer the cake out of the kitchen tin when they thought she wasn't looking, she'd flick her tea towel and nip their bottoms good and proper. She had such a great aim! You hadn't a hope in hell if you were a buzzing bluebottle fly."

"Sounds like they should have invented an Olympic sport just for Millie."

"She'd have won gold every time. Mind, she had a heart of gold too."

"May I ask why you refer to her in the past tense, Frank? If it's not being too inquisitive."

"Not today, Willow. I'm still processing my feelings... even if it has taken a fair few years. But I'm getting there bit by bit. We'll chat about it soon though, on a quieter afternoon."

"Of course, and I'm sorry for bringing it up."

"Not at all. The strangest of situations can trigger all sorts of random memories. And this one came courtesy of a man who can only be described as the world's most self-entitled git. It's quite remarkable really!"

Frank smiles and I have to acknowledge that the world truly does work in mysterious ways. I won't press him about Millie who, it's clear to me, must have passed away several years ago. And though I'm curious about his offspring and their whereabouts, I won't question him about them either. I'm just relieved the café is offering Frank the opportunity to reminisce and open up. How dare an uppity *pastel de nata* purist try to take that away? Who are we harming here with our little creative outlet? The guy said it himself, we are tucked away at the end of the pier, for goodness sake. I'm hardly touting my wares under the flashing lights of the amusement arcade...

WHAT AN OBNOXIOUS git!

Of course I can think of stronger words but swearing has never been my style. When one wants to use lexicography to highlight someone else's flaws, my wordsmith friend Reggie has taught me that there are more than enough adjectives and nouns to describe today's uninvited guest and his behaviour: mumpsimus, philodox and pish-monger all spring to mind.

And staying on the *of course* theme, now the perfect comeback enters my head (of course): that gold-framed Cristiano Ronaldo endorsement of custard, which is gracing the washbasin area of the loos. Why didn't I think to unhook it from its nail and show it to the idiot when he was snubbing my custard pairings? If his beloved Ronaldo thinks custard goes well enough with a fruit crumble, then as far as I'm concerned, that's carte blanche for me to create and sell (and for the customers to enjoy) every single custard tart variety on our shelves.

Blimming hindsight! Who invented a notion so useless?

I'm willing to bet it was a man.

I cheer myself up by remembering the two young women and the lad from earlier. It's either intrepid or delusional to follow up their request and visit the TripAdvisor website, but now I'm back home I can't resist taking a look anyway – because things can hardly get any worse – and I let out a giddy gasp as I read through the cluster of five-star recommendations listed under The Custard Tart Café, Weston-super-Mare. Not only have they, as individuals, taken the time to give the thumbs-up to my pastries and the venue (with some idyllic snapshots to boot), but I'm willing to guess they have chivied along every single customer present this morning to do the same. Even the sexist hi-vis jacket brigade!

I want to reply to every gorgeous comment with my heartfelt thanks but I know I need to keep things looking authentic. So many five star entries on the same day is a little suspicious, to say the least. I hope and I pray that those three guardian angel customers haven't unwittingly and telepathically shared their idea with the man whose shoddy behaviour has caused this giant act of kindness. The last thing I need is him adding his tuppence-worth to TripAdvisor, too. And now I am back to fretting over his snide remarks and those parting words of warning. Because that's what us creatives always do: forget all the wonderful, positive feedback, and zone in obsessively on the hater we failed to convince, stewing over their critique, wondering if we could have swayed them to like our little piece of art even a little bit.

It's several hours after the event and I am holding onto my cold cup of Ovaltine for dear life, staring vacantly out of the window, the magical twilight wasted on me. This is

Callum all over again. This is Rufus all over again. This is every time anybody has ever dissed my impulsiveness, innovation, and individuality all over again. *I can't do this.* Even in spite of the high praise. I will just have to see out the lease, give everybody notice, and return to a life of working behind the scenes; the life I was clearly destined for.

CHAPTER FOUR

I WAKE WITH a start, my temples beaded in perspiration. I wouldn't mind if this was thanks to a sex marathon (real or in a dream-like state, with a man as delectable as Antonio flipping Banderas, whose younger carbon copy in a certain marketing department is making my sister increasingly horny, and whom said sister can't seem to stop texting me about). Here's a summary of this morning's messages from Lauren:

Had a right moment with you-know-who in the uber narrow communal kitchen just now! Such a shame he needed to squeeeeeeeeze past me to get to the fridge while I was helping myself to coffee.

Making her own hot drink. Now that had to be a first...

But, OMG, even better than that was when the little hottie transformed himself from his work clothes into his football kit ready for evening training last night. Phwoar, what a bod, Bonsai! Those calves could give Jack Grealish a run for his money. Jamie was in our office at the time, and I have to say, I think it'll only be a matter of time before he ends up separating us. Boo! Antonio's playing it cool for now and barely takes any notice of me, despite the fact I am technically his boss in the

*hierarchical sense. Majorly green-eyed vibes perme-
ating the airwaves from my hubs, though he's
surrounded by young and pretty twenty-somethings
on his floor. Still, not one of them can compete with
the cool, calm gorgeousness of the new boy, and
doesn't Jamie know it? LOL.*

At least a couple of black coffees will have sobered her up.
That is something. Whilst her obsession with a certain
Hollywood star's body double seems to be growing by the day
(surely she's worked out the name of the new guy in the office
by now) thankfully there are no more outlandish mentions of
marketing campaigns starring Jen, Dave and *Friends*.

Come to think of it, now I stop to reflect on yesterday's
shenanigans, the jumped-up idiot who burst into the café
might have had a little something Antonio Banderas about
him, too. I can't put my finger on what, but he definitely put
me in mind of the actor – in his *Zorro* days, that is, not so
much as Shrek's nemesis, *Puss in Boots*. All of which is neither
here nor there, because my current physical state is the result
of something I thought I'd long ago put to bed; that
terrifyingly brutal recurring dream.

School play evening. The spring of my GCSEs. The
hopelessly amateur production of Bugsy Malone. I told you
I'd reveal all when the time was right. I guess home alone in
my bed on a Sunday morning is the readiest I'll ever be. I sniff
and grab a handful of the boxed tissues that are patiently
waiting on my bedside cabinet. Isn't it pathetic, the way a
distant childhood memory can pervade your adult life? A
shadow you can't outrun. It lurks ready to pounce when you
least suspect it. Unexpected stressful situations seem to trigger

it, and what with yesterday being up there on the EPIC level of tense, I know I am now in for several nights of torture. I really should see a hypnotherapist. Kelly would love that, not that I have ever shared this recurring nightmare with anyone in the waking world, it's bad enough reliving the real life events in my sleep. Or maybe I should sign myself up for some neuro-linguistic programming. But there are never enough hours in the day, and it usually stops soon enough by itself.

Anyway, where was I? Eugh, yes, my secondary school, Sandy Bay High, and its *eau de* boiled cabbage corridors. Sounds like something out of Grease, doesn't it? Although the fictional American high school would definitely fare better in the fragrance stakes, no doubt doused in the fruity nectar of bubblegum. But back to Bugsy Malone – I'd wanted to land the role for so long. No, not playing the main man,· nor dolling myself up as Tallulah opposite some luscious Bugsy. The role I'd crossed my fingers and toes for was *way* more exciting than that: spotlighting the stage, painting the background tableaux, sourcing and creating the twenties era props, swiping the mounds of costume-sewing out of the hands of the volunteering yet ungratefully grumbling mums. Aka my idea of bliss.

Instead I'd been lumbered with various doormat-style tasks; handing out programmes to the audience on arrival, plying Damian, our bossy scruff of a stage manager with cups of tea and biscuits, running between the dressing rooms to test my fellow student starlets on their lines before they made their stage appearances, and selling raffle tickets and ice cream to the hordes in the foyer during the interval. Then came the *pièce de résistance*: securing the painfully amateur art deco scenery in place before the opening scene of Act Two, and Tallulah's infamous song.

As usual, it took a little brute force to slot the giant clips into place at the left side of the stage. They weren't the best scenery boards, admittedly, but it was as far as the school's budget would go. I'd been briefed once and had demonstrated my competence twice, in an ordinary rehearsal, and then in the all-important dress rehearsal. But the clips on the right side were playing up big time tonight, our opening night. I was really going to have to give it some welly to wedge the damned things in place, or I'd be holding the scenery up by sheer willpower alone, until somebody else backstage cottoned on to my dilemma.

But those clips weren't the only thing playing up...

I tried to ignore the sensation at first, as I stood there, arms outstretched, trying to anchor the painted backdrop. The thrum of the expectant crowd behind the mock velvet red curtains built in intensity. The unusually oppressive late spring heat did nothing to help, a lone bead of sweat trickling down my temple. I watched Tallulah sashay into her place ready to belt out her number, I held my breath as the curtains opened on the fast-paced second half of the show. I waited for the orchestra to strike up the first notes of Talullah's solo, and I winced as Tallulah pursed her luscious red lips ahead of her lyrical outburst. I watched and I waited until I could take it no more. I just had to do something about that pesky, errant strand of hair and the way it wouldn't quit tickling my cheek. I carried out a quick mental calculation: *Could I?* Yeah, piece of cake! *But would my reflexes be quick enough?* They had to be!

No way was I going to be able to carry on like this for the next twenty minutes or so. It was one thing to hold the backdrop for an important scene in place with two hands. It was quite another to do that with a piece of hair irritating the life out of you. Besides which, I had not so much a stage to keep up, but a reputation to upkeep: the art of the flawlessly creative hair-do.

And that's when calamity struck. In slow motion. I needed both hands to unfasten the clip in my hair (the accessory that was currently holding up most of my Heidi milkmaid braids) and capture the stray strand, securing it back into place. For some unknown reason, my pea-sized brain had visualised me carrying out said hair maintenance move in a single, fluid motion before letting go of the giant stage panel. When faced with a split second decision between saving my hair-do or the show, there was never any question about my loyalty: the hair came first. I guess I figured the panel would just balance there on a knife edge for a second or two, patiently waiting for my attention to return to it, or at least one of my hands to grip it.

The point of no return dawned. Hair now secured, I lunged at the panel in vain, much too late to stop it catching Lauren sharply on the back of the head (Yeah, I couldn't bring myself to reveal Lauren played Tallulah until this point... Too painful, in every sense of the word!).

Our parents were in the front row of the audience. They captured the entire sequence of events on video camera, as if it was happening to another family and we might have a fabulous opportunity here to send the offending tape off to one of those TV shows that rewards you with two hundred and fifty pounds for sharing your hilarious hiccup with the nation. Dad adored that VCR recorder. Dad had no shame.

Even at the point when Caitlyn ran onto the stage to hug both of her big sisters and check we were okay, just as the flutist broke out in a spontaneously comical melody, still he kept the lens steady, capturing everything for posterity. I was sprawled out, face down, like a starfish by that point, but ever the selfless sister, Caitlyn didn't let that deter her from going in for a cuddle of teddy bear proportions. Meanwhile, the laughter levels in the school gym were off the chart. Lauren pushed Caitlyn away as she ran to her aid next, not before screaming, "How dare you ruin my moment like this?" at me at record decibels, and howling her way stage left, rubbing her head. I couldn't blame her then for reacting like that and I can't blame her now – although for obvious reasons, we never bring it up. She'd spent months preparing for her big moment and my impulsive behaviour had ruined it all. Damian's face was thunder, hair poking out in every compass direction as he pinned his eyes on my guilty face from the wings and my stage peers flocked around him to shake their heads in disgust.

"You had one job!"

I may not have heard Damian but I could lip read well enough, even if I was still impersonating a sea creature, flat out on the stage.

"You're a failure and a disgrace!"

"You've let the whole cast and crew down!"

The last thing I recall about that fateful night is my dear father (and this part is so wholly embarrassing, it's almost worse than my initial *faux pas*), marching up the steps to gather his girls in his arms, VCR still gripped in one hand. He turned to the audience to say, "Show's over, guys! You've had your laughs." But the curtains went down on his head, toppling him into the orchestra pit and onto the lap of the cellist, giving the throng one final, hearty guffaw.

It goes without saying that returning to school the follow-ing day was a scene plucked straight out of a Brothers Grimm book. "It'll be fine," Dad had assured me. "Like getting back on a bike after your first fall. You'll soon forget it ever happened and so will everybody else."

But I didn't – and nor did they. Naturally, Lauren didn't speak to me for weeks. And every one of my classmates turned on me, too. Even my best friends succumbed to the peer pressure and shunned me for days. And all of that was without anyone knowing the real reason behind me letting go of the scenery! I swear they'd have put scissors to my braids if I'd ever been foolish enough to reveal the truth.

If only my nightmare had stopped there. But history took it upon itself to give my teachers, fellow students and their parents a repeat performance later that summer term, and sadly I couldn't blame Damian's ineptitude as stage manager this time.

What can I say? There must have been something in the air. There was definitely something in my hair. Terribly bad joke at my expense. I guess I'm just trying – in vain, and in hindsight – to see the lighter side of the crappiest school term imaginable.

Now I may not have been an Olympian in the making, but I could knock out an impressive sprint when circumstance required. And the preparations for the annual summer sports day meant it did. As had long been tradition, the four school houses competed on the patchy green school fields to discover who would reign supreme, holding the shiny fake gold cup aloft on the podium by the cricket pitch amidst cheers of jubilation from a euphoric crowd.

Students battled it out in the athletic disciplines of track and field. Javelins were launched torpedo-style, shot puts were hurled with aplomb and long jumps were nailed, with new school records achieved in a number of age groups. Then came the finale and my part; the part which would put my schoolhouse (Tide) ahead of the perennial favourites (Rock). Yes, the four school houses had been baptised with the most imaginative of names way back when at the school's formation: Tide, Rock, Pier, and Sand. I guess they still embody Weston-super-Mare's chief characteristics, overlooking wannabe Ferris wheels and custard tarts…

I was number four in the relay team. I waited in my crucial spot with my fellow competitors, willing myself to think of nothing but the impending baton exchange with faster-than-lightning Fay Fox, relay team member number three. We'd practised our brisk handover every lunchtime that week. We knew it like the back of our hands – pun not intended but perfect. And I tried to ignore the encroaching irritation that threatened to knock me out of the all-important athlete's zone of concentration. But I'm sure you know how the story goes by now. A gust of wind came from nowhere and a wisp of hair escaped that sunny June afternoon's hairstyle. Can you believe I had made the fatal mistake of wearing Heidi milkmaid braids again? No, neither can I. I'm sure it comes as no surprise to learn it was their very last outing.

Even Dad refrained from charging to my rescue this time.

Only Caitlyn squeezed me hard later that day, after mopping my tears as I lay on my bed and stared wordlessly at the ceiling, hoping it might reveal why I had made the same mistake again.

"I get it," she'd tried to console me. "It's like... if one of my Barbies has a sticky-outy bit in her ponytail, I'll undo the whole lot immediately and start again and everything else will just have to wait. Even if Mum calls me for chocolate chip cookies or there's something amazing on TV."

"It's sweet of you to say so, little sis... but these things shouldn't even enter a person's brain when they're supposed to be focused on the vital task of grabbing a baton at the key point in a relay race, and their school house is currently tied with the favourites, so their very actions determine whether this year Tide might finally seize the victory. And they shouldn't cross their minds when they're supposed to be propping up a giant scenery frame on the opening night of a school play, either."

"Well, there should have been someone helping you with that scenery," Caitlyn sprang, as ever, to my defence. "And I'm not just saying that 'cos you're a girl and most boys have stronger muscles.... Or 'cos you're my sister and I love you. That Damian's a big stinky turd. He's lucky I didn't kick him in the arse."

Caitlyn had been right on that front. Damian was a dowfart; another word that had sprung up in conversations with Reggie ref. my poor choice of boyfriends (modern day translation: a lazy, useless sod). There should have been someone else there to help me the first time, but the second time my absent-mindedness couldn't be put down to coincidence.

If only both events that frightful summer had been a dream, like the bad one I'd just woken up from. But I couldn't even brush over things by calling myself clumsy. And nobody could label my obsession with my hairstyling as OCD. That is a whole different matter, a very complex different matter, which is all too often misdiagnosed and trivialised. At least on the dark stage I could run into the wings after my mishap. Out there on the open field, I was guilty as charged. Nowhere to run and nowhere to hide.

"And the legend does it again!"

That was Damian, who'd taken it upon himself to dart around me like the most annoying mosquito as I hobbled back to the changing rooms, head down.

"You had one job!"

And that was from my teammates, every single member of Tide from every single school year, the PE teacher, and Lauren – every single hour of every single day until the bell rang out for the holidays. Damian's catchphrase from the catastrophic Wednesday night production of Bugsy had caught on so beautifully, that 'you had one job' became my new name – often abbreviated to YHOJ for short. Even when I returned to study for my BTEC the next year. I could still hear the chorus of cackling kids as the teachers reached Willow Schofield on their registers.

I swear Caitlyn and I have a telepathic thing going on. My heart skips a beat as my phone rings, bringing me back to the relative cocoon of the present, and Caitlyn's name and number flash up. I take a deep breath. I'm grateful that I'm not still sitting at a wooden desk and using my exercise book as a tent to bury my head, from the shame I failed to live down until the day I walked out of the school gates for good. I look at the clock in my kitchen instead, realising I really don't have time to answer this call since I'm already running late for work.

But then I remember it's Sunday. Tim's running the kitchen on his own today. I feel guilty at getting him to shoulder that responsibility, without us knowing just how busy June's first weekend might be, but I let it ebb away. Technically this is the work call I should have made to Caitlyn when I came to my senses last night, anyway. I'm not cut out for running my own business and I need to let my sister know this morning, before she feels settled and sees this stint at the end of the pier as an annual thing. I need to let her down very gently and explain. This will be her one and only summer working at TCTC.

CHAPTER FIVE

IT DOESN'T TAKE long for Frank and me to have our quiet afternoon together. The post-lunch exodus, plus the pre-school pick-up lull, have left me with a virtually empty café. I can't say I mind. It's only mid-June but business has been relentless and it's a breath of fresh air – quite literally – to stand outside at the pier's edge and grab great lungfuls of sea breeze (and smaller intervals of sunshine) between serving a handful of customers. I don't even care if the gusts tangle today's bouffant 'power' ponytail.

"I'll fight tooth and nail over this blasted petition. How dare that arrogant so-and-so pull a stunt like this?" Frank cries, as he loops his arm through mine and escorts me back inside to the warmth of the café. He's arrived later than usual today for his tri-weekly visit, and it's as if he senses the place will be peaceful enough now for a confessional too.

"I'm not sure there's much you or anyone can do, Frank," I finally reply from my harbour behind the counter, weary of going round and round in circles over the subject that has rattled all of us for days. It just seems easier to admit defeat.

Now that I'm back inside the café, if somebody chooses to walk in and pelt me with grenades of verbal abuse, I can simply duck beneath my shelves of tarts and hide myself from view – or fly into the kitchen and lock the door. Reggie can cope with the workload, king of multitasking that he is, and Tim is sufficiently briefed on all things customer service to step in when things get mega busy.

I splay my (clean) fingertips across the countertop and, in a bid to convince Frank that battle is futile, I shrug my shoulders. They droop back into the slovenly position they've adopted (along with my downturned mouth) since a certain envelope containing a certain document slid itself under the café door. Quite why I bothered to fix my hair in today's feisty style, I don't know. The illusion of all that extra volume is pointless and does nothing to make me feel taller and braver.

"Although I do appreciate the sentiment," I add belatedly as I reach across the counter to pat Frank on the arm, before placing his customary three-tiered cake stand before him and setting to, adorning it with tasty treats. "The thing is, I'm a new business, an unknown quantity to the pier. Believe me, the last thing the management wants here is controversy, especially at such an important time of the year – and that's exactly what I've landed them with, regardless of who is at fault. I'm so decidedly out of my depth. I wouldn't even know where to start to challenge anything. I don't have the energy to think about it, either."

And I truly am in it up to my neck. My location at the very end of the pier is really rather symbolic in that respect.

"There was just something about that guy." I say. "He knew exactly what he was doing the day he came in, every move mapped out in advance as if he was playing that Battleships board game that my dad always tried to get us to join in with at Christmas." Frank nods in agreement, as if he's played it a few times himself. "I never stood a chance. If I'm honest, the petition to close us down hasn't even taken me by surprise."

Frank's brow creases, making him look unnecessarily ancient, and far too frail to tussle with anyone – in or out of a frigate.

He starts feistily enough, slapping his hand on the counter and saying he's not having it. "We'll fight on your behalf. I'll rally around more support than you'd think possible, lovie, to counter this ridiculous threat. The entire Somerset fire brigade for starters. These custard tarts of yours have the same cosy quality about them as a bowl of crumble and custard. That's what my beautiful Millie served me when I came home from my nightshift after... aft... af..."

But Frank is unable to continue with his story. His eyes water. My heart can't take this. I feel tears pricking and threatening to trickle from my own eyes. All I want to do is wrap him up in cotton wool and make everything better.

Maybe I should just get Lauren on board. She's definitely a bruiser. I'm sure that she'd have ideas to counter this unwarranted attack – some more orthodox than others. But I'm so fed up with her seeing me as accident-prone, someone she has to tower over like a protective pine tree. This was my time to shine. Aside from Muse Masters lending a helping hand with the marketing, I want to stand on my own two feet. I want to ignore the aggrieved words that idiot and Cristiano the pseudo-poodle pushed under the door; to call their bluff and carry on regardless – or to call time on my venture on my own terms. But the last thing I am prepared to do is add fuel to a fire and fight the stern words of the petition.

"I knew it was a sign when I read about this place of yours

in the local newspaper." Frank takes a measured breath. "It called me back, you see. There's something so comforting and grounding in the no-nonsense custard tart – even if you do jolly yours up a bit." I grin widely at that. "I couldn't quite walk all the way down here the first day you opened up – even with my cane for support. I had to hop on the pier train just to make the pilgrimage. But now I'm feeling strong enough to walk the whole way *every* time I visit you. That's a marvellous feeling, Willow. The panic doesn't engulf me like it used to. I've left the bad parts of the past in the past. That's the power of custard."

Frank chuckles lightly, before completely changing his tone. "And now that bastard thinks he can badmouth you, Reggie and Tim and your lovely pastries off the seafront. Well, he can damn well think again."

"Frank!"

Call me conformist, but I'm shocked to hear the strong swear word flying out of my friend's mouth. This is not the sweet-natured man I've come to know pretty well over the past month and a bit.

"Apologies for the cuss word. It doesn't suit the establishment, and I'm sorry. At least nobody else heard me, hey?" He scans the café behind him in case a customer should be hiding. "But he has no right to do this to you, or your customers. He has no idea how special this place is. He's just trying to be a food snob, like one of those stuck-up critics on television. Well, he's chosen the wrong place."

"Shall we?"

I gesture at the table nearest the counter, so I can dive back behind the scenes quickly if need be. Frank and I take a seat. Intuitively as ever, Reggie appears from the kitchen where he's been chatting with Tim. He fixes us up with a pair of teas and puts the finishing touches to Frank's assortment of tarts, carrying them over to us.

"You go first."

Frank nods at the tarts, and although I really shouldn't be pilfering my customer's order, I know it's the only way I will find out more about his backstory, so I plump for a rhubarb and custard, whilst Frank zones in on the rum and custard revelation, my latest joint creation with Tim. To my knowledge, Frank's not yet sampled this fusion of flavours and I find myself on the edge of my seat, in anticipation of both his story and his verdict.

It turns out that Frank adores the pairing of custard and alcohol, and it also turns out he was a firefighter in the local squad that dealt with the tragic Weston-super-Mare pier fire of 2008. He retired straight after. Although he'd dealt with many fires in his time, and all of the loss those fires entailed, the horror of seeing the building he'd so loved as a child go up in a fireball was devastating.

"You go through so much training as a firefighter. I thought I could get past it without counselling. And the last thing I wanted to do was open up to my family. How can you explain to them what you've experienced? Raking it all over again would only make them feel wretched, too. So I bottled it up instead. Of course, now I know better. A problem halved and all that."

I nod sadly. I can't imagine how mentally tough one has to be to join the fire service, let alone to tackle such an emotive blaze. It must have been a race against time, not only to save lives and livelihoods, but also precious memories.

"Fifty-two million, they spent on the pier's reconstruction. As far as I'm concerned, Willow, this café is an integral part of the phoenix rising from the flames."

Frank's words give me goosebumps.

"Wow. I did a lot of homework prior to setting up here, but I'd no idea the transformation had cost that much."

"Oh, yes. It took them the best part of two years to rebuild it."

This part I did know, but I don't admit it because I want to help Frank to help himself, to halve his problem by sharing it with me, to give himself a little more closure. I watch as Frank dives in for a plum and bay custard tart. We don't tend to sell so many of these to the younger crowd, but Frank and his generation are nothing if not adventurous.

"Well, then comes the saddest part of the story. The pier always meant my Millie to me. A weekly visit to the Grand Pier was part of my life growing up, and it's the very place where I met my sweetheart. Her mother used to be a cleaner here, whilst her father was in charge of the change booth, dishing out tokens, when he wasn't attending to various carpentry jobs along the boardwalk. I first saw Millie when she was enjoying the attractions with her brothers and sisters."

I take a cautious sip at my tea, even though I know it's not hot. Frank is like a fawn that could skitter away in these tender moments, and I don't want to distract him from getting his story off his chest. I sense that he needs to.

"Back then it was billed as the finest covered amusement park in the world. Which would make any teenager from 2021 piss themselves with laughter, in this age of instant gratification from YouTube, TikTok and Xbox – oh, I know all the terminology from my grandkids and our Skype calls." I smile at Frank, encouraging him to continue at his own pace, wondering where his grandchildren live if they have to video call one another.

"Even twenty years ago, that lofty claim would have seemed ridiculous," he continues. "What with Disney theme parks scattered all over the globe and daredevil roller coasters everywhere, but that was how small our world was in the early sixties. We lived in a big little snowglobe. It was more than enough for us. The excitement over progress was palpable. We valued everything and took nothing for granted. Things really seemed to be coming along in leaps and bounds, and the pier was our barometer for that, in a funny way. Games were upgraded, Wall's ice cream added new lollies to their menu, and as a fifteen-year-old lad in '63, I certainly appreciated a good-looking girl. I spotted Millie, next to the Laughing Sailor. Ugly thing it was. Out of all the romantic places you'd like to imagine first meeting your one true love, it is not next to a freaky-looking, coin-operated mannequin and his annoying peals of laughter. But there we have it. Somehow I swept Millie off her feet with a corny joke about the monstrosity, and it was me who had the last laugh, that old mariner never got a look in."

Frank stops to take a breath and catch up with his tart, so I re-fill our tea cups to give him a moment.

"It's an unusual meeting point – but as good a place as any for love to blossom!" I acknowledge.

"We swiftly moved on to the slot machines, chatting all the while," he continues. "And that's where I came into a little windfall, meaning I could treat us both to fish and chips on the beach. I guess she decided then that I was a keeper."

"Aw. I don't blame her, Frank, and I'm sure it was more than the money and the al fresco dining Millie was attracted to."

"Oh, ay. I guess I was a looker myself back in the day." Frank winks.

I sweep the flaky remnants of my tart to the side of my plate. I really should get back to work. Tim and I have a couple of *avant garde* fillings to experiment with this afternoon. One of them is so 'extra' that just the thought of putting it out for sale and a certain somebody deciding to barge back in here as if he owns the place, makes me want to cackle like a witch. It's unlikely I'll ever have the 'pleasure' of communicating with him in person again though. No, viciously typed words seem to be more his style...

"And that was our routine as we started courting." Frank draws me back into his tale. "Not the gambling, but taking a stroll on the pier on a Saturday night. Every time we walked those boards together, I felt more and more blessed at my good fortune. Never mind those arcade games, Millie was the real jackpot. The way those single lads out on the pull looked at us, I knew they were envious. It was just so lovely to wrap ourselves up in the nostalgia of that first encounter, every time we stepped out on the pier." Frank sighed, caught up in the memory. "We did it for years. We did it with the babies as they turned into boys, then loveable rogues, then husbands, then parents themselves. We did it for decades. We did it until the fire."

"Oh, Frank."

"I know you'd like to hear that we continued to do it after that awful day, after the pier was rebuilt. But sadly my Millie never got to see the end result. She passed in her sleep a week after we'd put the blaze out. The same week I retired. I know it was the fire that did it. Left her broken-hearted."

What do you say to that? Clearly Millie had loved the pier as if it were an actual family member, understandable really when she'd spent so much time with Frank and her boys there, and when it had provided her parents with the means to bring her and her siblings up.

"Everything changed after that. Peter and Paul – my sons, *our* sons – ran a very successful magazine business together in Bath. Millie's death, and my retirement, happened just a couple of months after they were given a golden opportunity to open up offices in Dubai, taking their wives with them. The business was too precarious to move back. Now they come over to visit when they can and they bring my five grandchildren, of course. But it's once a year at best. I don't hold it against them. They have their own lives to live."

"Could you visit them there once or twice a year, too?"

"I gave it a go, but I can't stand the heat in that part of the world, Willow. Truth be told, it reminds me of the intensity of a fire. I know they're all kitted out in the Emirates with state of the art air conditioning, in their giant luxury penthouses. But there's not much for somebody like me to do there, beyond sit inside and watch television or read. Nowhere in particular for me to potter about, or wander off to, without succumbing to heatstroke. Granted, it was good to see their set-up for myself, but all that opulence isn't for me. I'm a man of simple comforts. One night their live-in cook-stroke-nanny served us all up some kind of pudding topped with gold flakes that you could eat! If memory serves me correctly, it was only a Monday teatime and nobody was celebrating a birthday. It was very pretty, but as you and I know, nothing rivals a fuss-free custard tart."

"Except maybe a fuss-free custard tart with a bit of a surprise filling."

We both laugh at that. Never a truer word spoken.

Now Frank is off home again. My selfish wish has been granted, and I now understand my friend's backstory a little more. I know why nostalgia swept over him the first day he set foot in this place, and I understand what drives him to want to rip the petition – and its owner – to pieces. But I still can't find the motivation to raise my own proverbial fists. It'll be soul-destroying enough if the petition gets the right number of signatures to carry any legal weight.

"This is ridiculous!" Reggie had said a week earlier, waving the papers around in the air as if they were flags (thankfully the café was empty at the time). "It... or rather, *he*, let's not kid ourselves, cites 'an infringement of *geographical indications and traditional specialities*' as his gripe. He's saying it's misleading for us to let people think these are authentic Portuguese custard tarts. Next he'll be accusing the beach of trying to mimic the Algarve."

"And what part of The Custard Tart Café says Portugal in it, exactly?" I cried. "When have I ever claimed these are Portuguese per se? Where am I hanging the country's flag, either inside or outside of these premises?"

Damn and blast those blue and white tiles for turning up at all...

"Exactly, *exactly*!" Reggie's expression matches my outrage. "In any case, custard was probably invented by the Romans, they often added eggs to milk to thicken it. It's mentioned in Apicius." Sensing how lost I am, Reggie adds: "You know, the ancient Roman cookbook that was supposedly put together in the first century AD...."

Is there anything my friend doesn't know about the literary world?

"We aren't attempting to do anything controversial, like make our own version of Cheddar cheese," I add. "For crying out loud. Can't the man stop at humiliating me in front of a full café? To think that I gave him those complimentary tarts as well."

"Legally, we probably could make Cheddar cheese as the town of Cheddar is only ten miles away."

"You know what I mean." I shake my head in exasperation. "And I doubt even Cheddar would bat an eyelid in protest if we did. Canada gets away with it, after all."

"Canada doesn't claim their Cheddar is West Country Farmhouse Cheddar, though. That's the rub with the PDO." I shrug in response. Reggie is a walking encyclopedia. "That's foods with Protected Designation of Origin."

"Oh, Reggie, please stop taking us off on tangents! It's not helping me think straight."

"I'm sorry, Willow. I'm just trying to make light of his crazy idea. He hasn't got a leg to stand on. You must realise that?"

Well, that was Reggie's initial verdict, but he, like me, hadn't read many petitions at this point. No sooner had he done some homework on my behalf than Reggie assured me it was, in fact, a properly worded petition, not like some of the cobbled-together examples one might find floating around Facebook and Twitter. Nevertheless, the easiest thing for me to do is to go with the flow and stick to the path of least resistance. Aka bury half my head in the sand. Not literally. Although it has been tempting recently, with the beach on my doorstep.

Pants, though, isn't it? If only someone had warned me this is how it would all pan out, I would never have embarked on my custard adventure.

Anyway, Caitlyn took things remarkably well when I spoke with her a couple of days ago on the phone. You've got to love her Pollyanna optimism. "It will all come out in the wash," she said. "It always does." It's a nice sentiment but it also depends on The Opinionated Git not getting us closed down first.

I haven't yet got round to telling Reggie and Tim that their services soon won't be required. I just can't bring myself to do it. I'm guessing they think it's coming in any case. That wretched petition is a curse that's changed everything. Like Frank's story, it's doused the embers of the fire I had in me with ice cold water.

The dream is over.

CHAPTER SIX

A FRANTIC RAP at the door jolts me from my James Martin (recipe) binge – I wouldn't get up to open *any* door if I had the human version of my favourite male chef sitting on the sofa next to me. I open my apartment door to a pair of pacing Nike Airs, which would be put to better use on a basketball court. My eyes run the length of the man moving in front of me, taking in Reggie's troubled face beneath his mass of swinging dreadlocks, now set free from his work up-do. He's clad in his sports top and jeans as opposed to the more customary blue, white, and gold TCTC T-shirt.

"It's lovely to see you, Reggie, but couldn't it wait until the morning?"

If he wasn't such a longstanding friend, and with such a gorgeous girlfriend, I might have thought Reggie fancied me, randomly showing up like this of an evening.

"I've got a trio of things to tell you and none of them can wait until tomorrow when we're in the café," he says.

Crikey. I have genuinely no idea what this is all about and my stomach can't help but catapult at the possibilities.

"Well… er, since you put it so eloquently, you'd better come in."

I pull the door fully open, switch off the Prince track that's playing in the background and hope Reggie won't mind the mess. Not that it's anything of student proportions, but Reggie's house is immaculate. He still lives with his parents, but it's Reggie who vacuums the place twice a day, and it's Reggie who polishes tables and ornaments until you can see your face in them. Reggie is basically every woman's dream.

"I couldn't do this with a call, before you ask." Yikes. Whatever *is* up? He hovers next to the sofa and I realise he's waiting for me to move a heap of dog-eared cookery books – one of which is currently showing a rather graphic image of the TV chef James Martin looking at butter as if he'd like to take it to bed. I snap it shut quickly. Talk about being caught in the act with (food) porn. "And a WhatsApp voicemail message just wouldn't suffice," Reggie explains as he takes a seat.

Thank goodness for that. I've had my fill of those recently.

"So, you remember I told you about my weekend football match?" He leans forward and steeples his fingers. In a turn of events, I actually go and made a cuppa for him at last, and set it before him.

I vaguely recall Reggie mentioning something about an away fixture against a Bristol team, yes.

"I do. Go on."

"You're never going to believe this, Willow." He raises the mug to his lips and grimaces at the heat, braving it anyway and taking a long sip. "One of the players on the opposition looked suspiciously like the shithead who stormed into the café last week, the one who sprang the petition on us."

I hold my breath for a beat.

"How can you be sure?" My voice is embarrassingly high-pitched and flustered. "H-he had that cap pulled down right over his eyelids the day he came in to stir things up. We only saw half his face and the back of his head, at best."

"Oh, I'm ninety-seven-point-eight-two recurring sure, Willow."

"That's a bit precise, even by your standards. Sugar. I suppose the clues that he liked to kick a ball about were very much on show at the time, although I take it that Cristiano, that poodle of his, wasn't watching the match."

"No sign of the dog, no. But not only did it look like the same bloke, I also noted he was wearing the same childish green watch... until the ref reminded him to take it off: rules of the game and everyone knows that. He didn't look best pleased about it."

I cast my mind back and remember the brightly-hued watch. It didn't exactly go with his outfit then and it would definitely stand out with a football kit. Unless his team habitually dress as frogs.

"The question is: what do you want me to do about it, Willow?" Reggie continues. "I can easily arrange with Kane for him not to have a leg to stand on – or to kick a ball with – the next time my team plays his, here in Weston in approximately four weeks' time."

Reggie is referring to his younger brother, Kane, who has recently taken up professional boxing. I also know Reggie's not really serious. He's having a Reggie daydream moment. I've grown used to these over the years. They happen from time to time and unfortunately he tends to act on them – he's sent off a dozen applications on my behalf (and without my say-so) to programmes like *MasterChef, Ready Steady Cook,*

Great British Bake Off and *Come Dine With Me* (I feel queasy just thinking about the disasters I'd embroil myself in, on any or all of them). It makes Lauren's wild marketing ideas seem almost normal. Although Kane could easily take a swipe at the man causing this headache for all of us, he would never stoop so low, and in the real world Reggie wouldn't dream of asking him to either.

"I don't think violence is the answer, tempting though the fantasy may be. But I am soooo going to be there to spectate and spook him out, play him at his own game. Ha." I laugh at my rubbish joke. "I mean, what are the chances it really was the same guy who came in here that day?"

"Willow, *hello*? We've practically ascertained that with the lurid watch." Reggie's right. It's got to be him, hasn't it? "And well, I found out something else too, something rather juicy. That was point number two out of three, which I was about to tell you. I don't suppose you have any biscuits to go with this tea? I feel the need to dunk before we get to the next bit."

I sigh and shufty over to the kitchen area of my open-plan apartment, pulling a packet of uninspiring McVitie's Rich Tea from the cupboard. Reggie wrinkles his nose, clearly expecting something flashier.

"Those only allow four seconds of dunk time and taste like cardboard." He shakes his head as if I should know these statistics. "Add shortbread to your next shopping list, to avoid any future upset with your guests."

"It's the best I can muster up at *short* notice." I plonk the goods in front of him and Reggie eases a disc-shaped, paper-thin biscuit out, tutting at another awful joke. "Okay. It sounds as if I need to stand and take a seat again for this bit," I say, and comically, I do. "Are you going to let me in on revelation number two now... or should I add a tot of whisky to my tea to calm my nerves?"

Reggie dunks and consumes three biscuits before he is ready to break the news.

"His name is Tiago. Tiago Willis."

"Fu... uh... udge." I stop myself from saying the swear word that's sitting on the end of my tongue, remembering it's not my style. "I mean heck, that's rather Portuguese sounding! Well, not the surname, obviously... but... it really has to be him, doesn't it?"

"'Fraid so, my friend."

Reggie moves on to Rich Tea numbers four and five, and I tell him to take the packet home with him.

"Okay then." I clap my hands together. "I'm soooo going along to spectate at the home match so I can throw a custard tart in his face."

"Now that's more like it, and a far more acceptable level of violence. I honestly think a scenario with you munching on a takeout box of custard tarts in the stands could prove a big enough threat alone and see him scarpering off the pitch. Failing that, an actual custard pie in the face, in the manner of a practiced and professional circus clown, would make for some excellent journalism opportunities for the local press (and alternative publicity for the café), scaring him off for good from taking any further petition action." Reggie finishes the dregs of his tea. "Job done."

I let out a deep belly laugh. The idea is so perfect it's preposterous.

"I should really tell Lauren. It doesn't feel right to keep

this from her, what with all she and Todd have been doing to help us, but she'll take it to the next level and get the police involved. I know she will. I'm not up for that. If this petition thing is just a lame ploy to slate us all over social media, let him get on with it."

"Erm, Willow?"

"Yes?"

"You might need to do the standing up and taking a seat thing again. The other thing I found out about our mysterious mansplainer will probably come as a bit of a shock."

CHAPTER SEVEN

"What do you mean, he works at Muse Masters?"

But even before I've spat the entire sentence out, everything slots into place. So that's how he knew about the café. But perhaps worse than his underhand behaviour towards his employer (and my brother-in-law) is the fact that he is, without a shadow of a doubt, the 'hot new stuff' that Lauren is currently smitten with. I conjure up his face again from the day he steamrolled into the café and he really does have Antonio Banderas lookalike written *all* over him. Even with his cap pulled down.

What a mess… of Hollywood movie proportions.

"We left the car park after the match at virtually the same time," says Reggie. "But he was too wrapped up in post-match victory to sense anything untoward about my movements. So I took advantage and followed him around Bristol. Just to discover where he lives. Only he didn't go straight home."

I have terrible visions now of Reggie catching the guy in a tryst with my sister, and I await the inevitable revelation that he saw the two of them check into a city hotel together.

"He went to the marketing office in Clifton, where your Lauren works. Yeah, that place you just mentioned: Muse Masters. By the way, the night signage could do with some TLC; a couple of the lightbulbs were out and it looked more like a seedy bar than a sophisticated company. Anyway, I digress." Reggie takes a bite of his umpteenth Rich Tea. "I hung about in the car on the double yellows outside and hoped he wouldn't suddenly recognise me from the café. He came back out again within minutes carrying what looked to be a laptop bag, and taking a few too many glances over his shoulder. I guess he'd forgotten to bring it to training or thought it was safer to pick it up on his way home."

Now I have visions of this Tiago character donning gloves to sneak my sister's laptop out of the building so he can hack into password protected accounts and screw up certain marketing campaigns, although more likely he was simply taking his own laptop home to work on something. But then I recall some of the interim messages that had buzzed through that long night when Lauren was sending me her questionable marketing ideas. She'd apologised they were all via her mobile phone, because Jamie was the world's most paranoid CEO. He expressly banned company laptops leaving the building overnight. He was fine with it during the day, for meetings like the one Lauren had conducted with me at the café. But other than that, he did not want to encourage anybody sharing MM's top secret campaigns... or clients.

"Right. Where did he go after that?" I can't take the suspense.

"I don't know." Reggie waves a new biscuit in exasperation. "That's when the battleaxe of a traffic warden caught me."

Dammit. I really need to know where Tiago lives. How am I supposed to figure that out now?

"Oh, Reggie. I'm so sorry. Let me reimburse you for the

fine."

"Nah, you're all right. I sweet-talked my way out of it with one of those TCTC vouchers you suggested we always carry around with us. She let me off with a caution."

"Good for you!"

Well, that warms the cockles, if nothing else has so far this evening. Not that traffic wardens would be my choice of customer but they have to be fed and watered like the rest of us, I suppose.

"I'll just have to come along to the football match, then." I shrug. It's not like the universe is offering me up a more sensible suggestion. "And I guess I'll have to bring several custard tarts with me in case I miss."

"It would appear so, Willow," Reggie agrees. "If we're to keep Lauren out of this, and you're sure you don't want the police to get involved, then unless a miracle occurs, there's probably nothing else for it."

CHAPTER EIGHT

"OH, HUN!" CAITLYN runs in for a well overdue hug and I fight back the tears, realising how much I have missed my sister. "I can't believe what's been going on." She releases me and holds me at arm's length as if searching my face for damage. The weak sun streams through the window, shining a spotlight on her strawberry blond bob and smattering of freckles, all of which somehow makes her pewter-grey eyes appear emerald. "What an arse. Who is this guy? I'll set my javelin mates on him... and I can get the shot putters involved, too, if need be."

Caitlyn is studying for a sports science degree at Loughborough University. I snuffle back the tears and giggle instead at the vision of my little sister's athletic friends charging after the idiot who is out to destroy my business. It's the second time my allies have suggested a sporty solution to my problem.

"Believe me, I'd give you the nod if I thought we'd get away with it. But there's no sense in all of us watching our dreams go up in smoke, and some of your talented posse are headed for destinies bigger than mine. I'd never forgive myself if I saw them lose their places at the Paris Olympics."

Plus I'm planning to fine tune my own sporting prowess. Oh, yes! You read it here first: custard tart hurling – on a proper bona fide pitch – will soon be the big new thing everyone's training for. There's just the small matter of working out where and how to practice my aim. If only I lived next door to Ten Downing Street...

"True," Caitlyn acknowledges and I have to swallow down another chuckle because she's no idea she's giving the thumbs-up to the crazy thoughts circling my head. "But wouldn't it be satisfying?"

She looks off into the distance as if watching it all unfolding on a television set.

"Anyway, what are you talking about, with the dreams going up in smoke nonsense? Not going to happen under my watch!" Caitlyn is adamant. "What *is* going to happen is we are all going to pull together and work our butts off this summer to make The Custard Tart Café a roaring success. I've seen from the sidelines how much work you've put into making this business happen over the years and there's no going back now. This is a mere obstacle, and, like running water, we shall find a way around it!"

I open my mouth, to point out her wishful thinking may never undo the damage that blasted petition must have caused. But Caitlyn's on a roll, with yet another Schofield sister marketing idea tangent.

"Talking of my uni mates, they're all coming down to Bath next week for summer training – and they'll have the weekend off. You know what that means!"

"Do I?"

This already sounds as dodgy as her earlier suggestion...

"Beach day and carbs!"

"I'm not quite following. Is this some kind of athletics jargon?"

"Think fifteen top athletes descending on Weston-super-Mare, the pier, and most importantly, your café. All with highly active social media accounts in tow. Between them they must have close to a million followers." Caitlyn jumps up and down clapping at her own brilliance. I want to let out a low and sexy whistle myself, but that would be tempting fate. I'd rather put up the bunting *if* this outside-the-box idea is successful.

I guess the odds are in my favour – for once. Fifteen well-connected souls with good intentions, versus one irked idiot and his dogged determination (though Tiago's poodle probably hasn't put a paw print on that pesky petition, even if he was carried along for the ride). It's a battle of wills all right. And maybe, just maybe, it's a battle that Willow will win – with a little help from Caitlyn's friends, anyway.

I certainly hope so. Because it might just save me embarrassing myself by wreaking havoc with a custard discus…

Or maybe I actually should pace across the football pitch, spin, release, and let my custard shot put rocket through the air, smacking Tiago in the face, as I roar away all the tension of the past few weeks.

CHAPTER NINE

"COME ON. YOU know it makes sense," Kelly pleads. "Matt won't take no for an answer either. If *I* need this break before the summer season kicks in, then *you* definitely do… And as I said to Radhika, I'm not heading off to sunny climes without both of you there by my side!"

Well, as appealing as the thought of a holiday is, all of this is slightly easier for Kelly than for me. The ice cream parlour she and her partner Matt took over in Bath a couple of years ago is thriving, thanks to its plethora of fantastical flavours, and its central position on historic Pulteney Bridge. I doubt it has ever had to deal with a petition for closure – even if its previous owner, Giovanna Tonioli (Matt's cousin), initially set it up to annoy her parents after they allegedly cut her out of her inheritance. This just happened to be the family ice cream parlour, also based in the city… smack bang across the road from the one she opened. Yeah, talk about awkwardness. I had a lot of sympathy for the girl at the time when Matt recounted the tragic tale to me. Why does food so consistently evoke so many complex emotions in us human beings?

I guess it comes down to food being love, life, and the heart and soul served up on a plate, or in a cone. Food is everything.

I should have asked Matt for advice on how best to handle

things. If he didn't know the answer then he could have pointed me in any number of helpful directions, courtesy of his culinary contacts in high places. Matt and I have known one another for years, having lived in opposite houses on the same road from the ages of twelve to sixteen, even if we were at different schools. We'd frequently pop into each other's kitchens for whichever sneaky morsels either of us had on the go at the weekends, and when the weather was good, we'd head to Ellenborough park on the west side of Walliscote Road, our little dot on the map... Until his parents moved the family to a fancier abode in a cul-de-sac just off Sandy Bay, business evidently booming.

Nevertheless, we've always stayed in touch in a platonic and strictly just good friends way, and when he'd introduced me to his first steady girlfriend in years – Kelly – it had been besties at first sight. Kelly had come into Matt's life via the aforementioned Giovanna, and was seeking the solace of a good friendship at the same time as me (Gi had gallivanted off to Italy with her own knight in shining armour, and I'd been a perpetual social floater who was ready to be a bit choosier with my allegiances, settling down with a closer group of on-the-same-ish-wave-length-peeps). Radhika, despite being several years younger, had fit neatly between us when we'd just happened to meet her on the dance floor in one of Bath's trendy new nightclubs; this one was housed in a high-vaulted, neon-lit cellar, where our new friend was most unimpressed with the 'distinct lack of talent, given it was a Friday night.' Radhika is still most unimpressed with this issue wherever we go.

Anyway, I'm going ridiculously off on a tangent.

So, as we've already established, Matt grew up in Weston-super-Mare, like me. His family, and extended family, still own a bunch of of *ristoranti* in the South West, including two in the town; having unfathomably moved from the idyllic island of Capri to a not-so-idyllic, but certainly characterful, Weston – as you do. As useful as any of Matt's posse could have been to me, at least I now have a sketchy settling-the-score style plan of my own involving a footie pitch and some nimble circus moves. In my mind's eye, my very public custard tart nibble/lob has a fifty-fifty chance of working and scaring Tiago away from taking the petition to the powers that be. I won't say I am converted to the idea of staying open past summer, but I will say that, from now until I've seen the results of my attendance at the upcoming football match, I will try to chill out and simply go with the flow.

To an outsider, asking Kelly for advice might seem like the obvious plan, but this is the woman who once tried to convince me to serve my customers beetroot and eucalyptus-filled custard tarts; two of Kelly's iced delights! Yes, I know that some of my ideas are a little outside the box (I grimace as I recall the incriminatory words of the petition), but Kelly's culinary 'masterpieces' take things to a whole new level where commonsense doesn't always prevail. Even if they are always created in the name of health. In other words, much as Kelly and Matt's enterprise is a huge success, only half of it caters for mainstream customers' tastebuds – an area that is very much Matt's domain.

That's why I skirt around my petition worries with Kelly, mentioning only the bare bones, so as not to give her *carte blanche* for any ideas whackier than my own. And that's why

Kelly's brainwave of a girlie break in the Algarve comes as something of a surprise. It is out of character for my friend to even consider venturing somewhere so, well, *conventional*.

"Oh, I know what you're thinking," she chirrups, reading my puzzled expression. "Whilst we might have to do the nightclub in Vilamoura thing one evening, to appease Radhika, that's as far as I'm prepared to indulge in mass tourism."

"Right, I see."

I really don't, but there's no point trying to derail Kelly when she's got a plan.

"You don't need to worry about a thing, Willow. It's all taken care of. I knew you'd say yes so I've booked us all into this gorgeously authentic 'quinta' twenty minutes inland from the eastern Algarve." I rub my eyes. Clearly I am dreaming. I can't just up and leave the café for a week during my first season of trading. This is madness. Admittedly, the free publicity from Caitlyn's uni friends has been amazing, getting TCTC into the local papers, as well as boosting our Instagram following. We've even had our first experience of takeout queues spilling onto the pier. Reggie and Tim squealed when that happened! Emma and her team have also been and gone with the summer roadshow, so that's one thing less for me to worry about. In the end, although they were granted permission from the pier's management to broadcast the epic event from the café, it was with a limited audience for health and safety reasons. Bittersweet for us as it felt more like an intimate family birthday party than a large pop concert. But, while we may not have sold so many tarts, it was infinitely easier to manage and enjoy. I got to mingle with the hip and trendy locals who'd won the coveted places, and Emma roped in an impressive selection of West Country authors who read out excerpts from their brand new summer holiday novels on air, kindly adding paperbacks to our book trolleys.

"It's free cancellation up to a week before the holiday," Kelly crusades onwards, jolting me from my reverie. I bite my tongue, waiting for the spiel to end so I can finally make my excuses and worm my way out of it.

But Kelly could have been an aspirational travel blogger in a former life – a realisation I will definitely be keeping to myself since my friend loves nothing more than to bang on about the merits of past life regression (and, of course, numerology… but that's a whole other story). Basically, dang, she is persuasive when she wants something.

"It's well quiet, near the Spanish border side of the Algarve. For some bizarre reason, most people step off the plane at Faro and head for the commercialised west. But not us savvy ones." Kelly taps the side of her silver-studded nose. "Not only does the farmhouse have the most stylishly rustic rooms and a luxury turquoise pool flanked by olive, lemon, and fig trees…"

Oh, wow! That does sound good but I press my mouth into a firm line, determined not to take the bait.

"Not only does it have the cutest goats you ever did see meandering on its land…"

Help! I have always had a soft spot for goats.

"But Willow, get this: it's only got its very own *pastelaria* on site. They specialise in almond, carob and corn products, but for sure they'll make custard tarts. I mean, it's a given."

That does it. I'm hopelessly and irretrievably sold.

"No way?"

"Yes way!"

Kelly gets out her phone, tapping and swiping excitedly to reveal idyllic photographs of the unconventional accommodation. It's situated in a small rural town called São Brás de Alportel. I definitely can't recall the name from my family holidays to the region as a youngster, but then we did always cling to the touristy resorts on the coast.

"But what about Radhika? It sounds like her idea of hell, being so cut off from the action," I say.

"She'll come around once she realises how compact the Algarve is. She can hop in a taxi and be in Faro for a boogie in twenty-five minutes, if our compromise of one night out in Vilamoura's Strip isn't enough. Besides, who's to say she won't meet a hunky country dude? I've said it before and I'll say it again several times on this holiday: she's got to stop looking in all the obvious places. Romance doesn't work like that."

"Erm, Kelly? How much is all of this going to cost?"

Kelly raises her hand to stop my inquiry and shakes her head from side to side.

"All you need to know for now is that it's way cheaper than an apartment or a hotel in any of the main beach resorts. You'd be amazed, Willow. You can pay me back after the holiday."

And that is that. I leave Kelly to her expert negotiation skills as far as Radhika is concerned. I make a final check on the dates of the Weston-super-Mare versus Bristol grassroots city club – whose name I have already forgotten – football fixture. It's all good. The match isn't on until the week after the return date. Plenty of time for me to limber up my biceps then. Ooh, perhaps I can practice my custard tart catapulting on a beach where the sun actually makes an appearance, unlike our own version, whose skies have remained stubbornly plastered with thick white clouds for the past few days.

It doesn't take long to confirm the finer details. By the afternoon, Kelly has booked our taxi to Bristol airport from her house, as well as the flights and the rental car at Faro. In ten short days, we are Portugal bound.

•

CHAPTER TEN

ALTHOUGH IT FEELS like something of a risk, I know I need a holiday. Setting up a new business in the foodie world is a bit like one of those iceberg diagrams. The blood, sweat, and tears; the crippling self-doubt and the financial worries remain unseen by the outside world, below the waterline. Only the tip (the café or pub or restaurant or cocktail bar) gleams like a beacon that will cause the whole structure to either sink or swim. Hardly helped by uppity males of the Tiago Willis variety.

Lauren has messaged me with recommendations for swanky restaurants and wine bars that none of us have the budget to frequent; her memories of our family package holidays in fuss-free three star hotels with cardboard towels and empty minibars long forgotten. Mercifully, she has only mentioned He Who Shall Not Be Named once in the last couple of weeks. I suspect Jamie has moved Tiago to another floor.

Caitlyn is not only back in Weston-super-Mare for the summer and bursting with her trademark joie de vivre, but she's taking all the hours I can throw at her – I guess that's what happens when you are surrounded by all those focused and dedicated athletes on your sports psychology degree. She's also enlisted the help of some local student contacts who are in need of the extra money, negating the need for me to finally get around to putting out the ad for part-time summer staff that I have been seriously procrastinating about.

Tim's *natas* are as close to perfection as can be, and he's working at an impressively accurate and robotic speed to keep up with the growing demand.

Frank has told me this trip is non-negotiable (with an affirmative tap of his walking stick). I don't dare argue with that.

And Reggie knows the drill for everything inside and out. "All graft and little gratification maketh for one hell of a boring fart," he encouraged me in his unique way. "Relax. The café will be fine, even if this is a busy period. Besides, if you don't take this break, you'll only be green-eyed when I head off to Puerto Banus later in the season, and Tim takes his annual sojourn to climb a scary mountain in the autumn. Or maybe not, ref. the latter... I believe it's the Matterhorn's turn this year."

I physically tremble at the thought. Puerto Banus's attractions may be more Radhika's bling style than mine, but all those daytime DJ pool parties surrounded by influencers and semi-famous faces are a thousand times preferable to scaling a death-defying mountain. And to think my pastry chef willingly participates in this for 'fun' once a year...

In any case, the café couldn't be in safer hands as I jet off with Kelly and Radhika for a week in the sun. I haven't been back to the Algarve since I was a teen – a case of too many summers spent working – and I definitely plan to schedule in a few *pastelaria* stops, because this pastry chef never stops climbing the learning curve. It isn't every day that your holiday accommodation comes with a traditional confection-ery outlet in its rustic grounds, after all! My mouth waters at the prospect.

My last jaunt from Bristol airport had been with Callum for a long and difficult weekend in Prague. His impatience with my eagerness to try every quirky activity I could get my hands on flared up into one hell of an argument. Exactly halfway across Charles Bridge. Exactly halfway through having my portrait sketched, too. It was mortifyingly embarrassing. Evidently the artist had never seen anything like it, either, when I was forced to leave him with his half-finished sketch. I'll never forget the shock on his face. In fact, I tipped the poor man extra for his trouble... which was akin to throwing petrol on the fire of Callum's annoyance. Fair enough, my boyfriend would have had to find some way to amuse himself for half an hour (getting his own miserable head and shoulders sketched, appreciating the talent of the lone double bass player, and marveling at the mime artist trapped in an invisible box sprang to mind). But no. All Callum wanted to do was sit in pub after pub necking Pilsner after Pilsner. Then he'd hobble back to the hotel miffed at how much – which really was very little! – he had spent, then lord it over the flat screen TV, sprawled out on the bed.

And it had been the same the day before that, and the afternoon of our arrival in the Czech capital; me kayaking alone on the Danube, me wandering out on my tod to gaze at the beauty of Prague at sunset, and me heaving my weary legs to the top of the astronomical clock's tower to admire the fabulous three-hundred-and-sixty degree view, as my boyfriend tapped his increasingly impatient foot, back on the ground. Each and every magical moment was my gain and Callum's loss.

Had I known things would go downhill so fast, eighteen months after pulling him at the aforementioned neon-lit, high-vaulted nightclub cellar in Bath, whilst Radhika and Kelly got in another round of drinks, I would have spared myself the bother.

And as for Rufus, the toffee-nosed guy I had briefly dated before him, well, funnily enough that had ended after a trip from Bristol airport too. Me being me, I'd decided it was a good idea to tiptoe across the stepping stones of his parents' ornate swimming pool at their villa in the south of France (after a couple of glasses of red wine). Him being him, Rufus was far from impressed when I fell into the pool in front of his entire family and had to be rescued by the gardener since nobody else wanted to get their expensive clothes wet.

"Earth to Willow!" an excited Radhika cries, bringing me back, thank goodness, to the present.

"Oh, sorry. I…" I actually feel a little disoriented and grip the handle of my luggage tightly, unsure how I've fallen into such a deep daydream in an airport full of hustle and bustle. "I was miles away."

"Well, you will be soon… if you hand over your ticket and passport to that woman and get in the flipping queue. What are you waiting for? Snap out of that trance and let the holibobs begin!"

"Okay, okay." I giggle (although definitely not at the holibobs bit… if my friend really has to use an alternative word to holiday, let it be the slightly less irritating 'jollies'). I walk to the queue, and the butterflies immediately loop-the-loop in my stomach, just as they always do before I'm thrust into the air in what is essentially a tube with wings at two-hundred-and-forty plus kilometres an hour.

Kelly is already halfway to the check-in desk, eager to get to Portugal as soon as possible to inspect the eco accommodation she's secured. I hope the reality lives up to the hype. It certainly looked the epitome of enchanting and relaxed on the website, but then looks can be deceiving. And don't I know it?

We inch our way along the bendy orange-belted lines, doubling back on ourselves every time we seem to be forging ahead, until we finally reach the desks. The airline staff are either poised for their next customers or weighing cases beneath the long panel of glossy tangerine boards, and at this last hurdle, a British-style queue stretches ahead again, neat and orderly. Eventually it's our turn. We peel left and right to separate desks, and I hold my breath as my check-in official and I contemplate my luggage, which contains a tonne of hairstyling tools and accessories as per usual.

But it's Radhika who has to pay for excess baggage… or remove some of her stuff. She flings open her case with a mighty sigh, not remotely tempted to get out her credit card. It's painfully obvious she's overpacked, her case is bulging as if it's stuffed down a three course meal. It's all I can do not to laugh hysterically. Instead I put my hands in a praying motion to my check-in lady, assuring her I'll be ten seconds, and throw myself into mother hen mode, helping Radhika decide what to jettison and handing her plastic bags to put it all in ready to dump, ever mindful that if my eco-warrior friend Kelly were to see all this waste, we'd both be banished from the quinta before we'd even set foot in it.

Over my shoulder, I clock the exasperated expressions of our fellow easyJet passengers. My friend is now holding up hordes of people as she dithers over a fat tub of body glitter versus a family-sized bottle of coconut hand cream. Blimey, they look angry. And that's when I do a double take; the flash of a fire engine-red UWE Bristol baseball cap; the sense of a familiar-yet-unfamiliar frame; chestnut tufts of hair, and the collar of an expensive-looking polo shirt. My stomach churns, my pulse ratchets.

No. It can't be. I am stuck in yet another trance, imagining myself behind the counter of my café a couple of months ago, that's all. I snap my head back to the situation at my side, intent on living in the here and now, trying to leave all the stress that petition-issuing idiot has caused me miles behind.

Radhika finally sorts herself out just as I reclaim my passport and my own check-in lady narrows her eyes with a giant tut. I frog-march my embarrassing friend to the bins and she discards various bottles of shampoo, hairspray, sun cream and shower gel with another mammoth sigh, returning the plastic bags to me (in my defence, they are recycled plastic bags… and now they'll get another lease of life – one that is hopefully less stressful) before Kelly has spotted us in the distance.

"Utterly ridiculous." Radhika won't let the crummy start to the holiday go. "Now I'll just have to go and buy exactly the same bottles in the Superdrug store over in Departures. It's no secret how these places make their money."

She's sporting a frown that matches her environmentally conscious counterpart, Kelly, who has upped her disapproval to a glare and is marching purposefully toward us. "Great, no doubt madam saw all of that and will be attempting to fix me

up with local Portuguese honey and herbal toiletries instead."
Radhika grits her teeth at the highly likely scenario.

"So, then," says Kelly, mercifully glossing over Radhika's
current pickle. "We've only got an hour and a bit before the
flight, and getting through security is bound to take a while
given that it's summer. Let's whizz through the duty free shop
and on into Starbucks for an iced tea and a chill-out before we
board. I wouldn't normally go all consumer conformist, but I
must confess I have a soft spot for their Iced Passion Tango
Tea. It's got hibiscus and lemongrass in it which is giving me
some serious ideas for my ice cream."

Radhika screws up her face when Kelly isn't looking.
Whereas I make a mental note for once, wondering if I might
infuse that little pairing into custard. Unlike Kelly's usual taste
combo brainwaves, this one sounds sublime. And then I
remember my current quandary. A bit like the way you wake
up in the morning after something awful has happened the
day before, and for a few blissful seconds, you've completely
forgotten it… until the 'it' slaps you fiercely across the chops:
I have to double check if that man lurking in the check-in
queue was who I thought he was. Nah, it was probably just a
random person that had shapeshifted to the beat of my darkest
fears. Sure, any number of dark-haired men could have
bought the same hat. I've never been to uni. For all I know,
those baseball caps are handed out during freshers' week to
thousands of students.

I turn as furtively as I can to pan the scene behind me
again, but unless the red-capped male is hiding behind the
pillar, there's not a trace of him. Phew! The relief washes over
me like a power shower and I'm overcome with instant

happiness. I must have been imagining things. I take a deep breath, determined to get in the holiday swing. A relaxing break away in the sun in a beautiful destination has become such a rarity in my life, it would be a crime to fret about this. I owe it to myself, my friends, and everyone who is covering for me back at TCTC to enjoy every moment of it. Who knows when I'll get the chance to go away again?

Minutes later our water bottles are deposited in the bins (with Kelly understandably up in arms at the situation) before we join another queue to go through security. But despite my commitment to loosening up, I can't stop looking over my shoulder. Once again, nobody behind me fits the bill of my earlier 'vision'. Still, my fidgeting only increases as I get closer to the body scanner. I just can't help it. This is as compulsive as scratching an itch. An airport official homes in on me, and I don't need to be told I'll be taken aside for a thorough pat down if I don't nip my haywire body language in the bud. Which is precisely what happens when I reach the front of the queue, hardly helped by Radhika chortling at me in the background, now safely through. What a joke, with all the random bits and pieces in *her* travel bag. I'm sure she's got half of Boots in there!

"Let's hope the next queue is shorter," Kelly greets me after my completely avoidable ordeal, barely giving me a chance to put my sandals, scarf, belt, bangles, and rings back on.

"Guys, go on through without me and order me an iced coffee," I say as calmly as I can.

Kelly furrows her brow. She's a stickler for the three of us doing everything together as if we are a family unit of ducks.

"Honestly, I'll be with you before you know it." I wave her and Radhika off. "I just want to get dressed again in peace and quiet, that's all. Plus my bag could do with a complete repack after the embarrassment of the search. I can't bear getting on a plane and not knowing where all my bits and pieces are."

I could just insist that I need to pick up some lipstick or an eyeshadow as I pass through the non-negotiable shop that is strategically sandwiched between security and departures, but I never particularly bother with makeup unless I'm on a night out. Besides, that would only give Radhika ideas about adding to her own mammoth collection, and then Kelly will be drinking iced tea alone.

I also know I must be coming across a little weirdly by flat-out rejecting Kelly's suggestions. It's totally out of character for me – just as it would be for Radhika. Not because Kelly is bossy or a control freak. She's just always been the natural leader of the group. In a threesome, there is always one who makes the decisions.

Once my friends are a blur in the distance, I make another sneaky scan of the bodies queuing on the other side of security, and then dip into the perfume aisle, loitering over the various tester sprays, where I'm immediately pounced on by an eager salesperson. I feign interest and sniff at every thin strip of card presented to me, each of them dripping in heady fragrance. By my calculation, if Tiago wasn't a figment of my imagination earlier, and was a very real person standing in that queue – happening to be hiding behind a pillar when I last looked back at the easyJet line – then it'll take him around twenty minutes to pass through the shop. In other words, I have to find enough stimulation among the cosmetics, chocolates, and bottles of gin, to keep me here for ages, all without raising the missing person alarm with Kelly, or the shoplifting alarm with the store. This will be no mean feat. Small wonder that I end up panic-chatting my way into a makeover on one of the counters of the upmarket cosmetic concessions that are dotted about.

"Shall we go for an exciting change of style this afternoon?" the makeup artist asks. "I'm thinking of jewel tones to accentuate the striking colours of your eyes... It's not every day I get the opportunity to work on such an exclusive blank canvas. Apologies for my ignorance but what's the term for your... erm... eye colouring, erm, condition?"

"Heterochromia, and you're all right," I reassure her. "It's passed down from my father. For some reason I'm the only one of his three daughters who has it, though."

"Well, lucky you," she replies, and I know she genuinely means it.

Heterochromia is more than a condition. It's a quirk I have learned to love, but it has taken time. Thankfully, I never got ribbed about it at school. I guess my fantastical hairstyles diluted the effect of my eyes. On a subconscious level, I know that's why I went all out with the big, bold tresses, to detract everybody's attention from my face.

"Or would you prefer something a little more understated? I guess we should think about where you're headed today – is it a city break with shopping, dinner and wine bars, or will you be jumping straight into a pool?" the woman who is going to work miracles asks me.

"Erm, I'm not entirely—" I hold out my hand to count

the hours ahead of me, swiftly realising there's no time difference between England and Portugal, so I guess it'll be evening not long after we touch down, so I guess... oh, what the hell, let's go for the thing that keeps me on the stool the longest so I can find out if my suspicions about Tiago are correct. "Jewel-toned eyes sound great. Let's do it!" I say decisively.

"Okay, then. If you're sure. It's going to be quite a dramatic look for the daytime but hey, you won't need to do much to get ready to hit the town in... where did you say you were going again?"

"Dublin," I lie impulsively. I can hardly confess to staying in a rural retreat in Portugal now that I've been told I will look like a... actually, I've no idea what I will look like. Despite being *au fait* with the current hair trends of the fashion world, I haven't an inkling what any of these makeup terms are. Radhika only explained what contouring was to me the other day.

"Oh, perfect! Have a Guinness for me, won't you?"

The MUA has already closed one of my eyelids so she can cleanse it with a cotton wool disc, before I have a chance to reconsider what I've signed myself up for. I am now also realising that looking with just one eye for Tiago will not help me on my mission. As the MUA daubs one colour of eyeshadow across my eyelid, and opens up an alarming number of further eyeshadow compacts, I squirm and shift as best I can between applications. There's a handy magnifying mirror to the right of the dressing table so I cast my gaze into that from time to time too, even if it does mean jutting my neck out at a right angle.

"Are you okay?" she asks, concern creasing her brow. "Is the seat comfortable enough? Can I get you some water? It's just you seem a little jumpy and I'd hate to send you away with a wonky composition."

"Sorry, sorry. I'm er… just a nervous flier, that's all. Fidgeting helps to take my mind off things but I'll stay statue-still until you've finished up. I promise."

"Oh, I can completely sympathise," her voice rises an octave. "This one time when I flew back from Miami with my boyfriend, we hit the most awful clear air turbulence halfway across the Atlantic. Even the cabin crew lost all the blush from their cheeks! How everybody clapped and cheered when we finally landed at Gatwick."

"Thanks, that's… kind of reassuring. *You made it, yay…* and thank goodness… else you wouldn't be able to sort me out with this…"

But I cannot finish my sentence.

A flash of red cap catches my attention in the magnifying mirror. I hold my breath and the vision reappears, as if retracing its steps just for my benefit. This time it stands still, where it looks to be scrutinising the prices of the mini Paddington Bears on the aisle behind me. *Aw, that is so cute!* says my inner voice, mimicking Reggie's that fateful day when the man in my sights first set out on his mission to destroy my business. I can only see the back of his head but the slight kink to his dark brown hair looks eerily familiar. He may not be wearing that puffy body warmer today, but even from behind, I can tell that his style is preppy. The polo shirt is top quality and it's definitely the same navy blue one that I clocked in the queue. No doubt a Lacoste or something of that ilk.

"Fabulous makeover!"

The MUA provides the missing words and passes me a handheld mirror so I can inspect her handiwork. Despite looking in the magnifying mirror in front of me virtually every other second, I've been so consumed with spying on a certain somebody that this is the first time I have thought to properly look at myself. It takes every ounce of my restraint to do the polite thing and beam with satisfaction, but, oh, heck! *What has she done to me?* The eyeshadow, liner, and mascara are expertly applied, there's no question about it... but my left eye is cyan and my right one is royal blue. I look like I've come off the set of a music video for a pop song set in space. There's no other way to adequately describe my new look.

"Now then. I've priced up all the items we've used today." She sets an invoice on the company headed card before me. "And I'll just leave this here with you so you can decide if you want to add some of our hydrating cleanser, toner, and moisturiser. Skin that zings will really help your eyes pop all the more when you recreate this look for yourself. See, I've made a few notes here on the step-by-step process." Now she taps a pencil on her eye-wateringly long list. "And here's a link to one of our free makeup tutorials on our company website, where you can watch a video of one of our artists doing roughly what I've done. I'll just be waiting for you at the till."

"O... okay, thanks."

My voice comes out as a croak and I wish I'd taken the lady up on her offer of the complimentary water now, to get my money's worth, as well as to cool myself down. I'm feeling too guilty for the freebie of a makeover not to buy at least half of this list so I can get out of here quick-smart and track down the man. I hop off the high stool to hammer my credit card – hoping that Kelly is right about the affordability of this trip once we arrive at the unassuming São Brás de Alportel, and my eyes really do pop (which must be quite a sight, all things considered) as I come face to face with him. It bleeping well *is* Tiago!

"Everything OK?" the MUA notes my fingers gripping the edge of the counter, although it could just be that she is fretting over the state of my nails. "Don't forget to come and visit us again before your next journey and we'll work on your brows."

"Right, yes. That would be, um, incredible." I clench my teeth and will myself not to look at the slightly-too-perfect-to-be-believable templates arching above her own eyes. "Thanks, then!"

I turn to leave but my legs are jelly. I'm not sure how to play this out now. Which way should I go? What am I hoping to achieve? I shut my eyes briefly to ground myself. The answer comes quickly. I want peace of mind. Peace of mind that he is on *any other flight to any other place*. Surely that's not too much to ask? But how am I going to achieve that? Short of spotting him queuing up at a whole other gate to mine – and potentially missing my own flight – how can I possibly find out where he is going?

I had the good sense to scan the departures board twice before checking in and recall there are just two easyJet flights scheduled to leave in the next hour. One bound for Newcastle. One bound for Faro, the Algarve. But suddenly, more details about my fleeting vision of TOG (from now on I decide to omit the I and the A from Tiago's name, scramble the remaining letters up, and refer to him as TOG; The Opinionated Git) come to light. Namely, the giant suitcase TOG was propping himself against in the check-in queue, which hardly spoke of a fleeting city break up north. More's the pity.

Okay, stay calm. Even if he is on my flight, there's no way he'll recognise me this many weeks down the line, with this much makeup on. And actually, I further reassure myself, TOG really wouldn't have remembered my face in the first place – and definitely not now I have presumably gained a little Keira Knightly allure; at least that's the finish the posh makeup counter's marketing promises. Our slanging match that day on the pier had been short and sweet, his attention on my offending tarts.

Except… oh, sh… *ugar*!

I lift my hand to my head, swiftly acknowledging that I'm wearing the exact same hairstyle as I had the day that TOG burst into the café: the Dutch braided ponytail. What a horrible sleight of hand by the Goddesses of Fate! I have a system for my hairstyles. A different 'do' every single day for a month. From the power ponytail, which is typically how I burst into the beginning of the month, to the bubble ponytail (with bandana), which is how I end it; chopping and changing, subbing and swapping as new styles take my fancy, and depending on the behaviour of the elements, of course.

I can hardly tug the creation out now, to disguise myself. I'll look like I've been dragged through a hedge and back-combed, then TOG will definitely zero in on me – especially with my bizarre make-up.

I pretend to admire the star-shaped baby-blue bottles of

Thierry Mugler's Angel *eau de toilette* as I quickly calculate the rest of the non-existent strategies in my head. The size of that suitcase said it all, but I feel like I have the perfect opportunity here at least to confirm we'll be at opposite ends of the aircraft. He's still got that Paddington Bear welded to his chest… which means he's going to buy it… which means if I am stealthy enough, I can sneak into the check-out queue behind him, and peer over his shoulder to read the seat details on his boarding card… or make him drop it. I could even bump into him just as he's about to hand it over at the till to prove he's entitled to his tax-free teddy. He'd never recognise me with my space pop video eyes. The whole manoeuvre could be carried out in seconds.

But unfortunately, there's no time to ponder my dilemma any further. Something really strange is happening. TOG is inching his way closer to me. Today's hairstyle has let me down, the makeup counter's disguise has let me down, and *I* have let me down –wrecking my futile hopes for a stress-free holiday.

TOG seems to be chewing a grin. He makes a show of raising the peak of his cap as if to check me out in full, and I can detect his brow knitting together. Who does he think he is? Talk about a performance.

I need to think of something clever to say, because it's evident he's about to give me yet another piece of his mind. Instinctively, I pick up the Angel tester bottle and point it at him as if it's a loaded weapon.

"Freeze: don't take a single step closer."

A smirk spreads fully across his irritatingly luscious lips. Hand still clutched to the peak of his headgear, he raises an eyebrow as if to say '*seriously?*'

"Don't flatter yourself." His smile fades. "And I'd prefer that you kept my niece's birthday present out of your unnecessary self-defence tactics." He gestures at the stuffed toy in its iconic mackintosh and hat. "I'm after a bottle of the Calvin Klein that's right behind you, but if you insist on blocking my way, I guess Paddington and I will just take the scenic route."

TOG loops around the perfume gondola. Sure enough, he grabs a bottle of CK One Shock aftershave (and now there's no way he isn't the guy Lauren has been fixated on, if her olfactory skills are anything to go by) before turning to make his way to the till.

Oh, no you don't!

My mouth twists as I relive the recent anguish he's put me and my team through. Self-righteous prat. The very anguish I'm going away to try to forget. Life, it seems, has slightly different plans.

But I'm damned if I'm going to pass up the opportunity to challenge them now that it's here.

"Tell me you are not going to Portugal," I demand and he turns slowly to face me. I'm still pointing the spray at him and I realise I'm getting odd looks from the employee handing out thimble samples of Bombay Sapphire gin in the distance. I put the Angel back on the shelf.

It's like I'm looking at a whole different person, there's no trace of amusement on TOG's face anymore.

"Okay, so let me get this straight," he says. "Not only does she think she has the right to completely slaughter the Portuguese *pastel de nata*." My mouth forms the letter O at his awful choice of words. He makes me sound like a butcher. "She also thinks she has the right to decide who gets to set foot in *my* country." He removes his cap and fluffs up his hair in a wholly unnecessary move, because (of course) it looks salon-perfect, unlike most humans' mops, which would be pancake-flat after wearing that thing for so long.

I screw up my features, hardly caring what that must look like. How dare he! I clear my throat.

"The only reason I am standing in this airport right now is to take a well-deserved break from the stress that you, and you alone, have dumped so spectacularly on the doorstep of my café! So, yes, I do have a right to know your whereabouts, as it happens, because the last thing I want to do is end up bumping into you on a beach in the Algarve when I am trying to forget about the way you are seeking to destroy my livelihood!"

He bites down on his lip in a way which I refuse to view as sexy.

"You already saw me in the easyJet queue when, excuse me for pointing it out, you looked far more ravishing minus the metallic mermaid makeup." I wince internally but I am not prepared to show him that his disapproval of my new look has registered. "And if, like most people, you have glanced at the departure boards, you will have noticed they are going to two places: guaranteed sunshine… and not-so-guaranteed sunshine. I wonder…" He humours me and brings his hand to his chin as if deep in thought. "Which would I choose to jet away to, especially given the fact my family lives there?"

My heart thuds. I already know this to be true. But now there's no longer that 0.01% chance that he has a thing for cold northern cities. All I can do is look askance at him.

"What are you, a spy? Of all the weeks in the year, why did you have to go and choose the same one that my friends cajoled me to join them on?"

"I'm stunned you'd jump to that conclusion. I can assure you I have far more important and interesting things to do with my time."

"Oh, really? Didn't stop you prying into my company's activities and showing up there uninvited."

I attempt to arch a brow, then remember the vast swathe of iridescent shimmer coating each of my eye sockets, and cringe again at his earlier critique.

"Okay." He holds a hand up in surrender, while the other grips Paddington protectively. It takes me right back to his stance with his poodle in the café and a nervous giggle threatens to erupt. Does he always get into arguments when he's out and about with a furry prop? "I'll make a deal with you, seeing as fate seems to have thrown us together, whether we like it or not. Meet me mid-week – no need for all the theatrics though." He stops to wave his free hand in front of his face. "I might take you—" He stops again as if to weigh up his next words. "I'd like to take you out, that is to, er... to show you a proper *pasteleria* so you can have a true *pastel de nata* experience."

"You call that a chat-up line?"

Now I can't stop my brows from hitting the ceiling. I'm furious with myself for jumping to that conclusion – and the helix of pleasure whirling south from my stomach at the thought of some alone time with TOG. His smouldering eyes are doing wicked things to me, despite us being at loggerheads. But it doesn't half sound like he's hitting on me in some weird and warped way. I have never been so flummoxed by a male. He's contradictory, he's rude, he's pompous. *He's gorgeous.*

Stop. STOP!

Enough of the latter. I will not be swayed by good looks. I am not that woman, and I am not that easily won over. Nothing can excuse TOG's hideous actions up to this point and I will not roll over just because he's invited me out for a *pastel de nata.* Even if I do love the things.

I discovered them alone, quite independently from any egotistical male, fourteen years ago. I *know* what they taste like. They were the seed of my inspiration, for goodness sake. I do not need to be spoon fed. And now I hastily bat away the image of Bridgerton's Duke of Hastings and his spoon-licking scene from my traitor of a brain. I *will not* be Daphne, infatuated with a dashingly good-looking man!

"Of course it wasn't a chat-up line. Neither was it proposed as a date. Like I said before, don't flatter yourself." He eyerolls me and waves his cap about as if to indicate that I've totally misconstrued his words, to distract all and sundry from his invitation. "Whatever gave you that idea? That would be ridiculous."

Okay. No need to protest so much. I get the message loud and clear.

"I meant,' he continues. "So I can set you straight… so you can have a serious think about the way you've decimated the perfection that is a Portuguese custard tart. I assume you're heading to one of the tourist traps not far from Faro, having watched your poor friend display her overfull suitcase of bikinis and flip flops for everyone's delight. Then you can fly home when the week's up and change your menu immediately."

I blink rapidly, trying to process his spiel.

"You are unbelievable. Who rattled your cage?" He visibly flinches at my words. For a split second, time seems to freeze between us, like the individual frames in a movie. Although he tries to hide it with bitterness, he's not quick enough; I see the sorrow, I see the pain that is etched across his face. Half of me is glad, but the kinder, softer side of me – my aching heart – wants to take back my retort, however justified it seemed. I've hit him where it hurts. I may not know what that hurt is, but he's undeniably wounded.

"Fine. Don't say I didn't give you the opportunity to make amends." He clears his throat and my heart shrinks, my head taking over and brooking no more nonsense. "It seems to me that you'd rather see your business being forced to close."

"Oh, me and my business are here to stay," I yell at him because he obviously needs to hear it loud and clear. "I wonder what Lauren Masters will have to say, when she hears about the lengths you are taking to undermine not only her stellar marketing campaign, but her little sister's business?" I shouldn't have said that. Tiago's face turns a ghostly white. "I wonder if you'll still have a job left?"

I really shouldn't have said that. The last thing I wanted to do was bring my family into this in any shape or form – even if Lauren does work with the guy. Or give him any inkling that I'd been doing my background research and snooping on his movements. We had a plan, Reggie and I. A simple, real life version of that disgusting Hasbro game, Pie

Face, on the football pitch. We'd have had Tiago where we wanted him in seconds. Now I've been and aggravated the situation tenfold. "It's you who needs to get used to it, you... you..." suddenly one of Reggie's words pops into my head and I can only hope it's appropriate to finish off my sentence, "ultracrepidarian!"

Make that twentyfold.

Oh, well. What's done is done. Never mind custard tarts, that'll give him something to chew on. Honestly, though. The nerve of the guy! I have never ever met, or known, anybody quite like him. And thank God for that. Tiago looks at me blankly, as if waiting for me to explain the nineteenth century word for someone who is a know-it-all despite knowing nothing at all. Passengers are nudging one another now; muttering under their breath at what has probably come across as a 'domestic'. Staff are twitching too, especially my sales wizz MUA, whose name I never did catch. An airport shop is no place for war, no matter how much I've spent in the place, no matter how much I loathe the button-pusher standing before me, and no matter how far in the wrong he is.

I spin on my heel and leave him with a stupefied expression and poor Paddington Bear, who'd doubtless rather remain on the shelf than spend a two and a half hour flight with that idiot.

CHAPTER ELEVEN

"WHAT THE HECK?"

Radhika is awestruck. Judging by the inflection of the word heck, I'd say not in a positive way.

Well, at least Kelly is impressed "Oh, wow!" she says. "Who *is* this vision of loveliness? Willow, you look like you're headlining on the Outside Circus Stage at Glastonbury."

Radhika explodes into laughter and I know I will never live the episode down.

"Just ignore Rad, Willow. I *love* this new you!" Kelly's eyes are on stalks. "It's seriously inspired! Why didn't you tell us this is what you were going to be up to though? We've been worried sick that the security woman had arrested you after taking another look at the X-rays of your bag. And I'm afraid Radhika necked your iced coffee."

"I really think an airport arrest would be preferable to *that*," Radhika grits her teeth. "No offence, Willow, but this image overhaul," she says the words slowly and carefully, as if they are encrusted with thorns. "Well, it really isn't doing it for me. Yes, on the dance floor, but less is more in an artificially lit airport at four in the afternoon. I'm getting a migraine just looking at you, love."

I throw my blunt friend a sarcastic smile. That's it. I'm going to Boots for a pack of wet wipes so I can sneak to the loo and remove every trace of the Smurf I seem to have become.

"Uh, where are you heading, young lady?"

Kelly grabs me firmly by the wrist and I'm immediately transported back to the early nineties. My nan used to do the same thing when I sometimes escorted her into town. She might have been spindly on her legs but if I even thought of straying into a remotely trendy shop such as New Look, she'd yank me back into our sacrosanct bubble. And woe betide me if I had a hoody on that day.

"Our boarding gate's just been announced." Kelly points to the screen. "No time for shilly-shallying."

And no time for me to wonder if TOG is behind or in front of us now, as Kelly press-gangs me down the walkway for our gate, Radhika several steps ahead of us. All of which makes me sound a little bit ungrateful for this opportunity of seven days in a quaint quinta, when I haven't yet refunded Kelly for the experience, but in fairness, I didn't expect the jerk that is Tiago Willis to be on my flight, did I? *Great start to the holidays!* I guess I could just drown my sorrows in the drinks trolley once we're airborne, but I swear if I touch a drop of alcohol at this point, it will mix with the high altitude and make me cry like a baby.

"Here we go. Row seven. My lucky number." Kelly declares, as we make our way down the aisle of the aircraft to find our seats. "And I appear to be right in the middle of my girls in seat B. Unless one of you fancies swapping?"

I try not to think about that bizarre travelling phenomenon, when someone you've had a random eye-meet with in an airport ends up sitting in front, behind, or next to you on the plane. Because, on this occasion, there is only one face stuck like an earworm in my head. So I concentrate hard and frantically rewind to anyone else I may have seen in the airport. If I quickly insert a handful of possibles into my short term memory now, they just have to take the seats surrounding us. That's how it works.

"No way," says Radhika, penetrating my frustratingly blank mind. "I'm planning to pass out with my travel pillow glued to the window. And yay to seven being lucky but seriously, Kelly, this numerology malarkey is so flipping predictable. Everyone knows that seven's a lucky number, it's not rocket science."

"In the general sense, you're right. But there's far more to numerology than meets the eye and in this case I was alluding to the fact that both my birthday and Willow's are on the seventh and sixteenth of our birth months, respectively. Said numbers are ruled by seven in numerology, as well as the planet Ketu. So that makes these seats even luckier for us. Whereas your birthdate is the first of August."

"Oh, cheers. Why not let the entire flight know the rest of my personal details while you're at it?"

"Well, *I* could do with all the good luck available, so I'll cling on to that ray of light," I say, as I let the girls into their seats before me and dither at the end of the row to pack the overhead locker with all our paraphernalia.

I settle into my own seat at last and immediately grab the laminated menu, determined to try to forget about the perils of takeoff – and a certain somebody. All passengers are boarding the flight from the front steps today and I've still no idea if TOG is in front of me or behind me.

"This is so exciting, isn't it?" Kelly taps both Radhika's and my thighs. "I can't believe we've never been on a trip abroad together before. This was long overdue."

"And I can't believe I've signed myself up for another trip away with you, full stop, after that damned glamping fiasco in Devon," Radhika quips.

"Oh, for the hundredth time, that mix up was not my fault!" Kelly snaps. "How could I know the campsite was falsely marketing itself? At least the tent was up and ready when we got there and the loos were within one hundred metres. It could have been worse."

A sledgehammer of dread hits my stomach. I know I'm wallowing in negativity in general this afternoon, but maybe I should have done my own double-checking on this 'quinta', digging beneath the shiny veneer of the photos Kelly showed me. The glamping trip was a disaster, thanks to Kelly's misjudgement. Only later when I referred back to the campsite's website did I spot there was just one luxury cotton bell tent in the entire field. Luckily we only spent a weekend in Devon. *Please history, don't repeat yourself and make me and Radhika suffer for a week.*

With all my will, I focus on the menu's snack recommendations, but words and pictures begin to blur, my senses hijacked by a fragrance wafting like a warning on the air: CK One Shock. The same smell TOG squirted himself with from the tester bottle just before he picked his refill up. The notes of lavender, patchouli and musk tickle my airways.

Painfully slowly, I spot him in my peripheral vision as he shuffles down the gangway until he is standing right next to my seat. I feel sick. My heart races. I don't dare look up. I can feel his eyes on me, though. They're burning into the back of my neck, and the flash of his bright green watch taunts me from the corner of my eye. This is torture. I guess by the sound of his tutting that he's waiting for somebody further down the aircraft to put their bits and pieces in the overhead locker and sit the heck down in their seat. I'm going to have to hold my breath until he inches away.

Within seconds I feel a hand clamp down on the headrest behind me, tickling the stray wisps of baby hair at the nape of my neck. I force back a scream of horror movie proportions. So much for row seven bringing me good fortune. The woman who had been standing behind TOG is now at my side and that can only mean one thing: it's TOG's hand. He's going to sit in the row behind me. Oh. My. God. If this isn't scripted straight out of a romcom, I don't know what is. Except there's no romance to be had on this aircraft, of that you can be sure. My heart is pounding so loudly now. I'm paranoid that I won't be able to hide this from my friends, and I need to. Kelly and Radhika are mega protective. We may all bicker and banter but it's like a comedy show. We love each other really, beneath all that wordy soup. We pull the metaphorical drawbridge up for protection, or down for battle, as circumstance dictates.

I know there's a sixty-something male hugging the window seat in the row behind me. Which means TOG – oh, all right, Tiago, I feel childish abbreviating him so much, even if he is the embodiment of a rather giant child himself – will either have a prime view of my royal blue left-hand profile, or the top of my head. Great.

"Psst," says Radhika in a far too loud whisper across Kelly.

"Have you seen that sexy specimen behind you?"

"Not my type," I can't get my words out fast enough.

"Don't worry, I wasn't going to set you up with him or anything," Radhika snaps sarcastically. "Flipping heck, Willow, lighten up. I know you look like you're about to take to Instagram Reels with that makeup job but I'm not sure what's got into you," she raises her voice quite unnecessarily. I really don't need a public or private reminder that I look like a cross between a peacock and an owl. "You've been acting mega-weird since we checked in." Fabulous. I can already sense Tiago's head getting bigger behind me, his ego spilling over into the aisle.

In some respects, Tiago sitting behind me is better than him sitting in front of me: no irritating male-reclining-the-seat games. On the other hand, I'm one of those annoying passengers who needs to pop to the loo at least once while airborne, and it will be impossible not to see Tiago's face when I return to my row.

And I think we've already established the fact that I'm a nervous flier. Which means he'll see my hand gripping the aisle seat's arm on take-off too, and that's only marginally preferable to him peeking at me through the headrest gaps to watch me chewing ferociously on a piece of gum.

"The opportunity is wasted on you and we should have swapped seats." Radhika adds this afterthought to her rant. She twists her head to roll her eyes in the direction of the old man who is already snoring behind her.

"Is there a minute of the day when you are not thinking about your next conquest?" I snap back.

"Just as well that I am sitting in the middle of you two

today to split the energy. Enough already," says Kelly. "Radhika: If you don't meet a hot male of your own during this trip, I will personally organise a speed dating night in my ice cream parlour, like the kind Giovanna used to host. Bath is full of eligible bachelors, you just haven't met them yet. And Willow: your tension is melding into my aura, chill out!"

The plane begins to taxi to the runway, then the engines power up ready for take-off. My stomach performs its habitual plummet to the floor. The aircraft accelerates past the point of no return and I do my usual bargaining-with-God thing in my head, 'if we arrive safely in one piece, I promise I'll be a better human being; give more to charity; be more environmentally conscious, totally planting trees to cover my carbon footprint to Portugal and back; I'll stop eating so much fat and sugar; take up running; be more patient with Lauren... and avoid any arguments with the man behind me.' The last resolution is a new one but if it makes for a safe flight, I'm in.

Meanwhile Radhika is out for the count, oblivious. Kelly, I now discover, is one of those people who chatters incessantly at precisely the time when I need to zone out, cocoon myself in silence, and focus on us reaching the safe point of twenty minutes into the flight. I'm not sure if this is a statistic I have read about or one that I've invented. Either way it's always been my benchmark. It's around the time the cabin crew are in full flow with their drinks service and that scald of a searing hot cuppa always tries its darndest to make me feel like I'm sitting at home on my sofa curled up with a book and a decent mug of tea instead of hurtling through the air with dishwater. On this trip twenty minutes can't come fast enough.

The plane tilts and banks and Kelly jabbers on: "I was

thinking we could go on a guided cork trail hike. The countryside looks beautiful and it won't be too hot yet... blah-de-blah-de-blah." I indulge in a spot of nod-craft to appease her. The plane makes a weird noise. I know it's probably just the engine doing what it's supposed to do once we reach our cruising height, but the iron grip I've had on my scarf for the past fifteen minutes doesn't feel solid enough and I lunge at the meatier armrest, hardly caring that Tiago is behind me. I can face my embarrassment once we're safely on land. Some things are more urgent, like getting through this flight without screaming.

"You never told me you were a nervous flyer," Kelly says, her face a picture of concern as I quickly turn to reassure her I won't be having a full-blown panic attack.

"Oh, I'm not really... I've just got a dodgy tum today so I'm feeling the bumps a bit," I palm her off with a little white lie and she goes back to her guidebook.

But the truth is that my nerves have been getting progressively worse, I acknowledge as we hit a flurry of air pockets. Callum always had his earbuds in on the few trips we made together, his eyes closed, lost in the music. He never sensed the frightened female beside him so I wasn't as bad. And things were somehow different when we went on those family holidays in the noughties: Dad may not have been the pilot, but the plane just felt safer when he was in it... because he was my dad and dads are in charge (or like to think they are).

I close my eyes and focus on my breathing, trying not to imagine what Tiago is getting up to behind me.

"Would you care for any refreshments, Madam?"

The sound of the steward's question stirs me. She's directing her enquiry at Kelly – what with Radhika still being glued to her travel pillow – and before Kelly can turn her away, I quickly blurt out: "One tea with lots of milk sachets if you can spare them, and one of those blueberry muffins, please."

"Coming right up."

"What are you wasting your money on that for?" Kelly frowns. "You surprise me sometimes, Willow. You're a gourmet custard tart chef. How could you? Do you realise how many preservatives those things have sticking them together? It's the last thing you need right now. You should have gone for a nice restorative peppermint tea. It's the ultimate relaxant."

"Says she who went to Starbucks."

Talk about double standards. Kelly's nose, now out of joint, is soon buried back in her book. The tall, attractive blonde woman serving me shunts the trolley back a little. Talking of noses and cliches, I imagine Tiago won't be the sort to pay through the nose for food on a plane. I recall Reggie quoting from a newspaper article once. It claimed that items like the blueberry muffin which I have just removed from its wrapper, and which looks to contain a grand total of three blueberries, are marked up by some six hundred percent by the 'budget' airlines!

"A glass of champagne, a tub of Pringles, a cheese and ham toastie, and a Cadbury's Twirl," I hear a slightly Portuguese accented male voice behind me put in his order. Okay then, I am quite mistaken.

Why haven't they invented an airline teapot that doesn't boil drinks to volcanic temperatures? Never mind sipping my tea, I need mittens to touch it once I have added the paltry contents of the two milk sachets to it. But I bring it to my lips anyway, taking cautious mouthfuls and grimacing, as it is too strong as well as too hot. I take my mind off it with a nibble of the muffin. It's as salty as it is sweet but it's food and I'll stop all these mental complaints now. I'm going on holiday! Which is totally overlooking the fact that at some point on this flight, I'll have to face the man sitting behind me at least once, but just for the duration of this cuppa and this cake (of sorts), I will try to relax and reframe things and quit imagining all the imminent calamities awaiting me.

At least that's my intention, but as we head out over the Bay of Biscay and today's generous covering of rain-filled grey clouds, I bring my drink to my lips again and the plane bumps and shudders unexpectedly. As I spill a vast amount of tea on my lap and let out a massive 'arggghhh', I know that was just wishful thinking.

The flight attendant, making her way back down the aisle, quickly spots my anguish, inundating me with napkins.

"It's quite normal to encounter a little turbulence on this route," she says sympathetically. I feel like such a twit. I can just imagine the smirk on Tiago's face, the champagne bubbles helping it along nicely. Not to mention the one-liners he's thinking up after I got the last word in the duty free shop.

Why hasn't teleportation been invented yet? I want to be on holiday *now*. I squeeze my eyes tightly shut, to conjure up images of endless blue sky and pristine golden beaches.

"Goodness, you gave yourself a proper soaking there," Kelly says. "I hope you're not burnt though."

"I'll pop to the loo in a bit and take a look," I say. "I'm glad I'm wearing jeans, they've borne the brunt of it."

"Look," Kelly says quickly. "I know it's the last thing you'll want to be thinking of on holiday, which is why I'm bringing it up before we set foot on Portuguese soil: have you heard anything else after that *dreadful petition*? I'm not a violent person but I will wring the neck of whoever did that to my dear friend, if our paths should cross."

"You and me both!" Radhika is suddenly awake. "Something tells me it could only be a man." Her eyes narrow.

My hands shake at the thought of my two friends on the warpath... and the guy they don't know they're on the warpath with being seated right behind me. And I spill the remnants of the tea over my lap. Why did Kelly have to say that last bit so loudly. Why the emphasis on those words?

"Can anything go right today?" I blurt out pathetically. I really am playing right into his hands. This is so humiliating.

"Oh, my God! I'm so sorry, hun. We'll stay off the subject. Here," Kelly says, dabbing away pointlessly with her solitary napkin at my three-quarter lengths, which are now sodden.

Despite my current state, I can't help but think back to my friends' recent visit to the bakery, unable to believe they haven't yet put two and two together with regards to my even-barmier-than-usual tart ideas and the very reason for their invention, the clear and constant threat that said issuer of petitions poses, the fragile state of my mental health. Clearly Kelly and Radhika have been too preoccupied with the holiday.

How I had dithered at the front of the counter when they came in that day, one minute trying to shield my whacky invention, the next wanting to announce its debut from the rooftops:

"You haven't?" Radhika had peered at the tarts on the shelf once I'd finally decided to move back behind the counter.

"I have," I'd affirmed, unperturbed by her astonished face.

"B-but…" Radhika had tripped over her words.

And then I'd let out a few mini chortles, because I am only human.

"What's up?" Kelly had asked, cottoning on to the action.

"You don't want to know," Radhika replied, as if she'd just spied a rat scurrying across the tops of my *natas*.

Unable to resist the temptation, Kelly took a look for herself, gritting her teeth so hard once she saw that she looked like a ventriloquist.

"Erm, Willow? Have you completely lost your mind?" she finally said.

"You're looking at the prosecco and custard tarts," snorted Radhika. "Let me assure you, those pale in comparison with these." She waved a hand loosely in the direction of my newest creation and looked the other way, as if she couldn't handle viewing the offending items for a second longer.

"*Crisp tarts!*" Kelly shrieked. "Please tell me that's merely referring to their texture… and not the fact that you have stuffed them with potato chips!"

Well, now here Kelly was being a hypocrite. This critique was coming from the woman who thinks it's acceptable to offer her customers tahini and hummus in an ice cream scoop. "Fried slivers of potato covered in oil and topped with salt. Are you serious?"

"Not entirely, no." I came clean. "I did it to infuriate

somebody should they dare to set foot in here again."

Now I am snapped back to the present again, by my rather pressing need to visit the facilities. The food and drinks trolley has now returned to the galley at the front of the aircraft and a toddler and his mum have just vacated the loos, so the vacant sign is illuminated. I'm going for it. This can't possibly wait until we land.

I walk as elegantly and as nonchalantly as I can, bearing in mind I look as if I have already peed myself. Once locked inside the tiny cubicle, I frown once at the thin paper towel dispenser, which will do nothing to help my soaked crotch predicament, and I frown twice at my blue reflection. On second thoughts, it really does suit my current Eeyore mood. But there's no point trying to get rid of my new look now. I attend to my business and steel myself for the short walk back to row seven.

Oh, great! Brilliantly timed, Willow.

Of course, once I emerge, I am stuck behind the tax free goods trolley, and of course somebody in row six is all a dither, bombarding the flight attendant with daft questions about a watch that they might finally decide to purchase if they can be persuaded. This wouldn't have been so bad if it had happened in rows one to five, but row six is just a bit close for comfort ref. avoiding eye contact with Tiago. So that's exactly what comes next. I will so much for it not to happen, that my eyes look straight into his, fluttering their lashes with an agenda of their own. Yes, actually fluttering!

Not only has the smirking Tiago noticed, but Radhika is nodding too, chewing her grin and doing that eye narrowing thing again. She's onto me. I've got to turn this around at lightning speed once I get back to my seat.

"Who were you having eye sex with, just then?"

"Radhika!" Kelly implores. "There's a young child in the row opposite us. Keep a lid on it."

"Surfer dude at the back of the plane," I fire back.

"With your eyes directed at approximately the location of your headrest?" Radhika snickers.

"For the love of God, find something else to do besides attempting to pair up every singleton in your radius, Radhika. You've got too much time on your hands." As have I. I check my mobile phone, which is on flight mode, and see we still have another hour to go before landing.

Yet, as with all journeys, somehow this one comes to an end and before I know it, the captain is talking about us making our descent to Faro, where a balmy twenty-eight degrees and a light westerly breeze await us. Perfect. Hold onto that thought.

If only I could hold onto my passport.

But no. Me being me, I lose my grip on it just as I am rearranging, of all things, a strand of hair. My precious proof of identity falls to the carpeted aisle, and the passenger in front of me accidentally kicks it out of my reach as they twist and stretch to reach their small case in the overhead locker.

"Nooooooo!" I cry, but my anguish is muffled in the hive of activity that is the excitement of a Portuguese holiday with everybody around me rushing to get off the plane and into the sunshine.

"Move forward, Willow!" Kelly and Radhika direct me in unison once we are all in the gangway. "What are you doing?"

"I've dropped my passport and it's been shunted down the

aisle somewhere," I reply as if it's perfectly obvious.

"Knowing you, I'm sure it's in your bag," says Radhika. "Why would anyone get it out now anyway? We don't need to show it until we're inside the terminal building at passport control."

"Because I like to have it ready. I'm telling you, I dropped it! And I'm telling you I'm not leaving this plane without it!"

"And I'm telling you, you're holding up the plane!" screams Radhika, nudging her elbow past Kelly and digging it sharply in my ribs. "We'll keep an eye out for it as we walk. If you dropped it, we're sure to spot it."

I agree in principle but I am only prepared to walk slowly, combing every detail of the rows with my dramatic eyes, crouching down to peek beneath the seats. I don't care if everyone is huffing and puffing behind me. Let them get on with it. Besides, Radhika can hardly talk about holding people up, when she decided to rifle through her suitcase at the check-in desk, removing its heaviest objects at her leisure as opposed to thinking of her fellow passengers and opting for the speedier solution of agreeing to pay for excess baggage.

We reach the third row now, where a bunch of elderly travellers are seated, and my stomach turns to lead. I still haven't glimpsed my passport. This is a disaster! How do other people get through this hideous scenario without having the world's biggest meltdown? Surely I can't be the first passenger who's lost my passport on a plane? Just when I resign myself to having no option but to burst into tears at the feet of the pilot, who has come out of his cockpit to cordially wish everyone a good holiday and a safe onward journey, I catch sight of a rectangular flash of maroon on the floor.

But it's too late to yell for the old lady on the end of the row to pick it up. I take a deep breath and try again but my panic is lost amidst all the frenetic grabbing of cases and seat exit etiquette ('you go first', 'no, you go first... you've got your hands full there with those little ones'). I squat in the aisle now, and people complain behind me. I swear Tiago's voice is in the mix but I need to see where my passport is. Once I'm off this plane there might not be any getting back on it. Anybody would do the same in this nightmare of a situation. The little grey-haired lady's companion passes her a walking stick from the overhead locker, and I watch in dismay as it connects with my passport on the floor, somehow causing it to fly to the very front of the aircraft, undetected by another soul, until it disappears underneath the food trolleys in the galley.

"Willow! You're going to get yourself arrested! Stand up!" Kelly's voice means business. Rising quickly, I take in the curious stares of the pilot and two of the female cabin crew, who look far from impressed at my shenanigans.

Rabbit caught in headlights, I can't get my words out. They are lodged stubbornly in my throat, much like during my wretched French GCSE oral exam, when all my vocabulary flew out of the classroom window and onto the football pitch. Panic engulfs me. I'll be thrown off this plane within seconds if I don't say something.

"She's lost her passport and I think you'll find it's somehow been kicked forward from row seven all the way to the food trolley," says a deep, smooth and calm male voice behind me.

"We have a very tight turnaround, Sir." The pilot frowns.

"If that's the case then the passport needs to be retrieved within sixty seconds. I simply can't hold the next flight up any longer."

The pilot taps his watch as he replies to the guardian angel behind me, who I already know to be Tiago. But – to avoid a massive argument, to get my hands on my passport and to swerve ending up stuck in an airport like Tom Hanks in that movie – I will pretend it is the imaginary surfer dude I was eyeing up earlier. The pilot gestures now at the queue of outbound passengers through the porthole window, and I can feel the wrath of the scores of people waiting behind me, the panel of airline professionals standing before me, and the impatient travellers waiting to greet me when I do eventually get off the aircraft.

"Allow me." Tiago brushes past me and rolls up his sleeve. He removes his cap and lies flat on the floor, legs sprawled down the aisle. Radhika giggles and there's a grumpy hubbub from everyone behind us. I try not to ogle his incredibly pert buttocks as he wriggles and he writhes, using the peak of his cap to fish around, until finally, at the pilot's count of "fifty-eight seconds", he is triumphant. He quickly scrambles up, hand gripping the passport, which he places in my palm, refraining from all eye contact.

I am mortified yet relieved, embarrassed yet I have no more dignity to lose anyway. I am *so* many things. My hands are shaking.

"Are you not even going to say thank you to that incredible man?" quizzes Kelly, before yelling, "*Thank you on my very ignorant friend's behalf*," as Tiago marches off the plane and we follow suit. Kelly puts her hands in praying motion to each of the cabin crew and pilot in turn. I shuffle past, willing the Portuguese ground to open up and swallow me whole, the moment we walk off the steps to connect with our next mode of transport: the ubiquitous bendy bus. All those who have pushed past us in the height of my dilemma are now staring menacingly out of its window. I seem to have become famous for all the wrong reasons.

Tiago is glued to a pole at the other end of the bus and every so often the vehicle brakes spectacularly, flinging him forward in a move that can only be described as uncomfortable. I feel guilty for having secured myself a seat, even though he doesn't appear to have spotted me. I know it's pathetic, especially after all the terrible things he's done before today, but I feel tears gathering on my lashes at the selfless heroics back there on the plane and my dreadful lack of decorum and gratitude, so I quickly whip out my sunglasses. I'd never have retrieved my passport by myself. For one, my arms are too short. I guess I'd have ended up at the British Embassy in Lisbon, begging and pleading my innocence, missing out on the holiday, and, I don't know, possibly even finding myself in jail?

Where the hell could Tiago be staying? My mind runs through the possibilities as we continue to skeeter around the tarmac to be deposited at Arrivals. I'd plump for Faro, where we are now. Well, it has the largest local population so statistically it makes sense. Nevertheless, how can I possibly relax for a whole week when I don't know? I'll be looking over my shoulder, even on my sun lounger.

You do often see people you know when you're abroad on holiday. At least Mum and Dad did, when we used to do the package holiday thing as a family. It's the weirdest phenomenon. And in the good old days, with Bristol airport flying to only a handful of enticing destinations, you kind of expected it, because barely anybody would make a trek up to London to then head for the Med.

"Oh, hello stranger!" Mum or Dad would invariably get accosted by a hand on the shoulder or an eager 'cooey' in a departure lounge.

"Darn it... I thought I'd managed not to catch Mike from Accounts's eye when we passed him five minutes ago," Dad would mumble through his fake smile as he cheerfully returned Mike's greeting and marvelled at the 'good fortune' of an unavoidable chat with his work colleague.

"Fancy us not only taking the same week off but ending up in the same resort!" Mike would reply chirpily.

But even those kinds of 'surprise' airport exchanges are bearable, especially with the get-out-clause of whining kids needing food/a pee/a giant Toblerone from duty free to keep them quiet. How am I meant to enjoy my week away, knowing Tiago and I could end up at the same bar, on the same dance floor, elbowing one another out of the toaster queue at the breakfast buffet, or in the same patch of the Atlantic ocean (with me being royally trapped unless I want to parade past him in my shabby old bikini, the one I didn't get around to updating before we left)?

This holiday is a nightmare. The flight alone told me everything I needed to know. I should never have left the perimeters of Weston.

CHAPTER TWELVE

"I STILL CAN'T believe you! Not only was he luscious, and not only did you have the perfect opportunity to engage in some serious flirting with him on that flight, but then he retrieved your bloody passport like a trooper! What more do you want, woman? That was your cue to insist on taking him out for a thank-you drink… which would have led to, well, you hardly need me to explain that!"

"It's complicated," I shout back over my shoulder. Well, it's true. Not that I'm about to divulge to either of my friends that I already know quite a lot about the man who held the plane up to prevent me from facing the authorities.

Radhika is a dog with a bone. She tears across the car park at me as I try to keep up with Kelly, and we collectively stride towards the car rental office. In typical style, Kelly hadn't checked the small print of the paperwork properly before leaving Bristol, and it appears we have two minutes to pick up our car before the office closes for the day. Kelly will insist on booking with cheap and cheerful companies.

"But this can't be right. I opted for the eco-friendly, low emission Citroen C3." Kelly is already propping up the desk and wailing as the hire car desk's operator checks through her documents and hands over the keys. It makes for a welcome distraction from Radhika's constant interrogation, and I couldn't be gladder.

"And the last client opted for a convertible Mercedes but ended up with a Fiesta. It's coming up to high season, love, and we reserve the right to make substitutions as and when necessary," the Irish-accented employee replies.

At least we have a car to drive us far, far away from all the fun and games of aircrafts, airport – and airborne passports.

Kelly sighs and shepherds us into the car park, so we can clamber into our behemoth and sporty convertible Alfa Romeo Stelvio Quadrifoglio.

Hey, maybe things are about to look up.

I allow Radhika to take on the role of co-pilot in the front, where she continues to debate my baffling behaviour with Kelly, reclining herself as far as the mechanism will allow and massaging her hands all over the pristine leather seats. My eyes are quite happy to grow heavy, a catnap easing me into its clutches halfway through the journey to the farm stay, but the glimpses of countryside I do catch as we turn off the main road and head inland for the hills are of little picturesque houses and occasional villas scattered across the green rolling scenery. Not to be outshone, farms and rustic cafés put in an appearance here and there, and the hot pink bougainvillea is a glorious assault to the senses. Rows of cork trees, some already stripped of their flaky outer layers, stand like obedient soldiers guarding the road. That makes sense, the area is well-known for its cork exports. Hopefully it won't jog Kelly's memory back onto the subject of hiking in the heat, though. I'm not up for any of that.

The quinta's owner, Luisa, emerges from the stone building to greet us as we pull into the rough and tumble car park at the exact moment dusk seems to fall. I smooth down my own rough and tumble hair after that *al fresco* drive without a car roof, and Luisa presses keys, maps and leaflets into our hands – this being an eco-resort, presumably the latter are recycled.

Kelly and I share a room. Radhika opts to have her own space (aka no interruptions to potential bedtime action). Although we are all famished, we are too exhausted to contemplate the trek up the hill to the nearest restaurant. Luisa has thoughtfully left us with a welcome pack of freshly baked bread, a selection of Portuguese cheeses, sardine pate, nuts, dried fruit, water, milk, coffee… and most importantly, wine. We are sorted.

THE SOUND OF a cockerel wakes me earlier than I'd planned. I stretch my limbs, pasting half a smile on my face anyway, in the realisation I'm finally on holiday. I look to the side to see Kelly is still dozing in her bed, and just for a blissful moment it's like the flight never happened: we really did click our fingers and teleport ourselves to this haven in the sun. Except I have a sore head from too many glasses of red, and now the ticker tape in my head presses replay and the antics of yesterday return to haunt me.

As if she senses my thoughts, now stuck on Tiago's thoroughly squeezable derriere, Kelly stirs.

"Why did you have to let me drink so much last night?" I grumble.

"It was organic wine, Willow."

"That doesn't make it OK," I laugh, immediately regretting it and putting a hand to my forehead to quell the throbbing pain. "I think you'll find the alcoholic content of wine is the same no matter what kind of grape it's come from. I need coffee," I wail. "And I could murder a *pastel de nata*, obvs."

"You've come to the right place for that." Kelly sits up in bed excitedly, far too animated for this hour, rubbing her hands together. "I can't wait to carpe diem everything. Come on! Do you want to shower first or shall I?"

Breakfast is legendary and so is our timing: a flurry of excitedly chattering guests leaves just as we arrive so that we get the whole room to ourselves. Much as I always encourage each and every female on the planet to throw out the calorie intake 'rule book' that's been thrust upon us since birth, I know we are inevitably going to go home a few unwanted kilos heavier between us. But it's worth it. Bowls of mouth-watering morsels have been set out before us and I genuinely don't know which way to look or where to start. Juicy honeydew melon, Madeiran cheese, farmhouse yoghurt, more dried fruit and nuts, warm bread rolls, honey, butter, and homemade lemon cake vie for my attention. But for all the bounty, there's not a trace of the custard tart that my belly and heart pine for. I can't settle. Soon I'll have been in Portugal for twenty-four hours and still I won't have sampled one! That sounds ridiculous. Such a first world problem. Especially when I bake the things day in, day out. But I have to know how far I've truly come with my own pastries. I've been looking forward to this taste test milestone. I need to try an authentic tart here in the Algarve asap, to know I am on the right track. And, far more to the point, that Tiago is on the wrong one.

"So what excitement do we have on the agenda today? No, no, don't tell me." A thoroughly grumpy Radhika lifts a hand to stop Kelly churning out her plans for us all. "Mucking out the pigs, collecting hens eggs, and a dip in the stream."

We arrived late last night and nobody has yet seen any evidence of the alleged 'luxury pool,' so perhaps Radhika is right and a country stream is the best we could hope for to cool off.

"You won't find any pigs here," says the teenage waitress with the nineties undercut beneath her mousey-brown ponytail, who has appeared from nowhere to refill our coffee. Never mind swine, Radhika looks sheepish. "But you can help with the eggs if you want: you'll be saving me a job. As for the pool, I can confirm it does exist, and it is pretty sumptuous, despite its size. I should know. Its construction ate into my uni budget and meant I had to hang around here for a year out... and counting."

Wow, this is quite a bolt out of the blue.

"Oh, my goodness. We are so sorry for our friend's rude outburst," says Kelly, who is probably beginning to regret bringing either of her friends with her.

"And for your... erm, your predicament," I find myself adding, eyes wide, "although hopefully you'll get back to your studies soon."

Radhika looks on, cheeks candy-pink, hand that was going in for the lemon cake hovering mid-air.

"You speak amazing English, may I say," Kelly takes back the reins of this unexpected conversation, and Radhika and I both breathe a sigh of relief.

"Dad's from Liverpool, and Mum – Luisa, who did the meet and greet last night – is a local. São Brás born and bred. And Manchester will always be there." The teen shrugs. "That's where I'm headed next year for my chemistry degree. I'm Leona, by the way."

"Wonderful to meet you, Leona. I'm Kelly, this is Radhika, and to my left we have Willow," Kelly fills her in.

"Right. Hi," Leona considers each of us in turn as if committing names to faces. "Anything else you want to know before I head down to the coast for my other job today?"

"Ooh, what's your other job?" At the sound of the word coast, Radhika's curiosity is piqued.

"Nothing riveting," Leona replies. "I'm a part-time tout. I hand out leaflets for a nightclub."

"Are you kidding?" I swear Radhika is going to pull the tablecloth off and upturn the breakfast dishes in her enthusiasm. "That's really cool. Room for a little one to tag along?"

"Are you for real?" Leona knits her brow.

"Sorry, I shouldn't have imposed myself upon you. Forget I…"

"Of course you can join me." Leona half giggles. "As long as you're up for a bumpy ride down the hill on the back of my moped. Helmet not optional. And as long as you're prepared to hand out half of the leaflets so I can get home quicker and out of the midday heat."

"Am I ever!" Radhika belatedly turns to Kelly and me. "You two don't mind, do you?"

"If it gets it out of your system." Kelly eye rolls.

"Before you go." I raise my hand as if we're in class.

"Where's the nearest place to get a proper Portuguese custard tart?" I say. But Radhika is already speaking, wanting to know what do people do in the quieter São Brás for nightlife. Predictable!

"Surely you can ask Leona later, when you abandon us?" Kelly tuts.

"What a contrast in priorities," Leona smiles. She puts her tray down. Frankly, I'm amazed she's carried it for this long, as it's laden with empties from the early bird guests. I'm not sure my own biceps could perform as well, back in my own establishment. "So, you're basically here on the pull?" Leona gestures at Radhika, who nods uncharacteristically shyly. "And you're one of those foodies," she turns to me. I can't argue with the way she sums me up, so I nod my head too. "I'm guessing you're the peacekeeper, Kelly?"

I love this girl's bluntness.

"Something like that," Kelly replies.

"Okay. If it's decent-looking men you're after, Radhika, don't make the rookie mistake of thinking you'd be better off staying at one of the busy resorts. Cupid works in mysterious ways. Yes, the hot lads are two-a-penny there." At the turn of this phrase, we are treated to Leona's gorgeous Liverpudlian accent. It shines through every couple of sentences. "But it's quality not quantity we women want. I've met past boyfriends and girlfriends here in our humble São Brás. So my humble bisexual advice would be to stick around here as much as possible and see what drifts your way. You'd be amazed."

Radhika snort-giggles.

"You're still very welcome to tag along with me today, though. I sense it's the only way you're going to see what I mean."

This Leona is a sage. Never mind Kelly and her new age pearls of wisdom. Short, sharp home truths are this girl's MO.

"As for the tarts, step this way, please, Madam."

I follow Leona's command as if I'm in a trance. She leads me to the side of the quinta. In the dusky light last night, I hadn't been aware of any of this, which is silly really, given I had seen the photos online.

"It's more of a confectioners than a bakery but we do make *pastéis de nata* here a couple of times a week. One of those times just happened to be this morning. However, none of the custard tarts made it to breakfast as Mum has been on a cake-baking spree with the lemons and needed to showcase her infamous *bolo de limão* instead. Anyway, I'm waffling now. The point is, you're in luck."

"I should say," I reply as I take in my surroundings.

Leona dips behind the counter and plates up a tart for me, depositing it on the glass top. It seems impolite not to dig in immediately, but I have to take stock of the other wonders in front of me. As is so often – and frustratingly – the case in a bakery whose language I cannot speak, few of the products are labelled. Not that any customer could possibly be disappointed... unless they had a food intolerance, I guess. The fragrance is intoxicatingly uplifting; almonds, figs, honey, orange and lemon permeate the air. Piles of sugar-dusted treats lure me toward them. Then there are pastries in every shape and size, and dinky little morsels ranging from chocolate balls to candied fruits, elegantly glazed and nut-topped squares of plain and chocolate sponge, and a side table groaning with hearty rounds of carob cake and fig and almond cake. I'm in rustic bakery heaven.

I sift out a couple of Euros from my pocket to pay for the goods, but Leona assures me this pastry is on the house. It beggars belief that I can still find room in my stomach, after the delights of breakfast just five minutes ago. That's the power of custard, as Frank often reminds me. I take a small bite and I'm rewarded with a smooth, soft, rich vanilla centre, with the most delicate of pastries encasing it.

"Like I say, if you're looking for a traditional custard tart place, this isn't it. The closest and the best on the Algarve is in Tavira. IMHO anyway," Leona advises. "Just follow the hill back down to the coast, head into Tavira town centre and it's this little place right next to the river as you turn left at the bottom of the main street. You can't miss it. You'll know you're close when you see the kiddie's fountain with the stepping stones in it."

I will beg Kelly to go, of course I will. And if I don't manage to convince her then I will happily embroil myself in a spot of car-napping. But for now I am entranced enough by the sweet pleasures that lie in front of me, and I continue to inhale their perfume greedily.

CHAPTER THIRTEEN

"CAN'T WE LEAVE it until the middle of the holiday?" Kelly asks. "You've had quite the custard tart fill this morning as it is, greedy guts."

My request to head to Tavira isn't greeted with the fanfare I'd hoped for, but I suppose that's to be expected. Kelly chose the quinta for rest and relaxation, and this is only the first morning. Three has already become two, with Radhika about to depart for the glitz and glamour of the Portuguese seaside, and we've not even dipped a toe in the serenity of our own aquamarine pool yet.

"Okay, then," I surrender. I'm happy to fall into step with Kelly's plans. Much as I adore custard tarts, they are my working life. I really ought to be switching off here; swimming, sunning myself and reading, forgetting about the hiccups (and random heroics) of yesterday. Utter bliss. I ignore the kernel of guilt that has lodged itself unhelpfully in my brain, telling me Tiago might not be able to do the same, after I disclosed that he works with my sister. Still, it's not my fault he irked me to the max. He's brought all of this on himself, and I have no intention of passing on Reggie's discoveries about Tiago to Lauren anyway. Tiago doesn't need to know this, though. Maybe a week in the sun will give him a chance to rethink his impetuous behaviour and withdraw that petition from wherever it's been submitted. I can but hope.

Kelly readjusts the large sunshade to a position that's more to her liking, mindful of her milky, easily burnt skin, and I lie on my ridiculously full tummy, squinting at the first page of the latest Liane Moriarty paperback.

"See you later, girlfriends! Enjoy your day!" Radhika cries, making us both jump and gasp. Her yellow helmet zips past us over the top of the hedge which separates the pool area from the track leading to the quinta.

"I'm sure she's in good hands with Leona," I reassure an anxious-looking Kelly.

"You're right. She does seem like a savvy lass. I just hope we don't end up living separate holidays, that's all. This was meant to be a group trip and already we're fragmenting over plans."

"Oh, I wouldn't worry about that. Something tells me Radhika will be back with us before we know it."

I pull my sunglasses down to scrutinise the flurry of dishy-from-a-distance male delivery drivers toing and froing from the back of the confectioners to fill their individual vans with boxes of sweet treats. So that's what Leona was alluding to! Radhika must have missed them by seconds.

"Fancy a dip?" I ask Kelly.

"We'll sink. We've barely digested breakfast!" Kelly is horrified at the idea.

"We've got the pool to ourselves now. Who knows when the early birds we briefly encountered at breakfast will be back from their excursion. We should make the most of feeling like we're in our own private villa while we get the chance. Besides, if we drown, help's not far away." I tilt my head toward the confectioners with a knowing smile and Kelly's eyebrows ascend to the heavens.

"Radhika's a numpty," she affirms. "And that's coming from a happily married woman whose eyes don't wander."

Several hours later we are gathered around the wooden table on our joint balcony, listening to the soothing chorus of cicadas. We're also swatting at mosquitoes that are refusing to wither in the face of Kelly's homemade lemon insect repellent. I had to come up with every excuse in the book to avoid hiking through carob and cork tree countryside earlier this afternoon, thanks to Kelly's insistence that my morning swim was not enough exercise to cancel out my gargantuan brekkie. Then mercifully Radhika returned to the fold and Kelly was finally outnumbered.

"All right. You're off the hook for today and today only," concedes Kelly. "Group meeting first thing tomorrow though. We need to cater for everyone's tastes on this holiday. It's only fair. Radhika, you've already gone off and done your own thing," Radhika opens her mouth to discuss all the juicy titbits of her day, but Kelly is on a roll. "You can tell us all about it later. And not only that, Radhika, but we've already agreed to a night out with you on the Strip, which is a grand gesture on my part since my clubbing days are far behind me." Radhika rolls her eyes at the drama and neediness in Kelly's voice. "Willow: we've agreed to a day in Tavira so you can visit this custard tart place and tick that box."

"Oh, don't make it sound like a chore!" I protest. "There's plenty of culture in Tavira too. It says so in your guidebook. You could head up to the medieval castle, go to one of the wide sandy beaches, take a boat trip, pop into the non-touristy shops and sample the delicious local products, take yourself off to the marshland for a spot of birdwatching—"

"Yawn!" Radhika pulls a real one after she says it, starting all of us off.

"Aw, I love that we're so very different," I say. "Yet when it comes to yawning, we have such empathy and can all subconsciously agree that it just has to be done en masse."

"Yeah, all right. Can we get off the bloody subject now, please? I can't stop doing the damn Y word," Radhika replies. "Which is hardly surprising when we are marooned in boredom-ville in the middle of nowhere."

"Is that so?" I challenge, disappearing inside to unplug my mobile phone from its charger, click on the photo gallery, and push it across to Radhika so she can see this morning's excitement in close-up. Yeah, I know it was majorly uncouth of me to get snap-happy with those guys – and without their permission, too – but I couldn't help it if they just happened to be in the background when I was taking my touristy holiday pics, could I?

"Right," says Kelly. "*My one request* is that we all go on a hike together. I don't think that's too much to ask. The terrain isn't as hilly as you might think, and we'd be setting off before the extreme heat of the day. It will be an excellent way for all of us to blow away the cobwebs and move our arses."

"Oh, I could be persuaded," Radhika replies to Kelly's statement without knowing it.

"Great. That's settled, then. In principle we have three events booked to cater to our three diverse tastes: my hike tomorrow morning... in fact, I've already taken the liberty of booking it up at reception; they'll provide us each with walking boots, sunhats, a delicious Portuguese packed lunch and bottles of water."

"You what?" Radhika has only just twigged what she's signed herself up for and does not look impressed.

"Keep up, hun. You just OK'd it, remember?" I giggle, although I'm Camp Radhika on this one myself, and really don't want to expend that much energy.

"Willow's Tavira trip Wednesday, and Radhika's night out Thursday," Kelly summarises.

"Friday will have way better hot male footfall in the bars and discos, Kelly." Radhika sulks.

I know it sounds ridiculously presumptuous, but soon that consideration will be but a distant memory. I can already tell that Radhika will be enamoured with at least one of this morning's hunky trio by the end of the week. Assuming they return to the quinta for rustic cake reinforcements, anyway.

"Erherm. You heard what Leona said on the first morning: don't make snap judgements as to where and when the talent might appear," I chip in. "Look at the opportunity that passed you by today, for example."

"Whatever. Do I even have a choice?" Radhika bristles.

"Hooray! I'm glad we've got that sorted," says Kelly, too entrenched in her own agenda to have a clue what Radhika and I are talking about. "Although evidently we'll have our work cut out reaching group compromises in between our days out. Now we don't need to have tomorrow's meeting after all and we can sit back, relax and play a round of gin rummy... minus the gin and with a good old pot of the pu-erh tea I packed for such an occasion."

"Yay. Riveting," says Radhika as she gathers up the cards

in the middle of the table to cut them and we settle down to the wholesome excitement of Monday night in a remote Portuguese farm house.

CHAPTER FOURTEEN

RADHIKA IS IN a sour mood at breakfast and she can't even put it down to a hangover after last night's tame game of cards and the rather astringent hot drink that accompanied it. Not even Leona's hilarious anecdotes, about Radhika's flier distribution technique and chat-up lines over the most sumptuous coffee cake I am sure any of us have ever tasted, can force a smile onto my friend's face. I can't help but wonder if there is more to these mood swings than meets the eye; if they aren't simply a 'quirk' of her personality but down to something else altogether. They've certainly increased in frequency over the past year. Then I forget about my concern, as she immediately brightens up when she catches a glimpse of the delivery guys as we head back to our rooms to get ready for the delights of the hike. Maybe their presence at the quinta really could be a daily occurrence…

"Can you think of a plausible reason for me to accost them?" She knocks on Kelly's and my door, out of breath in her rush to coat herself in a bottle of Impulse body spray that made the flight to Portugal. "Ah, well, forget it." She takes in our clueless faces. "I'm sure I'll pull something out of the bag," she shouts behind her as she scurries off.

Kelly and I never do find out the result of her efforts. In half an hour all three of us are clogging up the small reception area of the quinta. Radhika has beaten me and Kelly to it and she's deep in conversation with the hike leader, and seems to have brightened up to saturation point.

Gosh, the wisdom of young Leona never fails to impress, and it's only day two. The potential for romance in this small countryside town is on a level with the likes of an episode of Emmerdale. Opportunities seem to abound here, just as they do in the fictional village in the Yorkshire Dales, and every male has something going for them in the looks department.

The rugged and really rather beautiful Santi introduces himself to us, saving a special beam for Radhika as they giggle between themselves that they are already acquainted and he hitches a brow. No sign of a wedding ring either. Frankly, it's hard for any of us not to be smitten with the man and his thick, brown, funky pompadour hair, that looks so effortlessly styled. He's all in khaki too, making me wonder if we are off on an African safari. Hopefully minus the scary wildlife.

Santi rounds us up and drives us by minibus to a layby, which surely defeats the whole purpose of an excursion from an 'eco' retreat. He leads us animatedly down a track flanked, unsurprisingly, by cork trees.

"Who wants to know some cool cork facts before we head into this mini *montado* – our local cork forest?" he asks enthusiastically.

"I know that pretty much anything can be made out of cork," says his number one student, Radhika. She looks pleased as punch with herself. What a fickle madam, though, it was only last night that she was dissing all alternative holiday ideas, and now here she is pegging herself as a flora and fauna expert.

"Almost!" Santi replies warmly with a twinkle in his eye. "But yes, you are right. You'll find evidence of that in the many shops we have in the area. They sell everything from cork fans to cork flip flops, cork table mats, cork wine racks, cork umbrellas, cork-encased torches, cork pinboard table lamps and cork backpacks. Cork is light, buoyant, and super insulating. Cork is biodegradable and a naturally waterproof building material. Cork is magic!"

I am immediately transported to the 'shrimp' scene in Forrest Gump, when Bubba Gump reels off the infinite and varied ways that his beloved shrimp can be cooked... ad infinitum. I stifle back my giggles. It's great this guy is so passionate. And it's not just the cork he's passionate about either, I acknowledge, as I watch yet another furtive glance pass between himself and my friend. Radhika has hit the jackpot, as Frank would say!

There's something so invigorating about going for a walk you don't want to go on, too; the realisation slowly creeping upon you that you are actually enjoying yourself, and you really don't want the experience to end. I suppose my strolls in Weston along the pier are marred by a mostly vigorous 'breeze' that does its best to tangle my hair into a matted mess before I've even set foot in my workplace.

As we walk deeper into the rugged terrain of the small forest, the meditative movement clears my head of its circling thoughts about Tiago as well. And I know it sounds like wishful thinking, but perhaps that passport drama has triggered some kind of long-lost kindness and compassion deep within him? How can anyone go back to the self-righteous, selfish and sour person they used to be, after employing such Herculean effort to help a fellow human being? How can anyone proceed with an evil petition? How can anyone deprive a town of custard tarts? I'm beginning to see a silver lining in my clumsy calamity. I'm sure it's given him second thoughts and that puts even more of a spring in my step as we march onward, admiring the warblers swooping overhead. The perfume of the forest lifts the spirits. Notes of lavender, fig and strawberry dance in the air. Iberian peonies and ferns stud the uneven ground, and ancient cork oak trees and olive trees dot the landscape artfully.

We stop for lunch beneath a fragrant canopy of carob and almond trees and I marvel at my phone having a signal out here in the sticks. Despite being instructed not to do so under any circumstances, I decide to make a quick call to Caitlyn to check in on the café.

"Everything's peachy here. Peachier than peachy, in fact," she enlightens me over a semi-crackly line. "In a move that's taken everyone by surprise, the council has agreed to a 'spotlight on local businesses event' on the pier."

"That sounds interesting. So what's involved?"

"We can take the opportunity to have a stand of up to one metre long this coming Saturday. Reggie took the executive decision to hand out free custard tart samples, as opposed to selling. As and when people acknowledge their delight at the various treat sensations, they can make their way down to the café with a discount card for ordering over a dozen tarts. He was petrified you'd go ballistic but I assured him I'd cover any costs incurred that you weren't happy with. That's how sure I am that it'll work."

"What's he like? I think it's a fab idea."

And good on the council for thinking outside the box.

With the success of Emma's roadshow, the bookish events, and Caitlyn's amazing friends, it's become impossible to quantify the effect of Lauren and Todd's marketing efforts, and I'm suddenly hit by a wave of guilt... followed by a tidal wave, when Caitlyn asks, "Willow? Is everything okay in Portugal? It's just that you sound a bit weird."

But I can't let on that Tiago is in the same country. It would take too long to rake up that particular story and I'm conscious that it's not only the trees in this forest who have ears.

CHAPTER FIFTEEN

MY PATIENCE HAS paid off and finally we are Tavira-bound. Even Kelly is enthused, having consulted her guidebook to find out more about the draws of the town that I'd already mentioned to her.

Radhika tried to wiggle her way out of today's excursion. Predictable. First Santi invited her to accompany him on another hiking trail, then two of the delivery guys asked her out for coffee… unbeknownst to each other and all on the same day. But Kelly was having none of it.

"You've got the rest of the week for that kind of gallivanting. And you did rather have Santi all to yourself yesterday. Don't think that Willow and I are fooled. We saw you having a crafty snog with him behind that cork tree. Portuguese country walks evidently aren't as boring as they used to be."

Radhika flushes but says nothing, resigning herself to the pact we have made.

"I think this must be the place," I say excitedly, pointing at the window of a bakery displaying rustic hillocks of imperfectly perfect custard tarts, after having meandered along several of Tavira's picturesque streets with my friends on my coattails. "We passed the fountain with the stepping stones back there and I don't see anywhere else that fits the bill."

"Cute," says Kelly. Swiftly followed by, "Erm, Willow?"

in such a way that I just know what's coming next, particularly as Kelly is pulling at her T-shirt somewhat excessively.

"*Yes?*"

"Do you mind if I leave you to it?" she asks, looking slightly abashed. "It's just that I've got my heart set on hunting out tiles while we're here and that castle looks interesting, too. I wouldn't mind getting a bird's eye view of the area from the top... and it would be awesome to check out some of the herbal shops to see if they've got any locally-made products for sale."

"And *I* wouldn't normally dump you either, matey," says Radhika, briskly jumping in with a behemoth smile now she's been given carte blanche, "but Miguel, Delivery Guy *Número Um* just texted me. It's *purely coincidental*, I swear: He's doing a few drop-offs to the restaurants and cafés in town today and wondered if I fancied a quick bite to eat."

Kelly and I narrow our eyes. "*What?*"

"I think you'll find that technically speaking, I have fulfilled my side of the bargain," Radhika's brow creases as she stands her ground. "I've accompanied you to Tavira. It's a fact that cannot be disputed." She opens out her arms, gesturing at the entire town to prove her point.

"Fine." I sigh in defeat. "Next time I'll get you to spit and shake on the specific details. But I have deeply unconventional tastes in dream day trips and I can't expect either of you to understand that. Go on your date, and go playing culture vulture," I tell the two of them. "I'll meet you at the fountain at four o'clock, okay?"

"It's a date," says Radhika, who clearly has only one thing on her mind.

"Deal," Kelly echoes.

My friends waste no time in getting away and I let out another sigh, but this one is of utter contentment. Finally I have some proper and precious *me* time, I realise, as they retreat into the distance, going their separate ways.

I'm not quite taken back to fourteen-year-old me, and my first experience of a Portuguese bakery. But something about the *pasteleria* I am about to walk into feels magical and otherworldly all the same. A strange sensation washes over me and I can't quite label it, other than to say it feels like everything will change when I leave this place today. It takes me a while to adjust to the darkness and the mahogany furniture that's so typical of these old authentic eateries, and see that the bakery is buzzing inside. Half of it is reserved for those who wish to stay in and enjoy their *pastéis de nata* at their leisure, and the other half is a thriving bakery counter selling, just as Leona had suggested, nothing but custard tarts. Selling them like hot cakes! They are plain, no-nonsense custard tarts. That goes without saying. But here in the palm of tradition it works. In fact, my own style of business would be inconceivable lining these streets.

"*O que você gostaria?*" asks the little old lady at the counter. She has inquisitive brown eyes and a bright red floral scarf wrapped around her low bun. It's a hairstyle I haven't yet contemplated and I am mesmerised by its simplicity and elegance. You simply don't see senior citizens attempting this kind of look in the UK, where everyone seems to go in for the standard granny vogue of short back and sides, stylish as that may look on some. The lady's two female sidekicks of a similar age look equally glam in their own right.

I open my mouth and quickly shut it again, suddenly realising I haven't even had the gumption to learn a few basic phrases in Portuguese. What a typical Brit abroad. I point at the tarts instead and show the lady I would like two; hopeful that the sign I am making with my fingers is not inappropriate in this country.

She smiles and scoops up a pair of tarts with a large palette knife, putting them in a brown paper bag, and passing them to me. I hand over my euros. Clutching the pastries to my chest, I am just about to point at the tables behind me to see if I might be allowed to savour my *natas* inside instead of on the street, when a burst of activity spills into the serving area through the kitchen door, all arms and gestures and streams of Portuguese, all male and moreish, all...

Tiago.

Tiago?

But no. It can't be. I'm mistaken. My eyes are playing tricks on me yet again. That, or I'm in a trance. Because his family is based in Faro. I know I'm in a *pasteleria*, and I know that some might say that was a slightly crazy place to head if I didn't want to bump into the guy. But this *pasteleria* is in Tavira. I made a calculated decision about today's trip. I looked at the map in Kelly's guidebook over and over, for goodness sake. The distance from Faro to Tavira is thirty-eight kilometres. That's like the distance between Weston-super-Mare and Bristol. It's as safe as houses, when you don't want to meet your biggest enemy.

I edge my way backwards in a flap. There's no way I'm sitting inside now. But it's too late. The little lady is determined to find me a seat, and won't have her customer leaving without the true *pasteleria* experience. She squeaks away in Portuguese and says something over her shoulder to the apparition. That's when I realise the man standing behind that counter is made of atoms and molecules, just like anyone else, because he ducks down to grab a plate, spins to pass it to his – his grandma? – our eyes meet... and the plate smashes.

Well, at least it's not always me who is the clumsy one, then.

Grandma huffs and puffs and Tiago just stands there as rigid as one of those Nutcracker dolls – minus the big hat and moustache. I find I'm doing the same, to be fair, with the little old lady in the middle of us both, arms everywhere, sharp tongue telling the inept young man behind her what she thinks of his waiter skills.

I'm too scared of her to run for it, so I meekly take the seat she indicates and consider tipping the tarts out of the paper bag so I can hyperventilate into it. This I had not expected. Spots dance before my eyes and I panic that I'm going to pass out. I hear china being swept, then the chink-chink of fragments being thrown in a dustbin, but I don't dare look up. I'll get some sugar down me and get out of here. Suddenly Kelly's castle expedition – or even playing gooseberry with Radhika and Miguel – seem like very attractive prospects.

Except I can't do that, because I sense somebody is walking toward me, and, like a real waiter in a café, his timing is impeccable: right when I have a chunk of flaky pastry lodged in my throat.

"You came!"

This cap-free version of Tiago, his dark glossy hair impeccable, immediately spots my predicament. He darts back to the counter, returning with a much-needed bottle of water which I knock back in one, spilling unsightly dribbles down my chin as I try to prevent myself from choking.

"Don't flatter yourself," I can't help but return his words from earlier in the week, wiping my chin with the back of my hand, in a most unladylike manner, thanks to the absence of a napkin. "I th… thought Tavira was no man's land, that's all."

Tiago's eyes light up and he takes the seat opposite me, lacing his fingers together and propping his chin on his knuckles.

"How so?"

He's so close to me, the scent of CK One Shock is acting like smelling salts. I can see the flecks of gold in his deep molten chocolate eyes. It's turning my insides into one hot pool of uninvited lust that's in danger of spiralling somewhere rather intimate, so I fiddle with the tart's pastry instead and will myself to simmer down.

"You kept on about Faro so I just assumed you'd be equally *far-oh* away from me. I guess I got that a bit wrong." I cringe at my pathetic play on words.

"To be fair, you never really gave me a chance to explain that my invitation was to come here: to my grandmother's *pasteleria*. When I was trying to work out where you were staying, I used Faro as a kind of drawing pin in the map of the Algarve. I mean our plane did land there, after all."

I pop a piece of the sublime *nata* in my mouth, determined not to show how much I'm enjoying it. It's all very well playing with my food but the sooner I eat this, the sooner I can extract myself from this hideous dilemma.

"Right. Erm, I suppose a belated thanks is in order for the passport fiasco," I say after swallowing my mouthful and ensuring history doesn't repeat itself by tipping back the dregs of my water. "So, yeah, *obrigado* for that."

"*Obrigada*," Tiago corrects me. "You're a woman." He lingers over the word and his eyes roam my face. It's not uncomfortable, and yet something about his body language makes it feel like the prelude to being whisked off to bed. "You say the Portuguese word for thank you with an 'a' on the end."

I know that really. Of the four or five words I've picked up in Portuguese, that tiny but important distinction is one of them. But of course I am under his spell, quite unable to defend myself. I resort to gritting my teeth instead.

"Anyway, what do you think of the *pastéis*? Amazing, aren't they?"

"A bit… yes."

"Oh, come on, Willow." It's the first time he's used my name and, although I'm reluctant to admit it, it makes my heart flutter. "You can't deny how fantastic they are. *Just as they are.* Which leads me to say something else now, that you'll either take as a compliment or want to slap me across the face for… but I'll take my chances anyway. You look fantastic too, without the huge sapphire and turquoise eyes. Not that it isn't your prerogative to have huge sapphire and turquoise eyes, but they are colourful enough without all that makeup. Oh, you know what I mean."

"Do you need this?" I pick up the fork and hand it to him, trying in vain to ignore the bolt of electricity that flies through my hand and up my wrist as skin brushes skin. "It's not a shovel, but it will help you with that very large hole you are digging yourself."

Something about the ridiculousness of all of this finally hits us both at the exact same moment and we break into unadulterated laughter. Belly-clutching giggles. Tears stream down my face and I marvel at the way human emotions can change so very quickly. Grandma is hovering at the edge of the table when I can finally breathe again; a sure sign to put a lid on it and make my exit, lest she be left with no customers. I rise to do just that but Tiago puts a gentle but firm hand on mine. We both look at each other, somewhat startled. Actually, my eyebrows feel as if they've taken off and are orbiting space. Tiago looks at least half as shocked at what's going on. And then Grandma totally throws me off my balance by saying:

"So, Tiago, I think it's time to introduce your *avó* to your *amiga*."

And just like that, any hopes of me making my great escape evaporate into thin air.

"Well, Grannie." Tiago's chipper confidence disappears in a puff of smoke too, his voice warbles. Evidently 'Grannie' is quite a matriarch figure in his family. "This is Willow... a fr-friend from England. And Willow, this is my grannie, Elsa."

"Ohh," Elsa crows. "And why didn't you tell me when you placed your order, *minha querida?*" She looks questioningly at me and I try not to flinch under her scrutiny. "I would not have taken your money had I known you were acquainted with my delightful grandson. Those tarts would have been a gift. Still, you are here now and I insist that you'll eat dinner with us this evening back at the house. I've got a *caldeirada de peixe* on the go."

I cannot get over this lady's English. Although heavily accented, her vocabulary is both extensive and impressive. And I can't get over that invite, either. No, though. As much as the idea of (what sounds like) fish stew is making my stomach rumble. Grannie Elsa's got the wrong end of the stick here. The wrong end of a very wrong stick. There's not a chance I'm going to be doing any of that. I open my mouth to protest at the same time as Tiago.

"I really can't, you see, I have to get back to my friends who I'm here on holiday with, but thank you for your kindness."

"She... Grannie, no. I mean we haven't known each other so long – we're merely acquaintances, that's all."

"Is that right?" Elsa looks pointedly at our hands. They appear to be waiting to be bound together in holy matrimony by a vicar. I deftly snatch my fingers from Tiago's grasp. And then I feel bereft. *Oh, for crying out loud, Willow! Get a grip. This is the man who is trying to put you out of business, you stupid, STUPID girl!*

"Okaaay," Elsa looks from one to the other of us, scanning our faces to see who will cave in and reveal the truth first. Which is pointless. We've both told her the facts. And yet our body language had an agenda of its own just then. "At the very least you will come into the kitchen so I can give you a little tour of the *pasteleria* and send you off with some fresh supplies for your friends."

At this, she tucks my arm under her wing and walks me behind the scenes into the busy kitchen. I feel like a show pony bustling past the other ladies, busy serving their customers. Tiago paces nervously behind us, hands upturned, eyes wide like a Pleading Face emoji when I turn to him for an explanation.

"Here we have the heart of the operation, the hub of the business. Allow me to present my youngest grandson, Eduardo, who is learning the ropes, and my husband—"

"It's her second husband so he's not my actual grandad," Tiago interrupts his grannie's sentence.

"He's been as good as, and you know it, young man. Eduardo *and Silverio*: say hello to our guest," Elsa sets Tiago straight and completes her introduction to the old man who is currently hunched over the very familiar sight of a tart mould.

Eduardo raises a hand, rolling out pastry so deftly that I wonder what he has to learn. Silverio doesn't look up immediately, as we watch him pour the last of a jug of buttercup-yellow custard into the pastry cases. Finally, he gives us a little wave, devoid of eye contact, his mind on more important things as he heads to the oven with the tray, briskly pulling two batches of beautifully scorched *natas* from the heady heat and setting them to rest on the worktop. It is a polished operation and I can tell straight away that this man would be as alarmed as Tiago is at the baking methods Tim and I use.

On which note, I really should make my excuses and go, before my culinary sins are laid bare for all to dissect at the kitchen table. I can already tell that Elsa will go ape... and there are far too many rolling pins on this worktop for my liking, all of them just lying in wait for her to strike me with. I remove my phone from the back pocket of my cut-off denim shorts and ask Elsa's permission to take a photo of Silverio's handiwork (with the ulterior motive of checking the time). *Sugar.* There's only half an hour left before I'm due to meet Kelly and Radhika. I'll have to slip away as quickly as I can.

As if sensing my desperation to leave, Elsa cracks open a bottle of port and sets out four mini goblets, plying her visitor first with what appears to be a non-negotiable tipple. I accept it gratefully... for medicinal purposes. I'm still in a weird state of shock, after all, unable to fathom how one thing has led to another so fast. The bitter blackberry and chocolate *mêlée* hits my throat and I feel my eyes glaze over. Then I watch Silverio quickly but carefully remove each tart from its piping hot mould. My back senses the heat from Tiago's body as he edges closer.

"Will you stay for dinner if it's just you and me?" he whispers in my ear, making me jump when Elsa, Silverio, and Eduardo are deeply immersed in their respective tasks, his lip brushing my earlobe ever so slightly. "I'll drive you back to your accommodation before midnight and I'll behave like a gent. You have my word."

What did he just say?

My brow furrows as if trying to work out an equation that doesn't add up. I wonder if I've somehow gulped down two or three glasses of this port without realising it. Okay. I've told you several times over that I don't swear, but now I am going to have to – if only in my head. *This is majorly fucked up.* All I came to Tavira for today was custard tarts, for a taste test of the most authentic local specimens I could find, so I could compare them to my own and decide, deep within my heart (and belly), if I am on the right track with my venture. *I am.*

And now I've got legs like Bambi's, a pulse of I-don't-even-want-to-know-what, and a dinner date that I definitely didn't see coming, especially given that I am dressed in an old T-shirt, frayed denim shorts, and a pair of sensible and totally un-sexy Birkenstocks.

Elsa, oblivious to the fireworks her enigma of a grandson has set off in my stomach, gets to work laying out cardboard boxes and a large paper carrier bag bearing the name of the family's business on it: *Pasteleria Pereira*. Before I even have time to answer Tiago with 'I really don't think so... this is not some holiday version of Pride and Prejudice," there comes a very English-sounding voice from the shop outside.

"Hellooooooo! Anybody there? I mean *olá...*"

Sugar. No, condiments won't do... *shit*. That's Kelly!

"Tiago, go and see to the customer, Susana and Carolina must have their hands full," Elsa instructs her grandson, just at the moment when I think I have formulated something kickass and get-out-clause-esque to quip back to him, in the wake of that proposition. But the next thing I know, Kelly and Radhika are trailing into the kitchen behind Tiago, all full of the wonders of modern day 'coincidence'.

"Well, well, well! This was obviously meant to be, wasn't it?" Kelly crows as we stand in a little huddle, with Elsa and her team beavering away in the background.

A ridiculous grin plasters itself across Radhika's face. "You're the epitome of a dark horse, matey... and a bloody good actress to boot. I thought I'd sussed you on the plane, but then you spun such a convincing yarn... and you weren't remotely grateful for this guy's heroics. I never could fathom that."

Both friends are staring at me. If there were an illustrated dictionary of the emotional states, I'd be top choice as the pictorial reference for *flustered*.

"Oh, no, no, no, no, *no*. This is not what it looks like at all. I couldn't possibly have known he'd be... don't go putting two and two together and coming up with... I thought he'd be in Faro..." And on and on I go, words spilling from my lips like a runaway train. I seem to have taken my cue from Tiago, digging my own very deep hole.

"You *are* allowed to enjoy yourself, Willow. It's been ages since Callum," says Kelly, quite superfluously. If I had a wet kipper to hand, I'd slap her across the face with it – and then some. What is she thinking? *Exactly.* She isn't.

"Can I borrow her for a little longer?" asks Tiago, eyes darting between the three of us. "I promise I'll look after her."

"Now just a minute." I wave at everyone, feeling over-whelmingly provoked. "Do I, as a twenty-eight-year-old woman, get a say in any of this? These two are my friends." I turn to Tiago. "They're not my flipping parents. I mean, not that I have to ask my parents' permission to do anything, or erm..."

I'm not sure where my protest is leading. Tiago's face does something familiar yet unfamiliar. It's the same bizarre expression that washed over him when things got heated in the perfume shop and I marched off. Somehow my words have wounded him. Again.

"It was written in the *airwaves*, guys," croons Radhika, bringing me back to the present and the very crossed-wire idea that has taken up residence in her head. "What a gorgeous love story you'll have to recount to your children, when they ask how Mummy and Daddy first met. Headline: 'Knight in shining armour saves princess from being locked up in Portuguese prison'. Aw, if it doesn't sound like one of those modern-day Mills and Boon titles."

Elsa's timing is impeccable. She bustles into our little circle of debate, lumbers Kelly and Radhika with bags of tarts (it's such a similar move to the way I plied her grandson with assorted pastries in my own café prior to booting him out, it is almost hilarious), and mumbles away in Portuguese, shooing my friends out of the door as if they're a pair of irritating wasps. Neither Kelly nor Radhika even attempts to protest, and off they go on a gale of high-pitched laughter. I am speechless at their desertion. I don't need to look at Tiago's face to know his injured look from moments ago has shapeshifted into a tiny smirk.

"Now then," Elsa says, rubbing her hands together as she returns to the kitchen, and Tiago and I stand there, wondering what she's got in store for us next. "Let's have some coffee and get to know each other better."

CHAPTER SIXTEEN

"I'M NOT BUYING it," Elsa insists as she pours out the thick Delta coffee, which is apparently the brand of choice in these parts. I panic when I realise there is no milk to dilute it. Eek. "There's something more than meets the eye about you two and I feel it's my duty to get to the bottom of it. In fact, neither of you will be leaving my kitchen until we do."

Nosey old cow!

I know I shouldn't be so harsh, in the light of this woman's hospitality, and I'm grimacing inwardly at my ugly thoughts, but I'm trapped in an unforeseen whirlwind here. Then again, to be fair, only half of me wanted to escape with my friends. The other half, the wicked half, wanted to see where things might lead if I hung around. Purely to preserve my café, you understand, and absolutely not because of any carrot-dangle of a romantic candlelit dinner – or what might be served for dessert.

Tiago takes a deep breath. Which is good, because I haven't a clue what to say to his scary grandmother, and instead will be investing all my trust in him to get me out of this pickle with the same gusto he got me out of passport-gate.

"Argh, it's a bit of a thorny subject, Grannie, and I really don't think it's fair on Willow to rake it up. She'd be so outnumbered." He gestures to the ever-silent Silverio, who has downed his tiny cup of elixir already. Then Tiago waves a hand to his cousin Eduardo in the distance, as an afterthought. "It's probably best that I take her back to her holiday accommodation now."

What? This guy is nothing but hot air. The last thing he said was that he wanted to take me out for dinner. Okay, to me only. But still. I don't know whether I am coming or going.

"I think I'll be the judge of that," Elsa sips at her coffee, winces and adds a cube of sugar.

Great, so the very scenario I dreaded will now come to pass; my custard tarts pulled apart and sneered at, an epicurean autopsy at the table. Remind me why I thought a trip to Portugal was a good idea again?

"Willow? Are you happy for me to drop you in it?"

"I'm not really following. What do you mean?" I mumble, avoiding eye contact. Has he set this whole thing up so he can shame me in front of his family, lulling me into a false sense of security with his empty promises of a reconciliatory dinner for two? Then BAM: the moment my guard is down, he strikes with cobra ferocity.

"I mean…" Tiago says, looking at me tenderly (but I'm falling for none of that now I know he's one big phony). "I can't really explain how we met without, well… explaining we met courtesy of *your major culinary faux pas.*"

See. The utter git.

Every inch of allure he might just have had has melted, faster than the butter in Silverio's custard. He's evidently got no qualms about me reporting him to Lauren and Jamie over the petition.

Not for the first time, I stand up to leave.

"Whatever are you talking about, Tiago?" Elsa hisses. "And please, you are our guest, Willow. You must finish your coffee," she insists, looking at me kindly.

"Oh, I'll tell you what I'm talking about, Gr—"

"No," I say firmly, the after-effects of the afternoon port kicking me firmly up the backside and igniting some much-needed confidence. "*I'll* tell you what he is talking about, Elsa, and then you can decide on the punishment to fit my heinous crime." I take a deep breath. "I make and sell custard tarts with fillings. In England, of course. I wouldn't dream of doing such a thing in Portugal, though it was down the coast in Vilamoura where I tasted my first *pastel de nata* and fell head over heels in love. When I say fillings, I don't mean the sugar, water, cinnamon, lemon zest, vanilla, milk, flour and eggs-only kind." I spit that last bit out so fast it sounds like a single word.

A lull seems to fall upon the room, stopping time. I fear I might suffocate, anticipating this gastronomical grannie's high-pitched shriek of a reaction, but the open door to the bakery is behind me. Thanks to all the speed-walking to work in the winds and weathers that Weston-super-Mare has thrown at me, I know I can be out of this place in next to no time.

"Good for you. I like a little innovation and entrepreneurship." Elsa finally speaks, her eyes twinkling unexpectedly. "So, what exactly do you put in them?"

"*Are you serious?*" Tiago cries. "And the question should be what *doesn't* she put in them?"

Tears prick at my eyes. Why have I let myself become

trapped in this spider's web? True, the alcohol hasn't helped. But I've been gaslit every step of the way by this wolf in delectable clothing. On my holiday, too!

Elsa tuts heavily, shaking her head. As if in disagreement with Tiago, and in solidarity with me.

"Life is evolution, Tiago! There is nothing wrong with a little change. Tell me about what you have done with our beloved *pastéis*, Willow. I'm sure it's quite lovely. And you, Tiago. Be quiet." I'm halfway back to loving her again already.

I gulp all the same, because she will soon change her mind when she hears just how far my twists and turns have extended. I'll be hung, drawn and quartered! I'll never leave this kitchen.

With trembling hands, I show Elsa pictures of my individual tarts from The Custard Tart Café's website. The website designed by the very company that the guy sitting next to me works for. It's the easiest way. She gasps. I panic. But when I spot the sweet little grin on her face, I realise it was a *good* gasp. She loves the idea… I think.

"Look, it isn't for me, or my generation here in this town." Oh. "But, having learnt English over the course of many summers in Oxford and Cambridge and Brighton and Bristol, for the benefit of tourist customers here in the Algarve – and for the benefit of Tiago's late father – and having understood a little of the English psyche, I think it's an excellent enterprise and I commend you, my dear."

Elsa turns on Tiago before he can protest, before I can process what she just said about his dad.

"Why are you so determined to put this girl's achievements down? You know full well that the Portuguese government fully encourages all of this culinary innovation. Take umbrage with them, if you must, but not Willow. Her love for the *natas* is pure. Innocent childhood memories that she's simply transformed in her own style. From the French croissant to the American donut, what cake hasn't had a makeover at some point down the line?"

"There are good makeovers – and then there are bad ones."

I know that Tiago is referring to my caking at the cosmetic counter all over again. Any snippet of sympathy I had ref. the late father comment disappears instantly.

"You're missing the biggest point, Tiago." Elsa shakes her head in exasperation. "Willow is doing this for her own people. Not the Portuguese! If people want to experience the tart in its pure form, they come to bakeries like ours instead."

"I couldn't have put it better myself. Thank you, Elsa."

"You're very welcome, *mihna querida*." Elsa lays a reassuring hand on top of mine. For some strange reason goosebumps fleck my arm. "Why can't the custard tart be the vehicle for all sorts of delicious fillings, eh? It's not going to make the standard *pasteleria* go bankrupt or become extinct." She finishes off with an elaborate "tsk".

I baulk at the mention of the word 'vehicle', itching to check that Lauren isn't drip-feeding this speech to Elsa through a hidden earpiece. It sounds exactly like the kind of thing my sister would say.

Elsa stands to clear away our cups, clipping Tiago playfully across the ear in case he hasn't quite got the message yet. "You know full well how it is with *farturas* these days, boy!"

I am lost. Bewildered. All at (Atlantic) sea.

"*Farturas* are like Spanish *churros*," Elsa explains. "Except fatter."

"My grandmother is insinuating that *farturas* have long been fiddled with," says Tiago. "Go to a fair or a public event in Portugal nowadays and it's virtually impossible to find a stand selling plain *farturas* with just a dusting of sugar or cinnamon. *As they should be.* Millennial vendors are stuffing them with all sorts of ridiculous fillings – from Nutella to jam... and Gen Z are all too happy to oblige and scoff them."

"Oh, you're living a sheltered life over there in the UK if you think that Gen X and the Baby Boomers aren't cashing in on the evolution of taste buds too," Elsa says. "Honestly, Tiago, it's precisely those generations of people who are selling funky *farturas*!"

Okay. I am fully back to loving this woman now. She's as cool as Leona.

"And the problem with that is?" I can't resist joining in and quizzing her grandson.

"There is no problem," Elsa replies firmly on Tiago's behalf.

CHAPTER SEVENTEEN

"Okay, so that's me told," Tiago sulks, flumping onto a bench next to Tavira's river Gilão. His face is the kind of resolute glum that not even the gorgeous sunset, pouring liquid gold onto the water's surface, can turn into a smile.

We have managed to leave the *pasteleria* at last. In other words, Elsa has shut shop for the day and finally accepted I can't take up her kind offer for dinner. I have to get back to my friends... don't I?

Then why am I still at her grandson's side when he has been so rude to me, when I could easily be making my getaway, when there's a taxi rank just down the road?

"I have a couple of unanswered questions," I say, surprising myself, delivering my own answer as to why I am sitting a little too close to him on the bench.

I squint at the arches of the Roman bridge that spans the river, then I pull my shades down from the top of my head and pop them on. I have probably already wrecked today's hairstyle, the power ponytail, whose vibe we know doesn't always follow through to words, actions, and deeds.

"Fire away. After what I put you through back there, you have a right to know the truth," says Tiago. Wow. I never thought he'd be so open to a grownup discussion. But indeed, after the carry-on this afternoon, he definitely owes me an explanation... or three.

"Why?" I start, then quickly change tack. "What I mean is, when your grandmother has made it clear she has no qualms about change and even the Portuguese government is giving the thumbs up to the nation's beloved *pastel de nata* being sold overseas... in various guises... how come you personally have such an issue with what I am doing? It doesn't make sense. I didn't know you before I set up my business. This isn't some kind of attack on you and your family. I put years of training and hard work and, above all, *love* into what I am doing. How could you be so callous as to try to destroy that for me?"

"I'm sorry. Grannie's home truths leave me under no illusion. I was probably wrong."

"Could you not have worked that out for yourself?" I ask patiently. Also, there is nothing *probable* about it. I am baffled by the guy. But this feels a little like the conversation with Frank back in the café weeks ago. Or, to put it another way, I could be one of those fishermen standing in a row to our right. Patience is everything, if I am going to get a bite and reel something juicy in.

"It's complex."

"Isn't it always? Well, I'm in no rush. You did invite me out for dinner, after all. Or was I imagining that bit?"

"You weren't imagining that bit."

He turns to look at me. Really look at me. Despite the shield of my Ray-Bans, I want to melt. That face is Antonio Banderas in *Take The Lead*. It's a flipping good job that I can't dance the Argentine tango. I'd be in it deeper than that river in front of us.

"I guess you heard my grandmother refer to my late father."

I nod slowly and sadly. He turns his attention back to the river, where a couple of little fishing boats are now chugging by.

"My parents died when I was twelve," he says. I inhale sharply. "Hit and run car crash in Bristol on the dual carriageway, about a mile from where we were living at the time. They were almost home from a night out at the theatre. *Phantom of the Opera*. I've never been able to watch it... unsurprisingly." Now Tiago takes a deep breath. "*Avó e avô* (Grannie and Grandad) were visiting us from Portugal at the time. Dad was British. Mum Portuguese."

"Oh, my goodness," I say, wishing I had something better to offer him... like the ability to turn back time and rearrange events.

"Mum met Dad when he was a holiday rep in Albufeira in the eighties. She followed him back to England when the travel company he was working for went bust. My grandparents were gutted but they understood. Mum and Dad married shortly after. My grandparents made a point of coming over to Bristol at least once a year. *Avó* – Grannie Elsa – embraced all things English so much that she'd always combine her visit to us with an English language course. It helped her communicate with me and my sister in both languages, it helped her communicate with my dad and, of course, it helped her chat to people from all over the world, not just British and American tourists. Many of them couldn't – huh, and still can't – speak Portuguese."

"Guilty as charged on that count," I fill the brief silence.

"In those days she would close the *pasteleria* for a month. Usually in February when it was quiet. The day after that fateful accident, she had to close the place for a year to help me and my sister get back on our feet."

This is so much to take in. I don't know where to start and I don't want to say anything remotely insensitive or inappropriate.

"Tiago, I'm so sorry. I didn't realise. H-how do you even begin to piece your life together after something so awful happens?"

"You can't. It can't be fixed."

He looks at me briefly then returns his attention to the water. A group of holidaymakers strolls past us. Tall and blonde. They look Dutch or Scandinavian. Maybe I'm stereotyping, but nine times out of ten I'm proven right when I guess nationalities in my own café.

"Time healing wounds is utter bollocks," Tiago continues, once the tourists are out of earshot, as if the words he is sharing with me are sacred and not to be overheard. "Scrapes and bruises, maybe. A broken heart, not so much. You just learn to live with it. That's all you can do. Learn to survive."

How I want to throw my arms around him and shelter him from all the hurt he's been through, but it's much too late for that. In both senses of the word. I just don't know where I stand with him. The best I can do is listen with an open heart.

"Grannie gave up her livelihood that year to come over and look after us while the house was being sold. School somehow carried on, paperwork and wills were sorted, custody plans were made. Grandad was still alive back then, and he came to help as well, but the bakery has always been Grannie

Elsa's pride and joy. I guess because she can switch so effortlessly between front of house, being the face of Tavira's *pastéis*, and then slip back into the rolling-up-your-sleeves mayhem of the kitchen."

I can't argue with any of that. The lady is a tour de force. I wish I had taken notes having seen her in action.

"Anyway, eventually they were allowed to bring us back to Portugal. So my sister Sophia and I lived with them here until I headed back to Bristol to study Business and Marketing at UWE. But Sophia stayed here. I think she almost felt duty-bound to look after Grannie when Grandad passed away – in the same way that Grannie looked after us. She's not set foot back in England since we left. I can totally understand that. She was older than me. She has more memories to haunt her."

"Didn't… couldn't your other grandparents give your grannie and grandad some respite… on your dad's side of the family?"

"Dad was estranged from his family. Biological and adoptive. I think he was very unlucky with his adoptive parents, who turned out to be just as incapable of looking after him as his birth mother and father."

Oh, my goodness. I'm awash with guilt for my frequent whines about Lauren. The truth is, I don't know how lucky I am to have had a stable upbringing.

"I've since tracked my biological grandparents down but it was too late; they died a few years ago. I established contact with a cousin on social media though. So that's something."

We sit in silence for a while. I wait for Tiago to speak again because I still I have no words.

"A nun from the Jerónimos Monastery of Santa María de

Belém in Lisbon chose to leave the order a long time ago."

"Oh?" I have no idea where this rather random statement is going.

"Do you believe in magic?"

"Sort of," I reply. "Not the trick of the eye, sleight of hand, illusionist stuff. But I think there's a deep magic woven into the fabric of the universe. So many things that can't be explained. I was always useless at maths, but having listened to Kelly, who you met earlier – and who just loves numerology – I can see that there does seem to be a numerical pattern to nature and the cycles, to life in general. Okay, that was a bit deep."

Tiago smiles.

"*Pastéis de nata* are ancient. Magically so in my opinion. They were first sold back in the 1830s in Lisbon but the pastries are believed to have been baked way before that. It's believed they came about by chance. Egg whites were actually mainly used to starch clothes in those days but the monastery would often have an excess. The monks and nuns would use them up by baking them. That's why you'll find little hatches built into the walls of monasteries in many parts of the world. They made sweet pastries out of the leftover egg whites, and served and sold them out of the hatches to passersby, to help with the upkeep of the monastery."

I know the monasteries-making-sweet-treats part of this tale and normally I would challenge this level of mansplaining in a heartbeat, but this evening I choose to keep quiet, sensing there is some alchemy to come.

"Knowing the great secret of the *pastel de nata* recipe, the nun on the run from Lisbon – the one I just mentioned –

decided she couldn't possibly take it to her grave. To cut a very long story short, my ancestors took her in when she fled to the south. They ran a small bakery back then – exactly where Grannie's is today. They mainly sold bread in those days, as other ingredients were thin on the ground, but they had a spare room and big hearts, so they gave the nun refuge when nobody else could or would. As a mark of her gratitude, and because she believed that religion kept too many useful secrets from the masses, she spilled the beans and shared what we believe to be the original *pastel de nata* recipe with them."

"*Honestly?* So those tarts from earlier derive from *the* real deal recipe?"

My heart races. This is so exciting. Like uncovering hidden treasure.

"Honestly, that's the story that's been handed down to a select few members of our family. You are the only outsider I have ever told." He lifts his hand and lets it hover above mine on the bench, then thinks better of it and takes it away. If I didn't know where I stood earlier, I am clueless now. "This is why I'm so fiercely protective of our *pastéis*. Not because I'm a bastard. But because these are not cakes to muck about with, as if you are some kind of Heston Blumenthal having a laugh. This is our history. Our culture. Do you get it now?"

And just like that he's walloped me in the solar plexus. All over again.

"Oh I get it," my fiery side kicks in, the rest of our conversation and my sympathy towards Tiago rapidly evaporating. "But anyone would think that I had stolen your actual family recipe, and set fire to it!"

I stand up. I can't be going round in circles with this man

all night. No matter how much I fancy him and detect more than a hint of the feeling being mutual. No matter how devastating his backstory. He has no right to make a metaphorical WANTED poster out of me. I'm just a regular girl with a dream who worked hard to achieve it. For crying out loud, Elsa has told him as much and given her blessing for me to go about my business without being hassled by her grandson, without being hassled by anyone. Isn't that how our conversation here on the benches started, with the 'so that's me told' line?

"I'm sorry for everything that's happened to you but I will not stop making custard tarts with exciting fillings in them. And that's the end of the conversation. Me doing so has zero effect on your grandparents' business. It's that simple but you are too stubborn to see it, and there's nothing I can do to change that, so I'm going home... well, to my accommodation in São Brás. Enjoy the rest of your holiday."

I turn to go, and Tiago makes no move to follow me, seemingly entranced by the river. That only makes me more furious. I want this to turn into a romantic scene in a will-they-won't-they movie, because I've totally earnt it in my humble opinion. What an afternoon!

Alas, Tiago is evidently not going to repent and sweep me off my feet with a passionate kiss, set against the backdrop of the now-apricot sunset, so I march forward towards the taxi rank. Typically, it is all out of cabs when I get there, the last one pulling off just as I approach. Great. Now what?

I turn round, steeling myself to walk past Tiago's sorry form on the bench, so I can get back to the square, because I have no idea where else to go. Gut instinct had better be right.

There has to be another taxi stand along this stretch of road, or closer to the centre. Damn it. Of course, he sees me walking past and turns, half-minded to stand, I can tell by the angle of his body, his legs looking poised to spring to action. He's got to be kidding. He will be getting no apology. I'm perfectly in the right to storm off. I quicken my pace and turn left, hoping my body language leaves him welded to the bench, But a taxi stand never materialises. The deeper I walk and the more twists and turns I take, the narrower the streets become until there is nothing but identical terraced houses, the occasional male-dominated taverna and dimming light. Yes, it gets dark late here in June, and yes, according to Kelly's guidebook, Tavira's crime rates are very low – but this particular street is decidedly shady. The tourists and locals wandering around earlier are nowhere to be seen, and this part of town is beginning to feel deserted and menacing.

I know I am lost, and the last thing I want to do is *appear* lost. But I take another wrong turn and find myself retracing my footsteps down the street where that group of men with the wandering eyes is swigging beer at an outside table. Walking past once as a lone female was bad enough. Of course it shouldn't be that way, but I'm taking chances in a pair of short shorts that leave little to the perverted imagination. Why is it that certain garments are acceptable in the day but not at night? I'm not even wearing heels, for goodness sake. And frankly, so what if I were?

Now I can hear footsteps behind me and they seem to be getting closer and closer. I should have begged my friends to take me back with them earlier. Correction, I shouldn't have had to beg! They should have had more common sense than to leave me with a strange man. This is a disaster. I pull out my phone so I can pretend to be in a loud conversation with my nonexistent boyfriend. Meanwhile, the steps get louder. Do I continue to walk fast and hope for the best? Maybe I can channel some of my teenage relay sprint technique, now that it really would make a life-changing difference? Or do I start to view those males in the bar as my guardian angels in disguise, and do a U-turn in this narrow part of the street, running back to them? Hang on a minute... What if my pursuer is one of them?

Everything happens in slow motion after that...

* A black taxi with a turquoise roof whizzes past, almost clipping me.
* I trip over a huge cobble, landing right in the middle of the road in a disoriented heap.
* The phone flies out of my hand and soars into the air, then lands and smashes into hundreds of pieces.
* The man from the bar (heck, I was right) makes a decisive move at me, his leery smile intent.
* I see my life flash before my eyes.
* Tiago lunges at the man from the bar, hovering over him with a raised fist and a face like thunder.
* I let out a delayed reaction scream. And then another scream. And then another. Front doors fly open and a crowd quickly gathers.

"You were following me too? You absolute idiot. You're as bad as him!" I scream at the world's most annoying man.

"I needed to know you were safe, but I thought you'd run

off if you saw me," Tiago shouts back "I… shit, Willow, speaking of running, we really need to get out of here—"

A voluptuous powerhouse of a woman has removed a rather frightening-looking stiletto heel and is running for me. *At me.* The look on her face suggests she has put two and two together and come up with eighteen. But I have categorically not been up to anything with her husband/boyfriend/lover! Bleugh, and in his dreams. Can this day get any worse?

Tiago grabs my hand and we sprint for our lives. Up and down streets, in and out of alleyways, and what feels like round and round in circles. Finally he slows us down to a jog.

"Of all the roads you could have chosen to end up on," he breaks the silence.

"You what?" I yell at him, withdrawing my hand from his iron-tight grip.

"That drunken letch was a few years above me at high school, here," Tiago shouts back over his shoulder, miraculously nowhere near as out of breath as I am. It's all the football, I guess, whereas evidently, my capacity to run like my life depends on it is nowhere near as impressive. "Tavira is a great place to live but even a great place has its town dickhead. You just had the pleasure of meeting him."

"Pleasure? I think not."

"And not only did you meet him, but his overbearing girlfriend-turned-wife. She was hard as nails at school too."

"Fabulous. So thanks to you I can never set foot in this place again, because she'll sniff me out and come after me with the heel of her shoe… or worse!"

"I'm sorry. I feel terrible for letting you go off on your own. I'm as much of a dick as he is. But less talk, more haste.

They're notorious for sniffing out a clash and their tight band of friends and family love to join in. If we keep up a pace until we get to the castle and skirt the edge of the convent then head back toward the river, we can do a loop to my apartment, and get ourselves out of this mess."

"I'm Dora, you're the Map," I reply sarcastically.

I jog-walk-jog-walk a couple of metres behind Tiago (my Birkenstocks unable to support this marathon much longer) until we reach the first of those destinations, checking behind my shoulder every few seconds in case we need to speed up again. Fortunately, we seem to have lost our attackers. Just as I feel like I can breathe easy again, we round a bend in yet another narrow street, and a tourist-loaded tuk tuk appears from nowhere, knocking me into the road.

Tiago puts out an arm to catch me but I am too furious with him and stand my independent ground. But resisting only throws me off balance, and I topple against the rough bricks of what I now realise is the fortress wall of the castle. It's not your Disney-style castle, I can imagine it must have looked forbidding in its heyday. Tiago loses his own footing in the process of trying to play knight in shining armour all over again, and now we are pressed snugly against one another. Gah.

I think briefly about sliding along the wall to escape, but with our mouths mere inches apart – mouths that are hungry despite the tarts, mouths that are thirsty despite the port – we are doe-eyed and helplessly entranced within moments. Tiago teases me with an electric brush of his lips on mine, before looking over his shoulder to check the coast is clear. Then he comes back for more. I reciprocate without a thought, letting out the moan of pleasure I've been wanting to make all day long, melting as he does the same… then again as he says my name mid-kiss before probing deeper with his tongue, each of us ravenous for the other. I don't think I've ever felt so firmly rooted to the present moment of my life. This kiss is certainly like nothing I've ever experienced before. It's tectonic-plate-moving. I know he feels the same, his hardness torture and bliss against me all at once. I want him now. All of him. And I'm not sure how I'm going to be able to wait.

"I promised I'd take you home," he says finally, gently biting my lip, the pair of us giddy as we come up for air.

"Then you'd better lead the way," I reply, letting him pull me along again, too dazed to wonder if this isn't the worst idea I have ever had in my life.

SOMEHOW WE MAKE it back to his top floor apartment without a repeat performance, both of us grinning like a pair of Cheshire cats who have got the cream and then some. But once we have walked up the exterior stairs and crossed the threshold of his flat, the mood feels strangely subdued. Maybe it's the harsh reality of the lighting? I don't even want to look at my face in a mirror. I just know that my hair is less ponytail and more cockatoo Mohican. Thank goodness I am not kitted out in that airport makeover to boot.

I follow Tiago to the kitchen and drop my bag on a barstool next to the worktop, the realisation that I am mobile phone-less hitting me again. I'll have to borrow Tiago's phone, as soon as I've worked out whether I'll be needing

Kelly to play taxi and come get me. I know I said I needed to upgrade my phone, but this was not what I had in mind.

"This is quite a place," I acknowledge, looking round the thoughtfully decorated kitchen, desperate to break the lull in communication.

Actually, it looks as if most of it came from Ikea, as is the case for most twenty-somethings (not that I know Tiago's exact age, but it feels like he didn't graduate from uni too many moons ago), but he's added touches of Portugal here and there. One of those iconic ceramic roosters sits by the window, vibrant in black, red, yellow, blue and white – the country's unofficial emblem, it's meant to bring its owner good luck. Vintage port and sardine prints artfully bring to life some of the whitewashed walls. And there are cork gadgets galore, from coasters to cork-handled utensils poking out of a cork pot. Even the bar stool has a cork top (okay, that one didn't come from Ikea). Santi would be in his element here.

"Er, thanks."

"So you own it and use it just for your holidays?"

"I'm only here once or twice a year. The rest of the time I rent it out with Airbnb."

"Nice. I bet it gets pretty booked."

We dance around each other conversationally as if the kiss never happened, as if we are mere acquaintances searching for any old thing to chat about. I suppose in many ways we are.

"Take a seat," he insists, so I move my bag to the floor and hop on the stool. "Grannie appears to have let herself in with a pot of the *caldeirada de peixe...* the erm, fish stew. There's enough for two."

"There are no flies on Grannie, are there?" I say, but he

doesn't reply, just gets on with the business of sorting out bowls and cutlery for the meal.

I drum my fingers on the worktop, trying not to think about the way they were sliding under Tiago's top only half an hour ago, for a jolly good rummage around that sleek torso. For the love of God, please tell me Elsa isn't lurking in the bedroom, though. Not that it looks like I'll be hanging out there myself anymore.

This is all so silly, like someone's pulled the plug from a socket. We were two different people out there on the street. It was, continuing with the voltage vocabulary, *electric*. He apologised for his behaviour. We couldn't get enough of one another. So when did Tiago's personality transplant happen? Not that I am exactly jumping on him. Well, I am a guest, after all. But I can't even sit here and scroll through my newsfeed on my various social media accounts to pass the time. This is hell!

Thankfully dinner doesn't take long to warm up because the ever-intuitive Elsa left it simmering on the hob... a bottle of wine and two glasses on the worktop next to it. I love the bond she and Tiago share and I can see how vital it's become to the mental health of each of them over the years, but two's company and all that.

Tiago sets a bowl and a spoon for me at the little round table in the middle of the kitchen, gesturing for me to abandon the stool. He produces a fresh loaf of bread on what looks suspiciously like a cork chopping board and sets it down, along with the casserole dish and the famous flask-shaped bottle of Mateus rosé – the stuff my parents sank every night on our Algarve holidays way back when. Nowadays it comes in clear glass, showing off its bright pink colour all the more effectively. I am stunned the locals drink it, considering how commercialised it is. Then again, Tiago is on holiday too I guess.

"Help yourself," he says as I settle into my seat, a renewed awareness of our proximity building. "Wine?" He puts a hand to the bottle.

"Thanks, but I think I'd best stick to water."

"Right. I... I get it." He runs his hands through his hair, looking stressed, and pours himself half a glass instead.

"I'm glad someone does, because I'm beginning to think I've morphed into a skunk. I know my hair's gone to pot and I'm guessing I could probably use a shower after all that running, but all the same..."

"There is nothing the matter with the way that you look. Far from it. I-I'm sorry for making a move on you earlier. It was wrong," he prattles as he takes his own seat. "I don't want you thinking I was taking advantage. I-I feel terrible about it." He takes a swig of wine. Now I decide that it'll be impossible to get through this with H2O alone, so I pour myself a glass too. A very full glass. "Ten minutes earlier and you were being pursued by a hideous creature who had God knows what on his mind. I feel like I'm hardly any better myself."

"Well," I say slowly. Okay, now I understand him clamming up on me the moment we set foot inside and it helps me relax. "The difference there is that I wanted you to ravish me, while we were sitting on the bench by the river. So I think I'll let you off. Besides, I didn't exactly protest when you finally got around to it."

"You didn't. That's true." Tiago treats me to a semi-smile

and then we are back to the weird silence again.

I sink some of the pink before tucking into the stew that has been ladled into my bowl. It's delicious. Full of flavour, hearty and warming. Not exactly the kind of dish I'd go for on a summer's night, but in the absence of salad I can't be choosy.

"It's actually good to get away from the girls for a few hours," I say, blurting out the first thing that pops into my head to fill the silence. "Kelly's had us hiking and Radhika's like a bird of prey... when she isn't panning the vista for eligible bachelors, she's planning her outfit to go clubbing later in the week."

"Not your idea of a holiday, then?"

"About as far from as can be. I'm here to relax and unwind. The only sights I want to see are foodie ones. Box most definitely ticked this afternoon... as well as tonight. This is excellent, by the way."

"I'll pass your compliments to the chef."

This is like watching paint dry. We know we have a spark (here I go, not so much ramping but amping the electrical jargon up again). I've just cleared up any doubts he may have by declaring how much I would have liked him to snog my face off earlier on. Why, then, does it still feel as if we are at loggerheads? How is a girl supposed to eat, when all she wants is to be devoured herself?

I can't help but wonder how Tiago would react if I was to instigate a game of footsie beneath the table, but somehow I manage to restrain myself. Call me old-fashioned, but I want him to make the first move.

As if reading my mind, he jumps up, clears the plates, and

places a tub of luxury ice cream in the middle of the table along with a pair of spoons. This is more like it. I dig in greedily without waiting for an invite, accidentally flicking a morsel of the melting Ben & Jerry's Chunky Monkey right in Tiago's face, giving the phrase 'ice breaker' a whole new meaning.

"Ow!" he wipes his cheek and sucks the ammunition off his finger. "There was a chocolate banana chunk in that!"

"Good!" I giggle.

"Oh, yeah? Come here and say that," he challenges, eyes twinkling with naughtiness. And suddenly we are back to a lust with the intensity of the tango.

I tease him with a spoonful of the refreshingly creamy ice cream, licking it from an upright spoon which might be a metaphor for something – erherm – else. The sparkle in his eyes revs up to a smoulder that tells me there is no need for further translation of my body language. Slowly, trying to ignore the flush of heat between my thighs now that we are very much game back on, I abandon the spoon in the tub, feeling ridiculously empowered, and get up from the table.

I let my messy hair loose from its band, walk over to him and fling a leg across his lap, so that I am straddling him on his chair. The two of us let our gazes flicker all over our respective faces, drinking in every inch of our mutual attraction. Tiago's pupils are sexily dilated. He seems pretty ready for another hit. His mouth dips to my collar bone, raunchy butterfly kisses trailing across the sensitive part of my neck and down to my chest. I weave my fingers in the enticing gaps between the buttons of his shirt, fingertips on fire from the touch of skin on skin all over again. He hoists my T-shirt off and tosses it behind him, deftly wrapping one arm around me to unhook my bra, caressing the small of my back as he lets his eyes rove over my naked body.

"God, you are so beautiful. I know it's the cliche out of every hot movie scene… but you are so," kiss "flipping," kiss "beautiful."

I am also a marshmallow. Every part of me is ready to comply with this man's demands. It's absurdly foolish given our backstory. My only hope is for Elsa to jump out of a cupboard to kill the passion in its tracks.

But on this sultry June night, fate has other plans. Tiago carries me from the chair to his bedroom, where we fall onto the mattress in a tangle of lust. Soon we are lost to Portugal, lost to my little café at the end of the pier, lost to the world… creating our own very private universe.

CHAPTER EIGHTEEN

THE QUESTION IS burning my lips. It's almost as hot as our lovemaking last night. Much like that final orgasm after round number three, I can't hold back any longer. I take a sip of coffee for courage. White coffee. Tiago may be half-Portuguese but the initial outlook is good. He has a bottle of milk in the fridge. Maybe this could be the start of something with a little longevity?

"So, are you going to drop the petition now?"

He butters his toast with a noticeably trembling hand and nudges the box of shop-bought croissants, urging me to take another, as if that might persuade me to change the subject. A lengthy silence stretches between us as I cut into my pastry and smother it with butter and strawberry jam.

"I, erm… What it is…" he waves his toast about. "There's no easy way of saying this."

My heart hammers. How could I have served myself up on a plate to this man? I'm already sensing this thing between us now has as much lifespan as the flavour in a stick of bubblegum.

"Please just say it!" I grip my croissant tighter.

"I sort of forged the signatures," he stammers so quickly that I'm not sure I hear him right.

With his free hand he runs his fingers through his hair.

Now I am sure that I heard him right.

"Wh-what do you mean?" I drop the sticky pastry I am holding back onto the plate.

"They're fake. Every last one of them. It's pathetic, I know. Look, I was never going to do anything with the petition. Not really. I just wanted to scare you into closing the café. Obviously I tried to make the document look as convincing as possible. I researched how these things are generally done... and then I," he frowns and closes his eyes, recoiling at how awful this is. "I kind of hoped for the best. But that was before I got to know you, before I developed fee—"

"Tiago, do you have any idea how totally unethical that is? And highly probably *illegal!* Why didn't you tell me last night before we... Why didn't you tell me yesterday afternoon?"

"I was desperate, impulsive, not thinking straight." He shrugs as if that makes it okay and is perfectly understandable.

"I'll say! *Flipping heck.* Why go to such lengths? You really despised me... Now that I've hopped into bed with you and partaken in all of the things we did last night, I'm guessing not quite as much, huh?"

"It's not like that. It's complex. I never wanted to hurt you. I can't help my history."

"Yes, I do believe we covered that bit yesterday." I sigh. "I have every sympathy for you having lost your parents at such a young age, believe me, I do... but that doesn't mean you can go around—"

"I just... I know it sounds crazy but I panicked for my grandparents. For the memory of my real grandfather, who did so much for me, for my grandmother, who has been my absolute rock. My sister, who you haven't yet met, has already expressed a huge interest in taking over the bakery with her husband once Grannie is finally ready to hang up her apron. She has a daughter too. That's who the Paddington bear was for. And you met her son, Edu, yesterday. He's so dedicated already at such a young age. It would break my heart for this let's-reinvent-the custard-tart craze to somehow backflip on itself, wending its way over to Portugal and taking the country by storm, so that the authentic places could no longer survive. My family would be destitute."

I want to laugh at the ridiculousness of such an idea. It would never happen. And, oh, so it's perfectly okay to attempt to leave me penniless instead.

"I love my grandparents too," I cut in, "but I'm sure I could refrain from issuing a petition to close down an innocent café in a humble seaside town in a whole other country. Do you have any idea of all of the hard work that's gone into it? Not to mention the fact I employ actual human beings with financial and emotional needs. What about them? You weren't just trying to put me out of business, but all of us. Then there's my customers. My beloved Frank, who donates tarts every week to deserving people – some of them homeless. People *need* The Custard Tart Café. It's become a haven for so many souls in such a short space of time. From the school mums to the teens, the pier workers to the tourists, the bookworms to the elderly, and everyone in between. You truly have no idea how much joy my quirky café brings to Weston-super-Mare."

Tiago's eyes turn glassy.

"You're so artistic, though," he gesticulates. "You could easily turn your hand to something else. It's not like you have to do what you're doing. Why not branch out? You clearly have culinary training. Besides, this fad might fizzle out. It's best for all concerned that you don't count on the popularity of custard tarts lasting forever; include them in your plans – why not? – but turn your place into a proper bakery that does a bit of everything. It's safer that way."

I've heard enough.

"Okay, Tiago," I stand up, unable to be here with him for a moment longer, pretending we are sharing a convivial breakfast. "Let's say I did acquiesce to your wishes: What are you going to do about the other reincarnations of the *pastel de nata* that have popped up in cities all over the world? Try and shut them all down? I can assure you that this is one game of whack-a-mole you will never win."

He has no answer to that. Which would be because there isn't one.

"I think I've heard enough," I say. "This was a mistake," I gesture at our surroundings, trying not to blush when I think of the way he so expertly tended to my every desire last night. "I'd appreciate it if we break all contact and go our separate ways. It was nice meeting Elsa. I enjoyed the behind the scenes tour and her hospitality. I enjoyed the tarts. But I should never have let myself be so duped by you. Nothing has changed, whether that petition has legs to stand on or not. You're hell-bent on trying to ruin my café."

"Willow, no. You have to believe me... *last night changed everything*. Absolutely everything. I just wanted to be honest with you this morning, since you asked if I was going to drop the petition. I like you. I like you a lot. But if there's any chance of a relationship between us, I need to start it on a clean slate."

What planet is this guy living on? "Relationship? You've got to be joking! One, I can't trust you... and two, you are still trying to get me to close or, at the very least, change my entire business. I am attracted to you, I admit it. I'm not the sort of person to jump into bed with a guy so soon. In fact, I don't mind telling you that last night was the very first time it's happened. But what you've just said changes everything for me. Yesterday afternoon, and last night, it felt like we were at the start of something. You opened up to me and explained your behaviour. I thought I got you. I thought could see where you were coming from. I thought we had turned a corner. There was logic behind your earlier actions and you seemed genuinely sorry for all the damage that had been done. But evidently I was being naive, seeing only what I wanted to see. There's no future for us. As amazing as last night was, it is what it was: a one night stand."

"Don't call it that, Willow! I can assure you it meant more than that to me. So much more. Can't we start afresh? I would love to take you out when we are both back in the UK. All I need is a little time... to stop feeling like a traitor to my heritage. It won't take long. I know it won't. The depth of my feelings for you already tells me that."

"You had plenty of time to come clean yesterday," I reply curtly. "I'm not putting my heart on the line, waiting around for you to decide that you want to be supportive of my career choices. That's not how a relationship works. Goodbye, Tiago. Enjoy the rest of your holiday."

This is too screwed up for words.

I grab my bag and walk out of the apartment, my eyes rapidly filling with tears. I probably look better than I did last night – I showered with Tiago's gel. Okay, not before he joined me for a quickie, soaping me up, and inevitably setting in motion round number four. But I wouldn't care if I looked like a zombie. All that matters is getting myself to the nearest taxi rank and back to the cocoon of the quinta, whose fortress I shall not leave until we fly back to Bristol.

CHAPTER NINETEEN

"WHY DIDN'T YOU tell us sooner? We're supposed to be your best friends!"

"Well, you're all caught up now on the disaster that is my life," I protest, having just info-dumped the entire events of last night and this morning as we lie by the pool.

"Radhika's right." Well, it makes a refreshing change for Kelly to say that, at least. Her hands are planted on her hips and her voice is ice-cold, her critique piercing me so much that I fold my arms for protection. "How could you keep such a dark secret from us all this time? Jeez. You think you know someone." Kelly shakes her head in disappointment.

"The nasty little shit who delivered you that humdinger of a petition was sitting behind you, *sitting behind us* for the entire flight... and you didn't think it important enough to let Kelly and me know? Oh, Willow. I despair of you!" Radhika adds her own thoughts with a shake of the head. She turns her back on me and picks up her sunscreen, applying it to her arms and shoulders.

My plan to sneak to my room, when I spotted both girls lazing around the pool enjoying the morning sunshine, was foiled the moment the taxi's tyres crunch on the gravel. No doubt Radhika thought I might be one of her love interests. If not for her sharp ears, I might have pulled off my furtive entree and avoided this Portuguese Inquisition until lunchtime.

"Because I knew exactly how you'd react," I finally reply, raising my voice several octaves and waving my hands around to make my point; increasing the curiosity of the other sun worshippers, the early bird family who are lazing on the opposite side of the pool. "*Like this...* and thirty-seven thousand feet in the air is not the best place for an argument!"

"That's as maybe, but you could have told us all about Tiago the moment we landed... and now you've gone and slept with him!"

Kelly is as incredulous as I feel, now the stark reality of the situation is beginning to ring out loud and clear. I am as bad as Tiago, for not coming clean in due time. She pulls repeatedly at the ribbon on her hat, a clear signal that she is stressed – and it isn't even her mess to be stressed about.

"Keep your voice down," I tell her hypocritically. "You had no qualms about me spending time with him yesterday afternoon, as I recall."

"That's because we didn't realise his true identity!"

"They really did break the mould when they made you," Radhika snipes.

"Do you know what, Rad?" She hates it when I call her that, but too bad, her bitterness is really uncalled for the morning after my giant mistake. "You're just about the last person I'm taking relationship advice from. You've spent the best part of this week not so much two-timing as triple-timing guys!"

Radhika looks like she's been hit by a truck, and I wonder what I am missing.

"Nice one," she mutters, turning her back on me and skulking off to dip her feet in the pool.

"To be fair, Willow can't really know the effect of her words. She wasn't party to last night's heart to heart, hun, was she?" Kelly says to Radhika's slender back in its gorgeous black asymmetric cut-out swimsuit.

"What?" I hiss. "What am I missing?"

"Oh, I'm not regurgitating my woeful tale to you as well." Radhika says over her shoulder, avoiding all eye contact with me. "Kelly can fill you in later."

"Right. Okay then. But what's done is done, as far as *my* woeful tale is concerned, and I don't ever want to talk about this episode again. Are we clear? Not a word to anybody when we get back. Especially not Caitlyn or Reggie. Very especially not Lauren. Promise me."

"We promise," my friends reply unconvincingly in unison.

"Great. I'm glad that's sorted," I say. "I'm going to have forty winks, do something with my hair." It's a two French plaits day today, but there was no way I was taking any extra time to tend to that at Tiago's place. "And then I'll join you back down here to plant my buttocks on a sunlounger which I don't intend to leave for the entire day... make that for the entire holiday."

"Talking of backsides," Radhika says, warming up a little along with the rays of the sun, "I don't care how cute that butt of his looked when he was stretched out in the aisle playing the hero card and rescuing your passport on the plane, he's a moron to seduce you, bonk you, and still refuse to rip that petition into shreds on the spot. *What an arse.*"

Radhika's actually come up with a half-decent joke there and I know from the twinkle in her eye that Kelly thinks the same, but since my friends have both insulted my discernment (or lack thereof) I am not going to laugh at it.

"The signatures are fake so that makes it meaningless anyway," I shrug. "But yeah, I thought that was the least he could do, too. I guess he wouldn't have had a copy of the document on him at the breakfast table, but he didn't exactly invite me to a burning-of-the-petition ceremony on Weston beach when we're back home, either."

"As I said, what a shit. Come out and party with us to-morrow night instead." Radhika is positively back to her old self now, but the idea makes my stomach lurch. I want to stay as far away from the Algarve coast as possible. "We've managed to blag a lift down to the Strip in Vilamoura. Twelve hours of hardcore partaaaaaying awaits us."

"Yay."

I don as convincing an expression as I can muster and fling my bag over my shoulder, trudging back to the room.

"I feel as enthused about it as you do, Willow." I feel my shoulders relax, hearing Kelly's semi olive branch and her sigh float across to me. "But we did agree to one event each and at least the place Radhika's picked has a cocktail bar serving sustainable and seasonably foraged drinks."

"Double yay," I reply, as my mind conjures up images of mushroom mojitos served by a group of wannabe Bear Grylls.

CHAPTER TWENTY

"SO, AM I allowed to know what's going on with Radhika, or not?" I ask Kelly, when she comes back to our shared bedroom for a siesta later.

"Oh, that, yes," Kelly replies with a dejected expression. "It's quite heavy to be honest."

"Ouch," I say. I settle onto my bed, hugging my pillow close in preparation, mind racing. What could possibly be up with our mutual friend?

"Arranged marriages don't have the hold they once did, but nevertheless, Radhika's feeling under immense unspoken pressure right now." My eyes grow wide. This does not sound good. "Her two younger sisters seem quite happy to be paired up with the sons of family friends – *approved and reputable* family friends." Kelly makes quotation marks with her fingers. "As you can imagine, Rad's bearing the brunt of it for showing no inclination to follow their lead."

"Oh, no! That's terrible for her. Depressingly so. It also explains her recent behaviour."

"Indeed," Kelly acknowledges. "It's nothing new, she says. Her parents, much as she loves them, have been dropping hints for a few years now. Not that Radhika's any age – she's only twenty-five. But the fact that Bhavna and Sumaira are in the throes of planning their weddings, to Gurdeep and Ritesh, is only adding to the stress. Her sisters' big days are all that Radhika's entire extended family can talk about. And the hushed whispers that she is being too choosy about potential suitors is making her uber-paranoid."

"No wonder she's constantly on the lookout for her own love interests, and no wonder she's so quick to snap all the time. I can't even begin to imagine how difficult all of this is for her. Especially as it's bombarding her from all angles. And she still lives at home. It sounds relentless."

"Let's just say Mr and Mrs Chandra have ramped up afternoon teas with friends and acquaintances in the West Country's Indian community, in a bid to help their daughter come to her senses."

Sugar.

This is such a culturally sensitive subject, rooted in family, honour, tradition, and heritage – and it's one I know hardly anything about. But I'm more than a little alarmed on behalf of my friend all the same. IMHO – to quote one Leona – Radhika should be allowed to follow her own path in this day and age. But it's not going to be simple.

"What can we realistically do to help?" I ask, somewhat pointlessly, because this issue is so much bigger than me. It throws my own current dilemma into much-needed perspective.

Kelly looks into space for a moment or two. "Just be patient with her. And maybe help her to realise that when the time is right, a brilliant and long-lasting relationship – one that she chooses to partake in – will come along, so there's no need to weigh up every male prospect so obsessively. I hate the way that last bit came out." Kelly shakes her head. "Radhika is beautiful, clever, fun, adventurous and uplifting. She shouldn't have to feel so... so desperate." Kelly sniffs and I embrace her.

And that's what we do, we cultivate patience.

By dusk I have shrugged off the mantle of fury and unease that is Tiago, replacing it with a cute multi-coloured halter neck dress and heels – the sole dress and heels I've packed for the holiday. Radhika showers her approval on me... a little less so on Kelly, who is clad in a green maxi dress and teeny-tiny knitted shrug, both better suited to the daytime. The dress is dotted with little Glastonbury Tors and sunrises. It would look cute on a toddler. Nevertheless, holiday rules are holiday rules and we have both kept our side of the bargain, supporting our friend in her choice of excursion.

Leona gives us a lift (mercifully in her car this time) to save us the cost of a taxi fare on one leg of the journey, and we head into Vilamoura, me feigning sleep as we pass the signposts for Tavira. Nevertheless, the hot and steamy things Tiago and I got up to unhelpfully replay in my head; strong, firm hands running the length of my body, the build-up of ecstasy so intense it is all I can do not to bite the pillow. Or the car's seat belt.

Stop it, Willow!

The venue on the town's infamous neon-lit street doesn't open until midnight, so we eat *al fresco* by the swanky marina, Radhika swooning over the luxury yachts bobbing about next to us. Every chocolate-haired male of a certain age that passes our little table on the pavement is Tiago and I find I have little appetite. Not even for a custard tart dessert.

As the sky turns from salmon and violet to blackberry, pinprick stars illuminating it, Kelly and I surrender to the inevitability of being dragged onto the dance floor for a boogie at the venue down the road. After 'doing our bit' for the handful of songs that I might have heard of, had I not had such great taste in *proper* music, Radhika allows us to slope off to the cocktail bar on the sidelines. The one that Kelly has been raving about. I baulk at the price list, which starts at thirteen euros a drink. It's all well and good us embracing one another's favourite pastimes, but you could eat at least thirteen *pastel de natas* for that price.

Kelly orders us a pair of Sea Dragons, made with rectified Scotch, tomato and peach, a combo you can be sure I'll never contemplate adding to my custard tarts. She brings the tumblers back to our table looking delighted, or maybe mesmerised, by the seascape of a garnish – a mixture of thistles and what I can only guess are some kind of beach flowers. I brace myself for a sip and grimace. This is making the herbal tea from night one taste good.

We watch Radhika's progress, like parents proud of their child's dance moves at a Butlins holiday camp. Surprise, surprise, she has somehow managed to get all of her quarries under the same roof this evening, seamlessly flitting from one to another on the dance floor. Santi, Miguel, and Delivery Guys Two and Three all seem perfectly happy with that. You could hardly label her technique a nineteenth century approach, and yet the treat them mean, keep them keen but at arms' length technique does have its similarities to the Victorian days of calling cards being presented (or not) to indicate one's interest in a suitor. Once again, I have to wonder if this is where I've gone wrong myself. It seems a better bet than jumping straight into one's enemy's bed. I take another swig of the Sea Dragon and wince, hot-footing it to the bar to pull in the next round on my own terms; the Gorilla is made with rose geranium rum, ginger, honeydew melon, and a 'splish-splash' of lager. Overlooking the fact the bartender is shoving a massive fern in each long-necked glass, things can only get better, right?

Alas, I've gotten ahead of myself. Far from anything in my current life pickle improving, things are deteriorating at one hundred miles an hour. For who is standing before me, smack bang opposite on the other side of the bar, but flipping Edu. Tiago's cousin! I knew we shouldn't have come near the coast tonight. Edu is in his late teens, for goodness sake. Of course the nightlife on the Strip will attract him and his mates, moth to flame.

I hide behind a pillar and now the barman has to twist his neck around it to ask for my payment. I try to communicate to Kelly that we have to go – like yesterday – by making a T sign. She shakes her head in disappointment and I realise she thinks I'm asking if she wants a cuppa instead of a cocktail. Not that Tiago is necessarily here, but I can't take any chances. This visit is all about catching up with his family, after all. It's getting awkward passing the barman my euros at such a distance, so reluctantly I edge out past the pillar – and that's when Edu spots me. His eyes light up as he makes the connection, regardless of the fact we'd barely acknowledged one another in the *pasteleria*'s kitchen. *Noooooo!* Now he's on his way around the bar. I abandon the money and the drinks without waiting for my change, without sampling another liquid foraged delight, and run out of the club, Kelly on my heels.

"What happened back there? Don't tell me you spotted Tiago?" She's out of breath when she finally catches up with me on Praia da Oura, the nearest stretch of beach, sandals in her hands to help her walk faster.

"Why? *Did you?*" I panic, my own breath rising and falling with a heavy crash in time with the pounding of the waves.

"I was too busy savouring the rest of my gorgeous Sea Dragon," says Kelly. "I reckon I could fuse that amazing amalgamation of flavours into ice cream. I can't wait to see my customers' faces!"

Hmm. The only clientele who'd find that special blend appealing would be those who'd lost their taste buds via Covid. But moving swiftly on...

"Not Tiago, no. His cousin. You only saw Edu's back, when you and Radhika were hauled in and then spat back out of the kitchen. He was busy making the *pastéis*."

"I appreciate the problem, Willow, but we can't just leave Radhika like this."

"And I can't go back in there!"

"Hang on a minute." Kelly holds up a hand to stop my objections. She fishes around in her handbag and pulls out a pair of binoculars.

"What on earth? Were you planning on bird watching this evening or something?"

"I put them in my case so I could use them if we went hiking, then forgot all about them until now. Might as well get some use out of them tonight, playing chaperone to Rad."

"Kelly! That's a bit voyeuristic."

"It's also saving your bacon, Willow. She's over on the benches with Santi... at least I think it's him. Seems like our services will soon be no longer required. We can find out what the lovers' plans are, then get ourselves the most environmentally-friendly looking cab back to the quinta for a lovely pot of herbal tea before bed."

I feel decidedly middle-aged at this announcement, and could almost run back to the hedonism of the club. I may be straight but I would love to watch the pole dancers in action. Callum and I never went to any raves or clubs on our Ibiza holiday three years ago, and it feels like a rite of passage in your twenties. But I remember how soft my bed is and how I have officially fulfilled my duties as babysitter to Rad – well, nearly. Once that's done, nothing is stopping me from submerging myself in every aspect of the quinta from now until our final day.

"Sounds wonderful," I say to Kelly with a massive grin, as we ignore the protests of our aching tendons and sprint through the rippling sand back to the lovebirds.

THE NEXT DAY we decide it's high time we venture into the local town proper. São Brás may not be as picturesque as other inland destinations on the Algarve (overlooking the gorgeousness of the quinta on its outskirts and similarly rustic properties dotting the surrounding landscape, and of course Santi's beloved cork trees) but it has a fabulous market. It's a wonderful place to spend a morning. Kelly haggles rather impressively in her pigeon Portuguese over plump red tomatoes and fragrant stuffed olives which we will take back to the quinta for lunch. And I pick up some mouthwatering cheeses and breads.

Radhika and Santi pace behind us in a gooey-eyed world of their own. It seems Santi really did win our friend's heart last night, not that I'm sure the criteria of his dance moves to Mambo Number Five can tell a woman much about a man. Don't knock it until you try it, I suppose. One thing's for sure, using that barometer I could have skipped my entire relationship with Callum, who had not so much two left feet as cold feet. Not once did I manage to lure him onto a dance floor, even though we met at a club.

I'm so happy for my friend. I am hoping she will overcome the inevitable challenges of a long-distance relationship, should the pair of them decide that this is more than a holiday fling. I'm also going to admit it: I'm more than a little envious too. Tiago didn't shy away from announcing he had fallen for me, an affirmation which totally got my pulse racing and blood pumping, but the compromise is too gargantuan. Being with Tiago in any shape or form would be nothing but a risk. Love shouldn't feel that way and I am DONE with anyone trying to thwart my creativity. As far as I'm concerned, he's just another life lesson, in what has turned into a very long line of people and scenarios trying to stop me from doing what I was born to do.

Jumping into the backseat of Santi's hiking company minibus with Kelly, the happy couple in the front, I vow to stop living in the past and keep myself rooted in the present, eking out every last rustic quinta pleasure from this holiday so that I can return to The Custard Tart Café refreshed and reinvigorated, ready to take on the summer season with my team.

Bring it on.

CHAPTER TWENTY-ONE

I'VE BEEN A nervous wreck all morning and I am properly forwallowed – yep, another Reggie word – that is to say, exhausted from tossing and turning all night. So much for those last couple of days of sun, pool, and cake feasting in the quinta's little bakery restoring my balance. We never got around to chatting about what day and time he'd be flying back when we hooked up unexpectedly mid-week, but it's pretty obvious Tiago will be on the very same flight as me this morning. Never mind those recurring dreams about being back at school, now I'm having recurring dreams about our night of passion together. Pfft. They are heaven and they are hell.

I'm dreading looking into those eyes again, reliving their burning intensity as Tiago undressed me at his leisure, taking in every inch of me – curves and stretch marks included – evidently liking all that he saw. Try as I might, I can't forget how turned on he was. Which means I am now a walking advertisement for blusher. Nobody would need to talk me into a makeover at Faro airport's cosmetics counters today. These thoughts seem deeply inappropriate in such a public place. I run my hand through the length of my knotted half-up half-down hairstyle (which I promise is hair art, and more elegant than it sounds) in a quest to distract myself from my shame.

Radhika and I wait patiently in the check-in queue in the airport terminal for Kelly to drop off the rental car and sort out the paperwork, saving her a space much to the annoyance of our fellow passengers. Then the three of us make our way through to Departures, thankfully minus the repacking drama this time. Keen to stock up on yet more Portuguese foodie inspiration for her future ice cream ventures, Kelly leaves us again to hit the small selection of over-priced shops. Please let her refrain from getting any Heston Blumenthal ideas about sardine ice cream...

"How are you feeling?" I ask Radhika, to take my mind off the constant urge to look over my shoulder. Initial signs are good: there is NO trace of my holiday fling. And who's to say he hasn't booked to be here for eight, nine, ten or eleven days? With flights heading to Bristol daily, nobody needs to restrict themselves to a mere seven-day break nowadays.

"I won't know until I'm back in Bath, I guess." She shrugs. "Something will give. It always does. He's a too-good-to-be-true package. That much is for sure."

"In my humble experience, there's no such thing, my friend," I try my utmost to reassure her, despite having no real track record to go on myself. "Santi's sure to reveal annoying habits, in time. Stinky socks lying around, the toilet seat left up, farts and burps... if you two decide to keep seeing one another, that is," I add tentatively.

"*If.* How I bloody hate that word. It needs to be banished from the dictionary," says Radhika. "He insists he'll be visiting once the summer season is over, though. And I've already booked flights for a trip out to see him in August, albeit I will have to do a lot of walking in crazy temps as it's peak tourist season so he'll be fully booked with his hiking trails. I guess that gives us hope, gives this thing – whatever it is – some legs?"

"Are you kidding? Of course it does! That's fantastic, and totally worth the sacrifice of wilting in the woods again for." I grab my friend by her shoulders and twirl her round with me, making both of us laugh like idiots.

On the third spin my giggles slow right down until they come to a very abrupt stop. I sidestep slowly until I am facing the café again. *No way!* Why does the universe have to test me like this? Goddesses of fate, I thought you were on my side?

"Willow, what's up?" Radhika frowns deeply, following my line of vision. "Ohhhhh," she says.

Yeah. Oh, indeed. Tiago is standing at a tall chrome table, leisurely tucking into a mass-produced *pastel de nata*.

"Somebody's lowering their standards," I snipe. "How can anything from an airport café possibly live up to Grannie's golden touch?"

And then I stop myself. Grannie Elsa is a diamond, my heart reminds me. She has to be a gem to put up with her grandson! It's no wonder he's protective of her baking in return. Then my head cuts in – *well, yes, to a degree.*

"I still can't believe both of us got laid on this holiday," says Radhika in such a casual manner, it's as if we're talking about the weather. "You've got to feel sorry for Kelly and the banality of marriage…"

"Matt and I are still newlyweds, I'll have you know," Kelly sneaks up on us out of nowhere, making us both jump. "There's nothing to worry about in that department, I can assure you. We may not follow the Kama Sutra to the letter but we do like a little role play and fantasy dress up from time to—"

"Enough!" I scream, covering my ears. I don't want to imagine either of the friends who make up this happy couple in a cop costume and accessories, or anything more unconventional, thanks very much.

"But the same person, forever and ever... until one of you dies?" Radhika lets that thought hang a little uncomfortably in the air.

If my *eventual* same person forever and ever (who clearly hasn't come into my life yet) made me feel the way Tiago did the other night (minus the accompanying fiasco) I'm sure I could live with that. I give in to the daydream and park myself on a chair in a bank of plastic seats facing away from him. The gates are in the opposite direction to us and with any luck he'll head straight for them anyway, meaning I can cocoon myself here for as long as possible until the final stragglers are boarding the flight, then run like the clappers to do the same. Or, so I thought.

"You're here!" a familiar male voice cuts through the daydream he's currently appearing in, taking me right back to the way he greeted me in his family's *pasteleria*.

Sugar, sugar, *sugar*!

My heart almost flies out of my ribcage at his sudden appearance and I swear somebody's cranked up a thermostat. Why didn't I plump for a vest top? I know it'll be at least ten degrees cooler in Blighty, but, well, we're not there yet, are we? Kelly and Radhika had better not have anything to do with this set up. I turned my back for literally all of half a minute. Now I find an incredulous-at-discovering-me Tiago blocking my view of the departures screen. He looks down at me with his warm chocolate eyes and my belly completely flips. I pull my legs up onto the seat and instinctively hug them to my chest like a child. Meanwhile Tiago just stands there, a huge smile lighting up his face, suggesting fate has brought us together again, when really it's the simple matter of an easyJet timetable.

"Unfortunately, so are you," I mutter under my breath, looking sideways out of the giant window to catch a plane taking off on the runway beyond.

"Willow, look, I'm sorry. Really I am. You have to believe me. I've been racking my brains as to where in São Brás you could've been staying. You never did tell me. I've knocked on the doors of all the hotels, bed and breakfasts, and even the Airbnbs, trying to find you."

Wow, okay. Now this is starting to sound like the Cinderella fairy tale – well, if you overlook the fact that it was the king's herald who did the dirty work of rapping at the doors with his trumpeters in tow... and this version of the story is decidedly more Birkenstock, less glass slipper.

"I realised as soon as you left the other morning that I was wrong. I should have come clean immediately about the petition being fake." Ha, more than likely only after Elsa gave you yet another stern talking to. "I've hardly been able to relax wondering how to get hold of you to apologise, to try and put things right between us so we might try to—"

"Well, now you don't have to," Kelly cuts in, her sickly sweet voice floating over the back of the chair so that I'm in no doubt it was she who alerted Tiago to my whereabouts.

"We'll leave you two lovebirds to it." She takes Radhika by the arm and they march toward the boarding gates.

"Oh, no you don't. I'm coming with you," I insist, rising quickly from the seat and grappling at my bag to chase after them.

"Willow, please give me the benefit of the doubt. I've been a jerk and an idiot rolled into one," Tiago pleads.

He looks so incredibly hot today; hair mussed-up, T-shirt just snug enough to reveal those glorious abs, and his topped-up tan gives him and the smattering of hairs on his well-toned arms a healthy surf-style glow.

"You can say that again."

"I've been a jer…"

"Look, I can't trust you," I interrupt him. "And I can't ever see that changing, so we can debate it until the cows *and* the Portuguese roosters come home. You have a hidden agenda. You're a control freak. You charmed your way into my bed."

"Technically, it was *my* bed."

"See. This is what I mean." I slap my forehead for added effect. "You have a comeback for everything. No matter how big or small. You always need to be right. You can apologise all you like but frankly, I never want to see you again."

I am talking out of my backside and the two of us know it, but I am done with this discussion. And for the love of God, why do we always have these showdowns in public places?

"I'll get down on my knees in front of the entire airport if I have to. I know I'm far from perfect but I opened my heart up to you last week. That took some doing. I thought you understood the reasons behind my idiotic behaviour. We have something, Willow. Something with the potential to become really special. You know we do. Please don't be too proud to recognise that."

"You're calling *me* proud? What a hypocrite. What you're offering me is too little too late, Tiago."

I grab my bag and run after Kelly and Radhika to join the boarding queue.

CHAPTER TWENTY-TWO

PHEW. THAT WAS intense, unnecessary and wholly unexpected. Unacceptable too. I settle myself into my slate-grey and tangerine-orange plane seat and turn my thoughts immediately to the laminated menu. I deserve a glass of something fizzy after such a hellish encounter, even if it isn't quite afternoon. And chocolate. Mountains of chocolate.

For some reason Kelly screwed up the pre-booked seating arrangements when she sorted out the return flight. But, though I may not be sitting next to Kelly and Radhika, I honestly don't mind... increasingly so as it appears everybody has now boarded and I have an entire row of seats to myself plus a hand-me-down magazine, courtesy of Radhika. Lush! Tiago is nowhere in my eyeline either. Now all I need to do is swiftly disembark the aircraft once the flight is over, without dropping my passport, and pray that my case is one of the first off the luggage carousel so I can make an equally nippy exit from the airport without bumping into him. I have no idea how cases are loaded into the plane's belly but I reckon there's a good chance that mine and Tiago's belongings will be spaced far apart, given we didn't check in at the same time. That comforting thought further relaxes me and I stuff my purse into the netted pocket of the seat in front of me, ready to purchase my tipple and treats when the bar service begins.

The engines embark on their warm-up routine. I am determined to enjoy every moment of this journey. I yawn and flex my arms, lacing my fingers together and stretching them outwards, focused entirely on the bubbles which will soon calm my fears at being seven miles high in the sky.

A member of the cabin crew walks down the aisle to do her final passenger and hand luggage checks before take-off. She stops suddenly at my row, leaning in to say something to me, so that I fear Kelly has ticked a box online forewarning the staff that I'm a nervous flier.

"Hi there, I hope you don't mind but I have a request... we have a family of three on today's flight who have unfortunately made an error whilst selecting their seats online, meaning a mother and her two young children are all sitting apart from one another. Since you have two seats free..." she gestures at the aisle and middle seat and I already feel like the world's greediest woman despite the fact none of this luxury was planned. "I was wondering if you would be so kind as to move to one of the seats the family is currently occupying. Of course, none of this is your fault or your problem, but we prefer that children be seated with their parents, ideally. The pilot is also keen that we take off in the next five minutes, so that we don't miss our landing slot at Bristol."

"Oh... of course," I reply, because what else can I do? Hopefully Kelly's annoying mistake won't now mean I am sitting next to a snorer with a tendency to fall on his neighbour's shoulder and dribble, or somebody who ate a pile of garlic bread last night.

"Thank you so much, Madam. Just bring yourself and your essentials, and follow me as quickly as possible."

We stride what feels like a walk of shame right down to the other end of the aircraft, passing a male member of staff going the other way with a mother and what can only be described as two teenage boys in his charge. My jaw drops at the way I have so casually given up my seat without proof of merit. These 'young children' are both taller than me, sporting facial hair that would impress Jason Momoa, and they are chewing gum with a total and utter attitude. In other words they're perfectly capable of sitting alone. I'll bet the mother has kicked up a fuss so they don't get served any alcohol. Talk about infuriating!

There's no choice now but to resign myself to my fate. I swear everybody thinks I'm a latecomer who is holding the flight up, when far from it, I am actually getting every single passenger on board home on time. I mouth a sarcastic "thanks" to my friends as I pass them and they raise their brows inquiringly. I was so deliriously happy on my own back there as well. Yes, this break has been wonderful, overlooking certain aspects, but I haven't actually had any me-time in seven days. Kelly and I shared a room and, since Kelly likes us to do everything as a family unit, being shacked up together so intimately put paid to that. Small wonder I'd quickly felt enthused about having the window seat (and entire row) to myself back there. Just me, and two and a half hours of blue skies, clouds, pointless gossip columns, and deep thought to clear my head and prepare for the return to my beautiful café, devoid of guilt for attempting to put every bakery in Portugal out of business.

The steward leading me to the rear of the airbus suddenly stops and I quickly realise I haven't spotted Tiago on my travels. That's weird. My seriously in-denial brain decides this is because he's flying to Porto/Madeira/The Azores today.

And then reality bites.

Once again, I upgrade the choice of cursing in my head, as seems to be so frequently the case in his presence. Of course, out of all of the one-hundred-and-eighty-ish seats on an easyJet plane, my new seat is right next to bloody Tiago.

"Hey," he looks up, and to be fair, he's just as stunned as I am.

"No, no, no, no. I can't sit here." I shake my head wildly, pleading with the retreating back of the cabin crew. "You don't understand… I know this man, and not in a good way. I cannot sit next to him for over two hours. I cannot sit next to him at all! Please find me another seat. Any other seat!"

"You'll sit the fuck down, love if you know what's good for you! I've got a taxi booked and waiting in Bristol and a shift at the pub for a very thirsty skittles team to be on time for tonight. On your head be it if we're late!"

I turn to scowl at the owner of the voice behind me, quickly changing my mind as I take in the snake-like eyes, ruddy cheeks and tangle of gold medallions of the unimpressed woman.

"Give her a break," Tiago snaps over his shoulder. "She's volunteered to swap seats because of somebody else's cock-up. I can't see any of the rest of you doing the same."

"How about you give me a break too." I hiss, sighing and sinking into my aisle seat. He does make a good point; I am the only mug here. Thankfully there is a middle seat between us, with Tiago sitting by the window. The battle zone is divided.

"Oh, good. I see you have your passport this time. I'm more than happy to look after it for you if you'd prefer," he can't seem to resist the opportunity to quip.

I channel the fury of my fellow female passenger and throw him a killer look.

My only way through this absolute nightmare is the aforementioned drink – although not too much, I don't want to let my guard down. That and burrowing into the gossip magazine, which is far easier said than done when you are intent on blocking off all eye contact with your fellow passenger, and when you don't know who the reality TV stars are; the ones whose alleged relationship antics you're reading about. In the end I am left with no choice but to hold the magazine aloft, giving myself serious arm ache, and frequent kicks from the charming female behind me who presumably feels I am ruining her view of today's flight experience. And so that's how it goes: bubble sip, read some gossip, kick... and repeat, until I have read the blimming thing twice over and my shoulders are in desperate need of a massage. Reluctantly, I stash the magazine in the seat pocket in front of me and pretend to doze off before Tiago misinterprets my move as his chance to resume communication.

I've not long rested my eyes when the captain's voice fires up over the tannoy system. "Er, good afternoon, ladies and gentlemen. This is Captain blah-de-blah speaking." I'm not too sure if he says Steve, Keith or Dean; why is it that all captains have that same monotonous pitch over the airwaves? "We will shortly begin to make our descent to Bristol, however, just to prepare you all – and there's absolutely no need for alarm," my heart skips a beat as I sense a *but*... "Air traffic control have notified us of some unseasonably strong and unexpected headwinds in the area and we can expect to be hitting them soon. For this reason, we won't be operating our tax free shopping service today. Apologies for that, but we'll need to do our final cabin check in preparation for landing a little earlier than usual, to ensure the cabin crew are all seated with belts securely fastened in plenty of time."

The delightful woman behind me mumbles several F words under her breath. She was obviously intent on splashing out on yet more jewellery from the duty free trolley. "Thank you for your understanding and thank you for flying with us today. We look forward to seeing you again soon and wish you a safe and pleasant onward journey."

Maybe let's get through this one first, shall we?

Naturally, as an anxious flier, the first thing I do when anybody – Captain very much included –tells me not to be alarmed… is to panic like mad, my brain calculating the worst possible outcomes and scenarios. But as the minutes pass by, I decide the best way through this is to shut my eyes until the *débâcle* is over. My decision lulls me into sweet oblivion. Nothing has changed. We're chugging along nicely. No oxygen masks have fallen from the ceiling. Everyone's in good spirits. The cabin crew don't even look remotely bothered. But then everything quickly shifts gear as I overhear the people opposite me say we are now banking over the city of Bath. This means we are lining up in the direction of the runway, nine miles outside the city centre.

Stormy is one way of describing our approach. No sooner has the plane changed course and the wheels have come down with the quintessential 'clunk', than the aircraft tilts dramatically from side to side. Immediately it feels more like we're traveling on a toy at the whim of Mother Nature than a large Airbus. Shrieks and gasps abound, kids scream, babies cry. Fucks and shits galore are emitted and I can only hope that parents are somehow covering their little one's ears. I don't dare pan the vista to catch the expression of the cabin crew. Once I perceive the faintest hint of fear on their faces, I am toast.

Tiago, the utter fool, unstraps himself and moves into the middle seat, putting his arms around me and pulling me close. It is only then that I realise I am one of the cursing passengers. I am also shaking like a leaf. My head stops analysing my behaviour and I surrender to the much-needed comfort of the embrace of a gorgeous man. Even amidst the panic it's incredible to feel the heat of his body, the reality of him in a situation that, to me, is filled with so much uncertainty, the sturdy frame of his chest, his heartbeat steady and in control.

"It's okay, Willow. I've got you. Everything's fine. It's just a bit of wind. These pilots are trained to land in all weathers. We're almost down. Then we're going to get inside that airport and I'm going to take you for a strong coffee and lunch."

"Please don't talk about food right now," I squeak.

"Okay, just the strong coffee then. Sounds good? Can you try to stay focused on that? We'll be on the runway," I swear he mutters 'I hope' under his breath, "before you know it. Close your eyes if it helps or if you want to keep them open then the best thing to do is fix them on something static like the back of the tray table."

"Sounds good," I agree. "Okay, I'll do it."

"And Willow?"

"Yes?"

"I meant every word I said. Today and the other morning. I really am sorry. I also really think I might be falling in love with you." He kisses my temple and I don't know whether to melt or scream or get in the brace position or pinch myself. This mix of high jinks and emotion is a little too much.

On and on the plane coasts and tips, dropping worryingly, then bobbing back up again as it hits the air pockets. This is certainly very different from any landing I have ever experienced in my life. It makes the Big One at Blackpool's pleasure beach feel like a doddle. It also reminds me of that heart-in-the-mouth video I foolishly watched a couple of years ago of a British Airways plane coming in to land in gale force wind at Gibraltar airport. Yeah, why did I do that?

Still no warning lights flash, no oxygen masks drop, and no authoritative 'brace, brace' comes out over the tannoy, and after a while I can feel my heartbeat slow down. This is the pattern, then; tilt, coast, bump and repeat... until we are on the ground. I can deal with this. I *am* dealing with this. I lay my head on Tiago's chest and quit the struggle, my breathing normalising. Regardless of whether or not I ever see him again once we step off the runway we are hopefully going to connect smoothly with very shortly, the soothing fragrance of lavender, patchouli, musk and whatever else is in his aftershave will forever remain with me. It will always bring me back to this moment of feeling strangely more protected than ever before in my life.

I wonder how Kelly and Radhika are dealing with this? Knowing Kelly she is lost in some transcendental music on her earbuds, whilst Radhika will be sound asleep, oblivious to everything. I peep at the window as we roll to the side again like a boat caught up in the waves, noticing with a wash of relief that the clouds have finally parted, ground is visible, cars are getting larger and larger: there's the reassuring ribbon of the A38, the car park. A final tip in the opposite direction, a realignment, and BUMP, we are down. On the runway and not the grass. Cheers and claps reverberate throughout the aircraft.

And just like that, the spell is broken. I pull away from Tiago, straighten up, fidget with my hair, and grab my bits and pieces – passport first – from the seat pocket, ready to run the moment the seat belt light goes out. Everybody on this plane looks as if they've been dragged through a hedge backwards, to coin the phrase both sets of my grandparents love to mutter whenever they can possibly throw it at a scenario.

"Hey, are you okay? We made it!" Tiago says, gently caressing my back, his fingers brushing deliciously against the back of my neck now, making tingles flood all over my scalp as they catch random strands of my hair. I'm left in no doubt that this man could give a mean massage.

"Fine. All good, thanks," I say, barely looking at him and his infectious grin.

I've got to stay focused. We've landed safely and we are snapped back to reality now. Daydreams over. Mercifully, both sets of steps come out for the plane this time, with passengers being allowed to disembark at either end of the plane, which is extremely handy when you are after a Speedy Gonzalez getaway yourself.

"Looks like we don't have far to go." I nod my head toward the passengers who are already scrabbling for their carry-on luggage from the overhead lockers and queuing (in a fashion) to peel off to the left of us. I am sitting with my back to Tiago and my front to the aisle, eagerly awaiting the prime opportunity to jump. "I can't wait to get off this thing!" I bleat overenthusiastically, cowering slightly at the daggers the red-faced woman now towering over me is dishing out.

I spot a gap, pretend to go left, then pace quickly right, throwing Tiago completely. I can already tell he has bumped into the angry female, going by the volley of expletives she has released behind me. Poor guy. I can't help but feel guilty. I could have just explained to him that I needed to get my bag from the overhead locker by my original seat and that I'd 'probably' see him in the terminal, I now realise – but I don't want to give him false hope. There will be no strong coffee. There will be no anything. I need that man out of my life for good and trying to disappear into a crowd is my safest bet.

I am petrified by what happened just now. I'm not even sure if it was a dream. One thing's for certain: I can't wait around to find out. It was the fear that had me acquiesce to his protective cuddles. That was all. I honestly would have hugged a complete stranger, I was that scared. I can't let that fear take over my rational thoughts. Tiago is bad news. How can he not be?

By the skin of my teeth – and my now-broken flip flop – I make it from aircraft steps to terminal, not helped by the heavens opening and leaving me like a thoroughly drenched rat. I'm then through passport control and baggage reclaim without a trace of him to set me off balance. I fling my case at the nearest trolley and push it determinedly. Tears gather on my lower lashes as I finally burst through the doors into the brightly lit Arrivals hall. Kelly and Radhika are by now trotting behind, struggling to keep up. For a split second I scour the many faces waiting for their nearest and dearest, wondering if Tiago's somehow cut through the red tape of security to re-enact a scene from Love Actually. But no. And why should he? I've made it perfectly clear I'm not interested.

Emerging outside into the cold, heavy, diagonally-slanting rain (the kind of wintery Weston-super-Mare weather that Reggie refers to as a thunder-plump), I abandon the trolley, heft my case onto its wheels and charge across the zebra crossing, racking my traumatised brain to remember where the taxi rank is, delaying for as long as possible the moment when my friends will grill me about what in the hell is going on.

CHAPTER TWENTY-THREE

"SHE'S BACK, SHE'S back!" Reggie momentarily abandons his tray of freshly baked banoffee custard tarts, jumping up and down excitedly at my appearance. I run in for a much-needed hug.

"Now, before you tell us how awesome and relaxing the week was," he says with a smile, "And before you treat us to a slideshow of your cultural pics, two things: firstly, sales have been incredible this past week. Like, the best ever." I know this already because Caitlyn texted me but I don't have the heart to rain on Reggie's parade. "I'll show you the figures in a mo... and secondly, the fixture for the Weston-super-Mare versus Bristol match has been brought forward to this coming weekend. Are we still game on?" His eyes dance with mischief. "Did you have a chance to practice *pastel de nata* hurling on the beach like you'd planned?

"Yay! That's excellent news and totally eases my guilt at abandoning you all for the week. Thank you so much for doing such an amazing job. And no. That won't be necessary anymore," I tell him in answer to both questions.

Reggie's grin slips away.

"I suppose it is the more sensible option," he concedes with a pout that tells me I'm a complete and utter spoilsport and he was looking forward to the action. "But Willow, you have to fight to protect everything you've worked so hard for. You can't just let that idiot walk all over you and knock the wind out of your sails. Hmm," Reggie looks pensive. "Evidently this holiday has made you a little *too* laid back."

"What I'm trying to say is there's no need for me to clown around at your football match and embarrass the hell out of you and myself, Reggie. It turns out the petition wasn't real. Tiago forged all the signatures."

"What the fuck?" Reggie cries. "But I did my research and everything seemed above board and kosher wording-wise, more was the pity. Not that I ever thought much would come of it. The accusations were tenuous at best. How could he sink low enough to pull such a stunt? Frank will be livid when he finds out."

I look around, startled, checking we have no early customers within earshot and breathe a sigh of relief.

"Sorry, Willow. I know I shouldn't curse in the cafe, but what a *loser* that Tiago twat is." And there Reggie goes again – not that I can talk after unleashing all of those expletives on a certain easyJet flight – but from his point of view, knowing nothing about Tiago's backstory, this verdict stands to reason. "It'll be all I can do to keep my mouth shut this weekend on the pitch with him, and definitely all I can do to resist kicking the ball at his tackle."

"He's dropped the petition and that's as good as it will get. There's no point in escalating the situation, tempting as it might be. Let's not tell Frank. Some things are best left unsaid. It's over."

"Willow?" Reggie queries, with folded arms.

"Yes."

"Why do I get the feeling that something else other than the petition is over, too? Something harking of undercover romance. How do you even know the guy's dropped the petition, more to the point?" Reggie's eyes look me over from left to right, searching for clues, and he plants his hands on his hips. "I know you well enough by now to know when something's up. *Have you been seeing him?* Lord, I hope not. I thought you had more common sense than that."

My old friend shakes his head, having put two and two together, and having, indeed, come up with four.

I surrender. This was all going to come out sooner or later, wasn't it? Besides, I can't let the anger eat Reggie up. I guess the same will go for Frank, inevitably, but only if he mentions the subject of the petition. There's no point rocking the boat (or the pier) unnecessarily.

"Fine. Let's sit down," I say. I've lost track of whose turn it is with the hot drink-making in times of crisis. I rise to fix us up with a pair of bolstering coffees but Tim pops his head out of the kitchen and beats me to it, serving us two rich and aromatic caffeine shots. This is an uncharacteristic treat, even if he's forgotten I take milk. I heap a teaspoon of sugar into my tiny cup, stirring methodically in mental preparation for the kick, hoping the sweetness will dilute it.

I pour my heart out to Reggie, though leaving out this, that and the other – he really doesn't need to hear about my bedroom antics – and then the first bunch of customers arrive. I don't recognise any of them but it soon becomes clear that they are on first name terms with Reggie and I feel a little nip of joy in my heart (the first hint of elation since I've been back) that this gaggle of quirky middle-aged women, and their accompanying sewing projects, have enjoyed at least one visit so much that they've returned for seconds already.

"I don't know what to say, Willow." Reggie turns his attention back to me as we tidy up our cups and plates (resistance to the aforementioned banoffee custard tarts proved predictably futile) and get back to work. "I feel sorry for the guy, but it doesn't make any of his initial actions forgettable. Forgivable maybe... and really, you're a bit of a saint if you can do that. On the other hand, maybe you should give him one more chance. It's obvious you two have a connection. He has apologised. You may regret it if you don't see where things could go. Argh, I'm contradicting myself, aren't I? I've always been pants on matters of the heart."

"I can't disagree with that, or you'd have persuaded me to ditch Callum sooner than I did." I roll my eyes. "But there's no way I'm interested in any romantic involvement with Tiago." Oh, thank goodness I'm not wired up to a lie detector. "Actions speak louder than words. His attempt to ruin me was off the charts. That tells me everything I need to know about his personality. He had more than enough time to think better of his scheme and admit the petition was a load of nonsense, and that's that."

"I hear you. You've got a very valid point there." Reggie chews on his lip. "Actions do speak louder than words."

I'm not sure why Reggie emphasizes that last sentence but it's neither here nor there. I have a business to run and a summer to get through, customers new and old to impress. I also have a big sister to catch up with on all things marketing before my little sister comes bowling in, excited to see me back. But then Caitlyn phones in mysteriously and uncharacteristically sick.

Now the morning rush is frantic. I yo-yo between the kitchen, to help Tim prep more of our smash hit limoncello custard tarts, whose Italian kick is going down a treat now the weather's hotter, and the never-ending take-out queue. Reggie, meanwhile, darts gracefully around the café, never missing a beat or a request for an order, a refill, or a payment. How will we manage without him later this year? The thought is as worrying as it is awful.

Once the rush finally slows down, at three o'clock, I make my long overdue call to Lauren. I'm hoping my guilt at having slept with the guy she fancies at work (which is plain ridiculous since she is married to a whole other man) doesn't betray me down the phone line.

"Oh, hi, Bons... I mean, Willow." What the heck? That's a first. Surely Lauren hasn't matured in the manner of a bottle of port while I've been in Portugal? "Hope you had a great time in the Algarve and visited some of my recommendations." Funnily enough, Radhika's nightclub turned out to be one of them. I shudder at the unwelcome memory of the extortionately-priced Heston Blumenthal-meets-Monty Don cocktails and the cheesy bop beats. "Listen, I'd love to chat but I'm up to my eyeballs here." Lauren sounds immediately distant.

"Yeah, it was great, thanks. Right, well... I erm... I'll make it quick then. I just wondered if you had any updates on the various bits of promo we discussed last time. Is there any news on the reaction to the TikTok video yet? Reggie mentioned you'd been in to film it last week, that the actors were incredible, the props imaginative." I'm such a technophobe. I really need to work out how to log onto TikTok to watch it, then I might have an inkling. In my defence, I've barely had time to breathe since coming back to work this morning.

"We've not had a chance to put it together yet, sorry," Lauren spits her words out quickly, and I can also tell she's covered her phone with her hand so she can talk to somebody in the background. I wait patiently. This is more than a little odd. Completely the opposite to the sassy sister who bounded into my café in May, brimming with ideas and enthusiasm. It's a three-sixty turn on her extreme ideas about Hollywood celeb endorsement, too. "Listen, I have to go. I'll call you when I'm free."

I say bye, but Lauren has already hung up on me. Well, I'm not impressed. Evidently she feels she has bigger fish to fry than those situated in the beige waters of the English channel. Looks like she has put me on the backburner. But none of her clients offer the world anything as tasty or essential as my tarts. And I am a woman on a mission. So it looks like I'm going to have to do this myself. I vow to swot up on TikTok tonight and beat her to it. How hard can it be?

Yes, summer business is booming, but I want more than that. Since my return from Portugal, and Tiago's infuriating suggestions that I switch from custard tarts to baking a bit of this and a bit of that – as if all of this is nothing more than a girlie hobby – I am hellbent on West Country domination. First stop Weston-super-Mare. Second stop Bath/Bristol/Glastonbury. I'm not going to be fussy. Where there's a clientele, there's a way. And this means I need to lure more outsiders to the pier. And that means the likes of

TikTok.

Why not attempt to replicate the famous Hummingbird Bakery's success while I'm at it, introducing the beautiful baking of one country to another? And why stop at the West Country? Why stop in the UK? Why stop in Europe? Why can't a woman become an international foodie business entrepreneur?

She can and she will.

CHAPTER TWENTY-FOUR

TWO WEEKS LATER and the positive effects of the holiday have totally worn off. I am the walking definition of depleted. Gloomy and tired. And I could throw my brand new mobile phone at the wall in frustration over how pitiful my TikTok attempts have been. My attitude is selfish when Frank and Caitlyn are trying their level best to cheer me up. Predictably, Frank brought the petition up within seconds of our first post-holiday convo, and so out came my polished yarn, and so up rose his brows higher and higher with every bite of his tart. Reggie's mates have stood in as extras for my video attempts, and Tim has been on everything faster than a Stepford Wife. And I know my gloom is selfish, when our customers are (mostly) rays of sunshine, all eager-eyed and watery-mouthed at the sheer variety of custard tarts one can enjoy on a seaside pier.

"No matter how you look at it," starts Caitlyn, pulling me aside and giving me a far too gentle shake one afternoon as we prop ourselves against the pier's railings and squint out to sea. "You inadvertently did what you had to, Willow. Serendipity arranged for you to bump into Tiago that afternoon, and if it hadn't, who knows, maybe he would have gone ahead with a real petition. As it is, we can forget all about the hideous episode and you can enjoy the fruits of your labour. It's only your first season and look how brilliantly things are going! I'm so proud of you." Her eyes grow wider in encouragement. "Speaking of brilliance, I've got tickets for us to see this amazing local band in concert tonight. You have to come. I'm not taking no for an answer. I paid for these with my hard earned part-time job money, after all," she says, removing the tickets from her back pocket with a wink.

Great. What choice do I have?

Later, as I'm getting ready for said gig, grimacing at the pinch of the skinny jeans that I hope I can soon donate to the charity shop, with bootcut or flares coming back to the high street at long last, I realise July has somehow merged into August. Reggie is depressing the hell out of me daily by reminding me that he will soon be off to pastures new (the sewing group have even made him a beautiful library book bag!). And that only further reminds me that Caitlyn will be catching the train back to Loughborough in the blink of an eye... Tim and I really need to recruit a couple of members of full-time staff. I should get a wriggle on and focus. If I don't advertise soon then our newbies won't get the benefit of training alongside Reggie and Caitlyn, and that would be a tragedy.

Hopefully tonight will help take my mind off things, reorder my priorities, and snap me out of this daft obsession with TikTok videos. They aren't the promo be-all and end-all that I am choosing to make them. There are a thousand other ways to globally market a custard tart café. Especially one that already sets itself apart with bookworm events. That side of things has evolved massively and magically. Emma's on-air 'call for authors' has brought us a list of incredible storytellers in every genre imaginable, all of them keen as mustard (or custard) to book a slot for our upcoming Tart and Tales Thursdays; an event that Reggie and Emma have coordinated to mark the beginning of autumn and all things cosy.

✧   ✧   ✧

AT SEVEN P.M. on the dot I try with all my might to get cosy in a totally different venue, but it's not going so well. A clarinet player with a goatee, a pinstripe waistcoat and a bowler hat sets up on the pub's little stage to my left. He clearly sees himself as the next Acker Bilk and he's swiftly accompanied by four more men, each of them clad in a checked cowboy shirt with a clashing colour scheme. The mere sight of this catwalk collection is headache-inducing and they haven't even warmed up yet. Two of the entourage carry ukuleles, two have violins. They all faff about with their mics self-importantly. I've heard their brand of we're-so-completely-rad-and-middle-class-but-different, so-Glastonbury-festival-fans-be-sure-to-watch-this-space music before. Total wheel-reinvention stuff. No modern day musician will ever have the diversity and panache of my beloved Prince. Caitlyn's been ripped off with these tickets. Well, it's her hard-earned money, like she said, not mine.

I gasp at myself then. Actually gasp out loud. What have I become? Prince would spit purple feathers at me if he were still alive and in this crowd. Such a Tiago assumption to make, without giving something new and creative a try. I am a hypocrite. I am despicable. Who am I, to sit here at this rickety wooden table, dishing out the same kind of critique that I myself seek to avoid?

Caitlyn returns to our prime viewing spot, snapping me out of my miserable musing. She places a pint of Guinness in front of me and her own half in front of her. I worry momentarily that my runaway thoughts are turning me into Kelly. Yes, you guessed it. I wonder for a split second if Guinness might find its way into a custard tart. And you know what? It really would work, in an acquired taste, bittersweet way. Ooh, that's the future Dublin café's specialty taken care of then, and I guess this evening's outing hasn't turned out to be a complete waste of my time...

"I'm concerned about you, Willow," Caitlyn sips the head off her small glass and studies me, taking me away from my daydream. I pat my finger along my lips to indicate that she has a cream moustache, but she doesn't take the hint. "I know there are a few years between us but I feel like you need me around until you are back to your bubbly self. I'm not sure I can start my new term at uni while you're this perpetually frazzled and blue. You're so unlike yourself, on a path to self-destruction." My eyes almost pop out of their sockets at that startling remark, and now she can keep her facial hair. "There. I've said it. In fact, everything about you right now is taking me back to your last summer at sch—"

"Don't say it," I cut her off. She's right. But I don't want to hear it. "I'll be fine. I am fine," I make a lame job of reassuring her. "There's no way you are missing the start of uni. I just need to get my head around organising new staff, and a new but affordable marketing company to pick up where Lauren has evidently left off..."

"Oh, Willow. You don't know the half—"

"Shh... don't speak. Do not utter another word!"

Unless I am seeing a mirage (and those are generally quite welcoming signs), Tiago has just walked past the bar and headed into the loos.

"I can't believe you!" I shout at my sister as the revelation sinks in. "You've set me up! What good could possibly come of this?"

"Well I had to do something!" Caitlyn snaps. "You two need to clear the air before you ruin the café all by yourself. It's obvious you have unfinished business that could lead to something rather exciting if you choose to let it. He couldn't be more genuinely sorry for what he's done. Every time he's called in to the bakery when you've been in the kitchen or out..."

"Tiago has what?"

"And *that's* exactly why I haven't told you! I knew the only way you'd not bite his head off would be a chance meeting at a social event, a bit of music... when you'd hopefully mellowed with a glass or two of fizz... or, erm Guinness." Caitlyn side-eyes the pint that I am rapidly sinking.

"The only thing that's fizzing is my temper," I retort.

I abandon my drink, grab my bag and charge immediately out of the hall before Tiago can emerge from the gents. In a minute I'm outside, into the sunsetting, sea-salty night. I seem to be making a habit out of doing this in coastal venues (huh, and apartments) where Tiago and his family are concerned.

Clevedon's beach is about as drab in hue as our very own Weston's. I plop myself on the nearest bench and wrap my arms around my knees, drawing them into my chest – my default mode for self-protection – taking in the cosy twinkly lights of the town's nearby pier. My surroundings have a certain and undeniable appeal. Low-key and humble. Perhaps not so very different to an authentic and plain *pastel de nata*. All of which makes me falter as I let out a shiver at the cool evening breeze. Maybe I am starting to see things from Tiago's perspective? Sometimes it's more than okay to let things be; custard tarts in their purest form, unassuming towns… Not everything requires an upgrade or an improvement when it is perfectly satisfactory just the way it is. Could I have done that all along with my café? Just offered what my enterprise's name suggested on its signage: no frills, no bells and no whistles, just custard tarts?

It doesn't take long for my sister to spot me on Marine Parade, illuminated by the garlands of white light bulbs that frame the rapidly darkening horizon. My thoughts flip on themselves again. Talking of lights, why should I dim my own to fit in with somebody else's idea of convention? What a boring fart of a world we'd be living in if we all did that. Even Tiago's grannie Elsa acknowledges the necessity of evolution, and we are generations apart. Isn't that all the reassurance I need that I am on the right track with my endeavours? The customer feedback more than backs me up, for goodness sake.

Why can't I just forge ahead without all of this drama, though? I hate it when my quirkiness – in its big and little forms – upsets the balance with my sisters. It did this at school, dragging them into my mishaps. And it's doing it now, in adult life – a time when I should more than have my bleep together.

"Okay," says Caitlyn, taking up the far side of the bench.

"I was hoping we could have this discussion back inside, but here will do fine."

"There's nothing to talk about," I sigh. "Other than the fact that me, myself and I need to take back control of my life."

"You are in complete control! Since when have you ever let anybody tell you what to do? Willow Schofield, you are officially the most independent person I know, and that's an accolade that takes some beating with my uni friends, as you can probably imagine. Listen to me for a moment, please." Caitlyn lets out a deep breath. "Tiago wasn't just meeting us this evening because I hoped there would be some chance of you two rekindling romance. Cherry on the custard tart though that may have been. He's here on business too."

I slowly turn to look at my sister, unable to process those latter words. And then she further enlightens me.

"I'm taking it upon myself to update you on the things that Lauren won't. The Custard Tart Café's marketing account with Muse Masters was passed over to Tiago, after he put himself forward to look after it a few weeks ago. If you want your business visions to become reality, you really are going to have to learn to work with the guy."

"*He what?*"

CHAPTER TWENTY-FIVE

"But that's ludicrous," I say. I feel sick and dizzy. My head is swimming. My pulse skitters. "I don't want him coming *anywhere near* my bakery – physically (which I understand has already been the case several times without my consent since I returned from Portugal), or mentally." I pause to take a deep breath. "Definitely not mentally. He can't be trusted, Caitlyn. You just don't seem to get it! In no way, shape, or form does Tiago Mansplainer Willis have the business's best interests at heart. Oh, why didn't I come clean and tell Lauren about the petition from the get-go? There's no way she'd have let him take over if she'd known about his devious intentions. I'm such a fool." I close my eyes and shake my head at my own naivety.

There wouldn't have been any need to buy myself a clown suit and a red nose, had I decided to go ahead with custard-gate at Reggie's football match. I already am that person. Just not in costume.

"Slow down," Caitlyn implores. "Let me explain the situation properly."

"How do my older and younger sisters know more about my business than me?" I bite back. "What a joke, when I am paying you both for your services at the moment. I am the embodiment of the typical middle child. Left out of every-

244

thing."

I am now on my feet, glaring at Caitlyn, who is shaking her clenched fists either side of her head, just like she used to when she was a frustrated little girl who couldn't get her point across to one of her big sisters.

"I may only have met Tiago a handful of times, but you know me, Willow," her voice goes all whiney. "I'm a good judge of character. I always have been. I see the best in people, yes. But I'm no pushover. Just a few weeks ago I was talking revenge-fuelled javelin and shot put tactics, don't forget! I can't speak for Lauren. I know she had a crush on him. It was you who told me that… but it turns out there's more to it than that. And it's not my place to say anything. She'll let you know more when the time is right."

My breath hitches in my throat, my heart thuds louder and louder in my ears.

"S-so what you are trying and failing to say is you know something really big and juicy and important that sounds as if it has a massive impact on *my* life. Something which sounds suspiciously to me as if Lauren's been romantically entangled with my man… with T… I mean *bloody* Tiago." I must be furious to let that expletive slip. "And you're just going to sit there and clam up. Unbelievable!"

"Argh, not at all. It's you who is making me stumble over my words, which is hardly a surprise when you are just so…" But Caitlyn cannot finish her sentence and I will never know what she was going to call me. For whatever reason, she stares in defeat at the sea.

We are motionless for several beats. Both of us know that the next words could wound deeply so it's best to call an undeclared ceasefire. I get up and start to pace around the bench, as if that might help. After a couple of minutes, a movement in my peripheral vision tells me the man in question is walking towards us, and closing in rapidly.

"Well, well, well. Speak of the devil."

"He really isn't, Willow." Caitlyn rediscovers her voice. "You've got this all so very wrong. If you could just go and visit Lauren, she'll set you straight. It's not something she can discuss on the phone. Certainly not in the office. The gossip grapevine in that place is something else and you know it."

"I don't want to speak to either of them." I stamp my foot in defiance as Tiago draws ever closer.

"We are going to walk to the car park – aka in the opposite direction to that hideous human being who I am entitled to call oh, so many things – and you are going to drive me home NOW!"

CHAPTER TWENTY-SIX

BY THE MIDDLE of August I seem to have miraculously snapped out of the self-indulgent doldrums, much to the apparent delight of everybody around me. And I say that not to downplay the awful subject of depression for those who are truly in a bad place. That dark hole of despair is extremely real, if all I have ever experienced is fleeting glimpses of it. In my case, though, I had simply forgotten to count my blessings, oblivious to the unending support of the crew I have always had around me.

But no more.

The weather has been consistently wonderful taking us into early September; I've found two hard-working and charismatic waitresses (Pattie, a recent widow looking to fill the day's long hours and get out of the house, and Ava, an eighteen-year-old taking a year out to save up for the steep expense of modern-day uni). Both have been doing a stellar job of shadowing Reggie and Caitlyn. Tim and I have also knocked up some epic Guinness custard tarts which we plan to trial in the autumn when the weather feels more appropriate for such hearty delights, and Tiago has barely crossed my mind.

Mainly because the moment he does, I sweep every inch of him under the carpet with an imaginary but very nifty industrial-sized broom.

All in all, everything is rosy as can be – with the exception of the lack of contact from Lauren. Still, as I recall, she made it perfectly clear she'd be the one to get in touch with me. I know she's been to Mum and Dad's more often than usual but I've managed to extract diddly-squat out of them. I would say it's weird that our paths have never crossed, given I visit my folks fairly frequently and we live in the very same town, but Lauren has rarely had much leisure time to grant our parents, so catching a cuppa and a natter chez Schofield HQ, Mum and Dad's old-fashioned semi-detached seaside villa, has long been a rarity for her.

Okay, everything is as weird as can be, too. In fact, the last five days have played witness to an unusual yet almost scheduled series of fortunate events:

- On Monday somebody from 'Nigella's team' happened across the café. I thought it was a joke to start with when the neatly coiffed young female asked if I'd be interested in one of our recipes featuring in Nigella's 'Cookbook Corner' on Instagram… until she handed me a rather official looking business card. I'm not saying such an honour is going to set the sky alight – it's just a footnote, and a very nice one at that – but the recognition means *everything*, and presumably Nigella herself has to give the thumbs up to such an endorsement.

- On Tuesday Peter Andre (I kid you not!) descended on the café with his kids after a spot of filming for a brand new fringe travel channel, and though I may not be a fan of his music, his aftershave, or the various reality TV shows he's chosen to grace over the years, it turns out he's the sweetest guy (happily posing for pictures with my customers, cheerfully signing their takeout boxes, napkins, and the inside of their arms) and a total foodie to boot (placing a mega order to take back to the production crew who were still working on the beach).

- On Wednesday I found myself ushered into the BBC Points West studios for an impromptu interview – and my first ever TV appearance –on a panel of local female entrepreneurs.

- On Thursday I was invited to take part in an upcoming regional food festival which will include a bake-along with... wait for it... James Martin! We are to share a stage in a tent packed full of expectant foodies, each of us battling it out to create the best custard tart. It's the stuff of dreams *and* the stuff of nightmares. I have no more words except for saying I will need to meditate daily between now and next spring to achieve any kind of dignity and composure.

- On Friday (today) #thecustardtartcafé is trending on Twitter and I only know so because Reggie has sent me a screenshot of the phenomenon, which Nigella herself has even piggybacked to retweet. I actually think I might faint! Never mind my usual injection of grounding caffeine in dramatic circumstances, by this afternoon I could neck a crate of Elsa's berry and chocolate-bolstering port to help me make sense of the week's shenanigans.

Now this is starting to sound like Eric Carl's book *The Very Hungry Caterpillar*, which is kind of apt given my wares.

"How do you think all of these things are happening, Willow? They're not random occurrences, you know." My younger sister tsks at me and then does a very rubbish job of hiding her told-you-so giggles.

Caitlyn is off to uni at the weekend (and Reggie has already left for his freshers week at Cardiff, sniff, sniff) so I know this is her last attempt at making me 'see the light' before she goes.

"I'm sure my Instagram stories have had something to do with it. I worked hard on them and they do look pretty enticing."

I also know deep down it's not them, Caitlyn's ungainly response of a snort confirming it. A hidden force is at play. The same hidden force that's been working behind the scenes for weeks now. The same hidden force that I stubbornly refuse to have a meeting with. Face to face or via Zoom.

"You just keep telling yourself that, sis."

Caitlyn winks at me, expertly twirling an afternoon tea cake stand full of glossy tarts. She saunters off with a cheeky grin to deliver the order to the family celebrating a birthday over at the prime window seat. Frank's seat. Fortunately, Frank has already been in today, all too happy to be the first to sample the rest of our proposed autumn custard tart highlights; the aforementioned Guinness tart, then a rice pudding tart drizzled with a ruby-red strawberry jam sauce, a Thanksgiving pumpkin and mixed spice nut tart, a whisky caramel tart and, last but not least, our zingy and moreish gingerbread eggnog tart. Frank rounded his feast off with that, and gave everything a resounding thumbs up, thank goodness.

Fortunately, and not so fortunately. Because there was something different about Frank that I just couldn't pinpoint this morning. A distinct lack of eye contact, for starters. And I'm not really sure if it is a good different or a bad different, which is worrying me.

But Frank isn't the only one acting out of character. Kelly isn't answering my calls (she vehemently opposes text messages so we have always operated in the old school way), and Radhika hasn't replied to my WhatsApp asking for a weekly summary of her life's events. In fact, she's not as much as batted an eyelid in response to mine. I know that she is probably preoccupied texting sweet nothings to Santi, but these are rather huge landmarks in my career, and, since Rad used to have a thing for Peter Andre, she really is being quite a *Mysterious Girl*.

So when I say life is good, yes, it is, and I have no complaints. But there isn't half a whiff of the curious in the air…

CHAPTER TWENTY-SEVEN

IT'S SEPTEMBER THE twenty-first. For a follower of the equinox like me, this means autumn has finally come. It means today is the day we can reveal our new seasonal tarts to the nation. Okay, one step at a time; to Weston's residents and tourists – who will hopefully shout from the pier's trendy and undulating roof top about them, the sentiment carrying on the breeze, enveloping Great Britain in a custard tart frenzy. It also means I have successfully navigated my way out of our busiest season of the year without having a marketing meeting with Tiago. I have proven my point: he can do whatever he is doing from afar and never the twain shall meet. It suits me just fine. Business is business and there is no need to make it personal.

Today's flipped ponytail with double braids swings from side to side like a pendulum in the fresh air. We had quite the downpour here last night but the sunrise this morning was spectacular and uplifting, its toasty tendrils quickly eating up the puddles. It's eight a.m. and the golden beams, although nowhere near the horizon where they dazzled me as the sun woke the seaside world up twenty minutes ago, continue to spotlight patches of the beach as though it's a dancefloor. It's a gorgeous sight. I'm almost tempted to hop over the wall and sashay my way to work along the damp sand.

Seagulls serenade me as I continue to march along the wide pavement that runs parallel to the seafront. And suddenly a helicopter flies in from the right and hovers over the beach as if this is quite the norm. I have no idea what it's doing, but it can't be dropping celebs off for a day trip. As lovely as this daybreak is, we aren't in Marbella. The heli circles high above the pier in a whoop-whoop that assaults the eardrums and then over to the beach on its left – the nearest stretch of sand to where I am walking.

The closer I get to where the helicopter is hovering, the clearer it is that somebody has gone to great lengths to do something arty-farty, seemingly overnight. My first guess at their spontaneous exhibition would be some of those sand sculptures, but the artists are usually clued up enough to make those near the promenade walls so they don't get washed away by the tide, and so they can cash in with monetary gifts of appreciation from passing tourists. The giant dragonfly in the sky bobs off again, and I guess it's looking for a criminal instead. Perhaps it has just ruled out the perfect hide-and-seek place under the pier, after taking thermal images and ascertaining that there's nobody down there clinging for dear life to the structure's iron 'legs'.

I squint at the distant remnants of the markings in the sand as I pass to turn left and onto the Grand Pier, unable to miss the conversation of the group of dog walkers who are pointing animatedly at the beach exhibition debris.

"Stories like that are pure chicken soup for the soul; the stuff of fairy-tales."

"It was proper lush. The hours it must have taken. Surely he couldn't have done it all on his own – not unless he was

Usain Bolt!"

"Who said romance was dead? Good luck to them!"

The high-pitched ring of my mobile phone breaks into my eavesdropping and I hurry down the wooden boardwalk of the pier, yabbering away to our flour and egg supplier to arrange today's delivery, completely missing my opportunity to peek to the left from my aerial view to see what all of the fuss might have been about. Tealights and shells dot the central seating areas of the pier this morning as I make my way to TCTC. I guess that's some kind of habitual installation to mark autumn. I haven't yet experienced all of the seasons here as a trader, so what would I know?

Once I'm inside the café I take over kitchen duty from Tim so he can have a break and a drink. Tim is a man of few words, so we tend to communicate by singing along to eighties hits on Spotify – peppered with numerous Prince songs – as we bake and prepare our custard batter.

But this morning I am taken by surprise when Tim immediately says, "You're not a morning news person then, Willow."

It's not even a question. He just leaves the statement hanging in the air, shakes his head as if he can't quite work me out and wanders outside to the pier for his ritual morning mug of tea. I pick up my whisk to get working on our ever popular espresso kickstart tarts. What was that all about? Too right I'm not one for the news. Pandemic essentials aside, I have never been able to accept the way the world's predominantly negative events are portrayed to us – morning or evening – endless doom with a little postscript mention of a ray of sunshine tacked on the end to try to cheer us up. It's massively distorted; a breeding ground for anxiety, despair, and the growth of one's own limiting beliefs. I suppose local news is a little bit chirpier but even that likes to dwell on petty crime, the town's lager louts, and road accidents. Okay, now I feel guilty thinking of Tiago's poor parents and the young family they left behind, who would totally be in need of answers and closure. I suppose in that respect I probably should tune in from time to time…

My thoughts drift to the fillings on my list. With the espresso kickstart mix poured neatly into Tim's perfect pastry cups, it's time to make a start on our exciting autumn treats before the first customers put in an appearance. In the background I can hear an incessant beep, beep, BEEP of notifications on my phone in my bag. I really should put it on silent. I hate it when the outside world interferes with my flow. I sing along with Prince's *Raspberry Beret*, determined to ignore the annoying intrusion.

"Willow, Willow, WILLOW!"

Well that didn't last long. I flinch, sending a spatter of batter flying at the back wall. I recognise that female voice but it doesn't belong to either of my sisters, nor my besties. Tim must have let someone in while he was outside. We're not open for another forty-five minutes yet. What's going on?

"I hope you don't mind but I *just had to come and see you before I start my shift at the radio station*." A beaming and very exhilarated Emma Hawkes peeps her head around my kitchen, jumping up and down, letting out 'eek!' after 'EEK!'

"Erm, Emma? What is it?" I ask, all thoughts of cleaning up my inadvertent coffee-custard mural disappearing. "Have you won the lottery or something? Do you want to sit down,

ISABELLA MAY

take a few deep breaths, and I'll get you a coffee and a *nata*? Our cherry and berry breakfast tarts have just come out of the oven so you're in luck… well, as long as you blow on them, they're as piping hot as those notoriously volcanic McDonald's apple pies. A hundred times tastier obvious—"

"Really?" Emma folds her arms, knits her brow, and comes over all headmistress-like. "Do you honestly mean to tell me you haven't seen this morning's news?"

"What do you mean?" I laugh nervously, fear rising inside me as to what on earth two news mentions in such quick succession could possibly imply. "I don't have time for things like that. We're launching a new range of custard tarts today and even if we weren't… the answer would be no… I'm not a sensational, blown-up and over-exaggerated story sort of person. Never have been. Can you imagine the negative energy my tarts would be fused with, having the news piped through these walls? I do love listening to *your show*, of course." I skim neatly over the fact that I turn the volume down as soon as Emma's interviews with fascinating people, or her talk about books and all things interesting, come to an abrupt halt when she is duty bound to hand the mic over to the newsdesk or the weather reporters.

"Oh, Willow. It's not me who needs to sit down! Here, let me take over that whisking while you have a little look at this." Emma makes a couple of adjustments with her mobile phone then places it on the kitchen's one and only wooden chair, barely able to contain her enthusiasm. The instruction seems non-negotiable. It won't hurt to swap places for a few seconds just to placate her, I suppose.

"Okay." I shrug. "But you'll need to cover your hair with

a net, thoroughly wash your hands and pop an apron on." I point to the drawer, the kitchen sink, and the hook on the cupboard door, showing Emma the order to be followed. She sets to it immediately, pressing her mouth into a firm line as if trying to hide a giant smile. Monday mornings don't usually tend to be this eventful around here. As soon as Tim is back I will gently but assertively shoo her out and off to her day job. Tim always gets jittery when more than a pair of people are in the kitchen. "Two's company," he always says, with no need to waste his words on finishing that sentence.

Once I am satisfied that Emma's ready to go near my precious mix, I sit on the chair and pick up the phone. The screen is paused on a video. Nothing can prepare me for what I am about to see.

I press the triangular play button, instantly sucked into the twilight as the footage reveals somewhere very familiar to me and my heart: the beach outside. A man in a beanie hat crouches on the sand laying out pebbles and shells, weaving fairy and tea lights in and around them. It looks pretty, though it's clearly freezing, droplets of rain hitting the screen for added effect. And it looks like part of a plan – a pre-prepared message. The first letter is large, practically the height of the man should he lie next to it. It looks like the letter F. The man has his back to the camera the whole time, practically every inch of his flesh is hidden, even his hands are in gloves and the hat completely covers his hair and ears. How can I even tell it's a man? Somehow I can sense it from that scant flash of jawline. He works faster and faster to add more and more letters to his piece of art. The video speeds up and the next thing I know he has spelt out seven whole words:

FOR THE BEST CUSTARD TARTS IN THE WORLD

Who is this?

Don't tell me... it's somebody Tiago has employed, in his efforts to outdo any of my own organic marketing. I wouldn't put it past him. Although, I suppose it could also be a mystery diner who wanted to review us somewhere other than TripAdvisor. But there's no way any helicopter pilot would be entranced enough by a café recommendation to hover over it, even if he or she was a custard tart fiend. Out of the corner of my eye I see Emma paying less and less attention to her task, peering at me instead, but I am too intrigued to worry. She can't overbeat the mixture anyway, she's putting in nowhere near enough elbow grease. The recording continues and now begins the intro to a song I know (and love); Prince's Starfish and Coffee. *Oh my goodness.* The tears well up. I don't even try to stop them. Whoever this person is, *they see me.* Like really see me. My interpretation of Prince's lyrics in this song are of a unique girl whose creativity shines through when it comes to food and its pairings. It always has been, since the day I first heard it. Others may disagree but Prince's 'breakfast song' has always kind of summed me up. How could this person on the beach intuitively know that?

In between seeing the letters build words and the words build sentences, there are tasteful stills of (oh!) *me* – on my recent holiday, and thankfully not in my bikini! – as well as some particularly toothsome shots of the tarts, and the customers enjoying them in the café. If I'm not mistaken, said clientele looks suspiciously like Reggie's friends, the ones he'd drafted in as extras for that TikTok video of Lauren's that never was.

The footage returns to the beach, speeding up once more to show the rest of the letters being added shell by shell, pebble by pebble to make a massive, illuminated statement in the sand, until it is finally complete and reads:

FOR THE BEST CUSTARD TARTS IN THE WORLD...
VISIT WONDERFUL WILLOW'S CUSTARD TART CAFÉ
AT THE END OF WESTON-SUPER-MARE'S GRAND
PIER!

There's a twinkly red arrow pointing to the pier too – just in case anybody should think they're being directed to Brighton or Llandudno.

P.S. I MIGHT BE A BIT IN LOVE WITH WILLOW.

P.P.S. OK. A LOT IN LOVE.

P.P.P.S ALL RIGHT, WILLOW IS THE LOVE OF MY LIFE!

I blink rapidly and go to open my mouth over and over like a goldfish but nothing comes out.

The words are so large, they can be seen from the air. Yet this can't be Todd alone working his magic with the drone. As if on cue, the man whose back has been facing me – facing all of the viewers – turns slowly at last, removing the woolly hat from his head and I let out a gasp of utter shock.

"Who else could it have been, you silly sausage?" Emma finds this reaction particularly hilarious. "I didn't mean to alarm you... but what a dreamily gorgeous surprise on a Monday morning, hey? You and this café have become something of a national sensation, and just wait until America wakes up. The US networks love a good underdog romance story."

The sheer effort this harebrained plan of Tiago's must have taken! But what possessed him, when I have consistently made it clear that there is and can never be an *us*? My eyes glaze over and a lump forms in my throat, but I battle to keep watching the recording to the end and see Tiago's bow of a finale. Then I make Emma replay the video, pausing at specific intervals and zooming in on some of the background characters who appear to be helping out with this romantic quest.

They are Caitlyn (hang on a minute, she's supposed to be at uni right now!), Reggie (ditto... although I suppose this was filmed on a Sunday night and maybe neither have lectures until this afternoon), Kelly, Matt, Radhika, Frank... *Frank* (*what the heck?*), and some other little helpers who appear to be wearing purple Loughborough uni tracksuits.

How am I meant to take all this in? It's too much. I crumple to the kitchen floor and bawl my eyes out. I can't help it. Emma could be filming me now, for all I know. At the very least she could choose to recount this part of the story over the airwaves to today's radio show guests. My guard is down at last. I love Tiago too. Proper, all-encompassing, love him. More than words can say. Which is ironic seeing as he's just spelt his feelings out for me in the most public way. But it doesn't change a thing. It's not meant to be. If it was, the universe would never have delivered us so much friction from the start. We'd soon be at each other's throats in a relationship. It could never, ever last the distance.

✧   ✧   ✧

I HAVE FINALLY regained a normal breathing pattern, coaxed Emma out of the door with a humongous box of custard tarts to be shared with her workmates and interviewees, and carried on in the café as best I can – which isn't the easiest task in the world when every second person walking through the front door (not to mention Pattie and Ava) is questioning me about the 'romantic message in the sand' and reeling off yet more media and social media platforms that are sharing it with their millions of viewers. And I can ignore my own queue of phone messages no longer. I'm gearing up to give several meddling people a piece of my mind when Caitlyn's incoming call beats me to it.

"Forgive him."

What a way to greet one's older sister after she's had the shock of her life.

"Why should I? Or you, for getting involved in all the silliness," I snap back predictably. "It's a few pebbles and shells. Big deal."

And grr. I hate it when my little sister is right. Now I know how Lauren must secretly feel... perpetually. Hehe to that sentiment.

"Because I have never known anybody go to such soppily romantic lengths – and neither have you. Because even my Loughborough sporting buddies said they would have struggled to find the stamina to lay that not-so-little lot out in the middle of a rainy English night, hence all of us getting together to help Tiago in shifts. The guy's probably got hyperthermia now!"

I go to open my mouth and say something to halt this stream of a one-ended conversation but once again, I have been rendered a fish gasping for air.

"Because there's only so many times anybody can make these gestures and there's only so long that anybody can be expected to wait," Caitlyn goes on. "Because if you don't give him a chance and stop denying your own feelings, you will kick yourself for the rest of your life. Maybe not today and maybe not tomorrow, but one day this stubborn decision of yours will bite you on the arse. It will be too late then. He'll be with someone else, a cute couple of kiddies… the both of you secretly settling for second best and morally unable to do a thing about it."

Caitlyn's made her point. But does she seriously think my own thoughts haven't gone there?

"Okay, *okay*. I'll think about it. Are you happy? Now please, leave me alone so I can finish up service with my team and shut shop for the night. It's been a long day."

"Tell me about it." I can perceive Caitlyn's glare down the phone line. "At least you had some slee—"

I know I shouldn't, but I hang up on my sister. I can always blame it on a demanding customer or a bad connection when she lays into me in the next few seconds with an angry text. I put my phone in my bag, zip it tightly to halt any further interruptions, but unfortunately none of this stops the replay of Frank's same but different words from earlier when he'd visited for his thrice-weekly afternoon tea package:

"Granted, he didn't come into your life with the most conventional of chat-up lines, but if there's one thing I have learned, Willow, it's this. We have to grab our opportunities for happiness with both hands and savour every moment of them because we never truly know how long they will last. I know my first encounter with Millie on this very same pier was slightly more idyllic, forgetting that ugly laughing sailor dummy tittering away behind us… but you can't say that Tiago hasn't tried to make amends. Yes, that damned petition was as tasteless as Ryvita. He's fiercely loyal to his family, that's all. Moving forward, if you do decide to give him the benefit of the doubt, is that really such a bad trait?"

Hearing these Oscars-style speeches from my sister and Frank, two human beings at the opposite ends of their life journeys, I have no choice but to digest and accept the truth. I don my own woolly hat, put on my snug bomber jacket, sling my bag over my shoulder, check that Pattie and Ava are happy to lock up tonight, and make the short pilgrimage to the beach.

As soon as I step out onto the pier though I realise what a klutz I am to think that I can visit the spot of Tiago's sandy spiel. The tide has more than covered it. The video is all that I have now. So I change tack and head to Tesco to buy popcorn, a bag of donuts that I know will taste more like bread than cake (but one lives in perpetual hope) and a new tin of Ovaltine because I'm running out. At the till, I spot Tiago's message emblazoned across the front page of the *Weston-super-Mare Mercury*. I pull my hat further over my eyes and quickly pay, bagging up my treasures to take them home, where I plan to change into my Winnie the Pooh onesie and watch the footage on re-run until I have made my decision as to what to do next.

But before I can do that, when I get home I pick up the

giant pink envelope that is lying in wait for me on the doormat. Surely I haven't sleepwalked my way into Valentine's day too? Nothing would surprise me anymore. I dump my bag and gingerly tear open the envelope to find a confirmation print-out for a luxury spa inside. It details a rather luscious-sounding list of treatments... all paid for by Kelly and Radhika. What on earth? I call Kelly for clarification, knowing that this time she will pick up, since she is one of the many people who has been leaving me messages all day – although in true Kelly avoidant style, her voicemail this afternoon was a mini podcast pleading with me:

Please forgive me, Willow. And please forgive Radhika, too. We know that what we did to help Tiago on the beach last night can only be classed as meddling, but our hearts were in the right place. Once Reggie and Frank contacted us after getting their heads together with Tiago to come up with a master plan, well, we could hardly refuse. Frank was such a trooper. It was amazing to meet him at last after everything you'd told me about him. He's so generous, too. He parked himself under the pier in his deckchair and blanket and plied us with custard tarts all night. He must have spent a fortune in your café to help us keep our strength up. Oops... I've totally dropped the boys in it. Bye for now!

Forgiveness. It definitely seems to be the theme of the day.

Kelly picks up after the first ring.

"It's nothing. Just a token gesture. There's no need to

thank us. You didn't exactly get much space in Portugal and you haven't had much time to think since you've been back, so Radhika and I clubbed together. We thought a spa day would do you good." I look all around me to check for a hidden camera. How can Kelly tell I have even seen the envelope, let alone opened it? "I checked with Tim before we arranged it and he said he'd work you harder today so there would be plenty of tarts ready tomorrow, so you're all covered to take the day off."

"But Tim has no way of knowing how busy we'll get… the extra trade is building like you can't imagine, thanks to all today's publicity. We'll have to turn customers away at this rate! I can't just leave Tim to it, not so soon after my holiday. That's not fair."

"All right," says Kelly with a deep sigh. "I wasn't going to say anything but my Matt is going over to help Tim for the day. You know how amazing he is with pastry. The ice cream parlour is quiet now the weather has turned so it's no biggie."

"Right. Thanks," I reply, feeling a little relieved. Matt is more than capable when it comes to patisserie. "That's very thoughtful of you but really, Kelly, there was no need for you and Radhika to do this. I can reach a decision about my love life without being caked in mud and smothered in rosehip oil. Lovely though I am sure it will be."

"Just go and don't even think about trying to get out of it," my friend screams. She sounds exasperated.

"Kelly?"

"I know exactly what you are about to say and I can hand on heart promise you that Tiago will *not* be waiting to pounce on you in the Jacuzzi."

"Or anywhere else?"

"*Or anywhere else.*"

Oh. My mouth turns down at the corners. Which is ridiculous given the guy has made it crystal clear that he *is* ready to pounce on me anywhere and anytime, all I have to do is give him the nod.

"And on the subject of Tiago, despite the fact that this is your decision to make, I do think you'd benefit from a few words from me, your older, wiser, and most spiritually in-tune friend, so I am going to give you them."

Great. I could really do with being in my onesie already with that popcorn by my side. I feign a cough so I can open the bag of sweet and salty Tyrells kernels without Kelly realising, and greedily pop several pieces in my mouth. This could take as long as a full-length movie. "Okay, that message on the beach was a bit corny," Kelly informs me. "But your heart already knows it was the biggest, most passionate and credible apology you have ever received in your life. Would Callum have gone to such lengths?" I almost choke on my popcorn trying to conjure up that image. "Tiago's gesture was so vivid, Willow. Like the Great Wall of China, you could probably see it from space. It's given me some awesome PR ideas for our ice cream parlour... I'm thinking of festive floating environmentally-friendly wooden letters topped with waterproof LED strip lights, shimmering down the River Avon in the run up to Christmas. The business is by the water's edge, after all... and I'm sure I could pay somebody to dress as a snowman and stand on one of the barges to point a sign at our building on Pulteney Bridge. Tiago's a bit of a genius."

Once Kelly's speech is over, I finally climb into my onesie, make my Ovaltine, bite into a donut (it's surprisingly cake-like, hurrah!), switch on the TV to reassure myself that my love life is no longer the talk of the town (oh, heck, they might have moved swiftly on at the local ITV studios but now they're debating it on BBC's The One Show), toss the James Martin cookbook I am re-reading onto the carpet, so I can curl up on the sofa without the pointy corners of a hardback poking my toes, and watch the video again, trying to gauge the amount of time and effort that went into Tiago's message; sensing every ounce of that man's love for me. I flick my gaze back to James, whose top shirt button is undone, and who is looking at me as if he'd like to undress me, too. His expression has the same intensity as Tiago's actions. And that's when I finally realise it probably doesn't get better than this.

The ball is in my court. I have Tiago's phone number, after all. But speaking of clichés, there's one slight fly in the ointment when it comes to conducting any kind of relation-ship with him on English shores.

Lauren.

How on earth do you solve a problem called My Big (Entitled) Sister? And given Caitlyn's mysterious hints that night at the folk music gig, how can I be sure that nothing has ever gone on between Lauren and Tiago? I'm going to sabotage my entire relationship with her, if I claim my stake. She'll die a thousand deaths, of anger and embarrassment.

CHAPTER TWENTY-EIGHT

AFTER SUCCUMBING TO the soothing effects of Ayurvedic massage and reflexology, I take myself to the beautiful turquoise pool of one of Somerset's top spas to flex my muscles and swim a few lengths. The Jacuzzi and steam rooms overlook the stunning kidney-shaped lagoon, where I am now doing a few leisurely laps. Mental note for the future when the business is making serious money: Tuesdays are a great day to visit this place. I count just four other people in the pool. All are minding their own business, allowing everybody to relax in their own space, taking in the jawbreakingly beautiful chandelier suspended dramatically above us, the stunningly patterned tiles, and the magnificence of the giant arched windows with views onto the lush green West Country fields. The two messy buns of the people languishing in the Jacuzzi rest on the edge of its squishy-looking tiles. I think I might just have to drag myself there next, once they have vacated.

Another figure emerges from a treatment room fringing the far side of the pool, with an uncharacteristically messy bun of her own. I say 'uncharacteristically,' because I know this woman and usually her hair is perfect. I stop swimming mid-length and hold onto the pool's edge. There's something else that's different. My older sister is in a swimsuit (what happened to the tiny bikinis?) and, if I'm not mistaken, she's sporting a tiny pot belly where formerly there was a wash-board stomach.

I guess all of that wine consumption, and the inevitable hangover munchies, could only be kept at bay for so long. Not that I am knocking the pot belly look. I definitely have one of my own, and would always prefer it that way. A life without my daily intake of custard tarts is unthinkable.

Lauren turns and waves at me, completely unperturbed. She makes a knife and fork gesture and then jabs a manicured finger at the floor. Okay then. I guess I am going to give it twenty minutes to ensure we don't bump into one another in the changing rooms, and head downstairs for lunch, where it sounds very probable that I will meet her.

"HEY," I GREET her and dive in for a kiss on each cheek. "You're looking... great. Erm, what are you doing here?"

No sooner are the words out of my mouth than I know that Kelly and Radhika have set us up.

"I'm sorry for not telling you before. I felt awkward... and more than a little dumb. I don't think either of us needs to talk about the person who links us in that respect; in fact, I'd appreciate it if we could pretend those conversations and messages between us never happened."

I nod my head and close my eyes because I cannot bear Lauren in humble mode. It doesn't suit her.

"I'll be honest, I wasn't sure of his motives when he put himself forward to handle your account, but well, he's certainly getting The Custard Tart Café noticed for all the right reasons – not that Jamie or I completely condone the way he's mixed business with pleasure… but I suppose we can overlook that just this once." Lauren quirks a brow. "It's clear the pair of you are smitten and you deserve to be happy."

She stops for a quick sip of her drink and clears her throat. "What I'm trying to say is, things have changed. Everything's changed, Willow." She puts a protective hand on her tummy. Oh, my goodness. Get the flags out, Lauren is calling me by my actual name… without even faltering over a letter B before doing so… and wait, *what*? That hand gesture. Surely…

'Yes, I'm pregnant, Willow.'

Oh, so that's what the pot belly is all about! My goodness, talk about me missing a trick. "It's time for me to start taking my marriage seriously," Lauren says. "Jamie too. No more eye candy for either of us. You're going to be an auntie!"

"Wow! That's amazing! Congratulations!"

It also explains all the recent secrecy and strange behaviour. That definitely wasn't a conversation we could have had on the phone.

"Look: water, not bubbles." Lauren nods at the tumbler in her hand, raising her glass, at which point I realise mine is still empty. A waiter comes over to take my order and soon we are tucking into a bowl of parmesan truffle chips (mine washed down with Bolly) while we wait for our grilled fish with lemon and samphire.

I COULD DO what I am about to do next from the comfort of

my humble home, but I have decided to make the most of the beauty surrounding the spa. So I take myself and my (third) glass of champagne outside to a quiet corner in the grounds. There's a quintessentially English country vista of meadows and cows. Hopefully none of my companions will start mooing or pooping while I make this momentous call to the man I am very much hoping might be the love of my life.

I take a bolstering sip and exhale deeply as I wait for Tiago to pick up the call. I feel like I'm not really here. It's such a surreal thing to have punched his phone number into my mobile, waiting for him to answer. I am not waiting for long.

"Where did you get all those pebbles and shells?" I ask breathily, without even introducing myself. "Because Weston-super-Mare's beach is predominantly known for its mud. And how many trips to Ikea did that tangle of lights entail?"

Tiago laughs. Nervously and huskily. I can practically smell his cologne and I knock back another glug of champagne, relishing the fizz as it slides down my throat.

It's not the most original opening, but I'm genuinely curious about these things.

"It's a long story... and the fact that you've called hopefully means you'll let me tell you in full, over dinner."

"Lunch," I cut in. "If we're going to explore the possibility of us, I want to do that over a stone-cold sober meal with no temptation of beds."

"That's a shame. I was hoping to re-enact some of our last moves in that department, but I can be patient. I'll just have to undress you with my eyes as we quaintly sip our orange juice and nibble our French fries."

"Tiago! You are incorrigible."

Tiago, you are also making me cross and uncross my legs. I am grateful for the sudden breeze to cool me down.

"Seriously Willow, thank you for giving me another chance." His tone matches his sentiments and I just want to melt. "I guess I got ahead of myself during that bumpy landing. Once you'd scarpered, I genuinely thought all was lost, other than a potential marketing meeting. I'd be lying if I claimed not to have an ulterior motive when I asked to take over TCTC's account. Mainly though, I just wanted to do everything in my power to help right my wrongs and turbo-boost business for you."

My heart swells. This is the point of no return, I realise, and I surrender to it with a small and floaty sigh.

"Your marketing techniques have certainly made an impression... to the point I'm not sure how we can cope with the demand." Both of us laugh at that. The dust settles between us, the bubbles floating to my lightweight head; I have always been the same with gassy drinks. "It's a nice problem to have, though."

"I can help you with that particular hurdle too. My background is in business and marketing so I have more than a few ideas."

"I'd be interested to hear them." I swirl my glass flirtatiously, regardless of the fact the cows are my only real audience.

"I..."

"You..."

We both go to speak at the same time and are reduced to fits of giggles again. Tiago must be at work at the moment, so

I hope he can take this call outside. Not that Lauren will be listening in, of course.

"I just wanted to say what amazing friends you have." Tiago goes first and to be honest I have completely forgotten what I was going to say anyway. "Reggie kind of made himself known to me after our last football match." Ha, I'll bet he did. "He admitted that although he wasn't my biggest fan, something that would take a miracle to change, he could read between the lines and sense there might still be a chance you would forgive me... but that it would probably take more action, and fewer words."

Tingles flood my spine. Reggie had made a point of reiterating those words during one of our conversations, hadn't he? "Reggie gave me a right – and totally deserved – dressing down, reminding me that if I had the nerve to pull off my original stunt of waltzing into the café and causing such a scene – an act that was as absurd as it was unwarranted, since the Romans invented custard – then I needed to dig deep and find the same kind of spirit to prove that you're worth fighting for. That your café is the bee's knees."

We both fall silent for a moment as I take all of this on board.

"I know without a shadow of a doubt how you feel about me," I finally say. "But the thing I am struggling to wrap my head around is that you *truly* rate my custard tarts... which reminds me... you never did give me the verdict on the ones I gifted you that day; the tarts that were paid forward by Frank."

"You really want to know?"

"Oh, I really, *really* want to know," I reply, bracing myself for everything now to go spectacularly pear-shaped, but I want nothing short of authenticity moving forward.

"Okay," Tiago sighs deeply. "The fact is... although it pained me at the time to admit it... and this doesn't mean I don't love my grannie's plain and simple *pastéis*, by the way." I wait with baited breath for his verdict. There is bound to be a 'but' coming. "I'm going to be honest with you, Ms. Schofield... you are *creative dynamite* and every single one of those tarts set off fireworks on my tongue. I'm insatiable to try more of the things. I must admit, Frank has been a lifesaver in that respect, funnelling me regular supplies so I can enhance every aspect of marketing the little gems. Your autumnal ideas are a revelation, by the way." My mouth falls open in disbelief. I am so glad we aren't doing FaceTime. "And now I deserve a Golden Globe for my acting skills."

Oh, so he is lying out of his backside. I knew it was too good to be true. This is how it goes with me and relationships. Every. Single. Time.

"Have you any idea how hard it is to suppress a smile when all you want to do is be furious with someone because they're such a culinary goddess? From the moment I first laid my eyes on you and your tarts, I was infatuated," he says.

"I suspected as much," I fire the words back quickly and matter of fact, hoping they mask my delight. "Cristiano rather gave you away when he sniffed so appreciatively at the air in the café that day, bless him."

"Hmm, I'll have to have words with that dog later. Clearly I'm not the only one with a soft spot for you."

EPILOGUE

YOU WIN SOME, you lose some in the game of life, and the game of love. Days after defrosting my heart and gingerly agreeing to a daytime date with Tiago (at the neutral yet gorgeous setting of the Ivy in Bristol's Clifton district, where it took me a while to stop looking over my shoulder for a waiting-in-the-wings Grannie Elsa), I knew my gamble had paid off. We waited until dessert, and then unable to hold back any longer, Tiago leaned over the table to kiss me and I fully obliged. It was a kiss not so dissimilar to custard, funnily enough. A kiss with the heat, moreishness and delicious familiarity of custard. A kiss which very nearly saw us thrown out of the brasserie! On the subject of Elsa, I swear she put something in our port that day in Tavira. When you think about it, why would the family's mysterious nun lodger stop at handing down secret recipes for *pastéis de nata*?

It would be such a stress-free world if we could simply fall in love over the presentation of a rose or a long and starstruck look, but it would also be a boring one. I like to think that our initial stumbling block of a story only served to make us stronger. Because all of that was two years ago now. I've just turned thirty, can you believe it? And Tiago and I are going strong. Stronger than strong.

So strong in fact that we work together, too! I know...

After our first date that September, after I finally accepted that Tiago was best placed to run the Muse Masters' marketing campaign for The Custard Tart Café, things really took off. And he took off too, leaving MM to follow his heart and set up his own marketing business. A business with just one client: me.

Everything happened so quickly after that. Weston-super-Mare's chamber of commerce got in touch to help us expand the premises, still keeping the flagship pier bakery, of course, but setting up a further base in the town. Next came an outlet in Bristol's trendy harbourside, and a prime location in Bath – unbeknownst to me, Matt and Kelly had been keeping their ears to the ground for a while, and then the perfect spot came up just a stone's throw from the tourist magnet of the Abbey and the Grand Pump Room. Stuff of dreams or what?

We haven't quite made it to London yet, but one step at a time. *Who am I kidding?* We haven't made it to the Big Smoke, but we have made it to Portugal! After accepting our joint invitation to spend her annual February sojourn in cold and rainy England (at the Schofield-Willis *pied-à-terre* in Weston-super-Mare), Elsa was so bowled over with our business innovation and success, that she returned to the Algarve to invest in a spin-off business of her own. Nowadays she fuses the modern with the traditional. Grandson Edu helps run the contemporary *pastelaria* in Vilamoura, luring overseas holidaymakers away from fish and chips with fantastical custard tart fillings. Meanwhile, Elsa and Silverio continue to do what they do best, baking and selling simple and delicious *pastéis de nata*, infused with the ancient wisdom and secrets of the past.

"As long as there are human beings with appetites, there will be a demand for old and new," Elsa declared that first February of our official coupledom, giving a thumbs-up to our brand new red velvet Valentine's custard tart as she shivered in her mammoth woolly scarf at the window seat overlooking the milky coffee (or in Portuguese, *galão*) waters of the English channel. She was sharing an afternoon tea platter with Frank, who nodded his head in reverent agreement.

Elsa had no idea of the perfect timing of her words that day, but she soon did.

I had literally just opened the most exquisite invitation, to Radhika and Santi's June wedding in Portugal! To cut a long story short, Radhika's parents came around more quickly and easily than she'd ever expected, accepting that sometimes traditions can change with the times. Especially when they are new ways of celebrating love.

Love of people, or love of food.

Tiago wound his hand around my waist as we looked on from the counter, and when nobody was looking he rubbed my stomach affectionately, whispering tenderly in my ear:

"I so want to tell those two oldies about *our new addition*."

"Me too," I replied. "But you know that such a momentous occasion requires an equally momentous accompaniment: custard tarts!"

And with that, Tiago took my hand and we joined the sages at their table, where Elsa was already rooting around in her giant handbag to swiftly pull out a small bottle of port which she proceeded to pour into three empty tea cups.

"None for you, my dear." She looked me up and down with a knowing smile. "Not for at least another seven months."

THE END

ACKNOWLEDGEMENTS

There are always so many people to thank for their help before, during, and after the writing process. Needless to say, thanks to absolutely EVERYONE who has bought and read any of my previous books: your kind words definitely keep me going!

I am indebted to Fiona Jenkins and Sue Baker, as ever, for their phenomenal support. I would also like to thank my amazing editor, Alice Cullerne-Bown, blog tour organiser extraordinaire, Rachel Gilbey (and all of the brilliant book bloggers who have devoted their time to take part in the tour), and friends Heidi Catherine and Lizzie Chantree for helping me out across the miles, often at the drop of a hat!

The Fiction Cafe and TBC reviewers groups have also been super generous with their time and lovely comments.

Heidi Swain definitely can't be forgotten in this list...

Mum, Tina, and Auntie Pat – you all rock and your support is sooooo appreciated :-)

And then we have the wonderful Emma Hawkes, who has a character named after her in this book! I hope I did you justice, Emma ;-)

Three lovely ladies created some very unique custard tarts which all appear in the story, and Willow's cafe certainly wouldn't be the same without them – neither would Tiago's blood pressure:

Tara Lyons – *Potato Crisp Custard Tarts.*

Carmen Guthrie – *Matcha Custard Tart flavored with*

vanilla and honey, drizzled lightly with dark chocolate ganache...
garnished with a piece of dark chocolate, blood orange and
almond bark.

Andrea Pole – *Lemon and Thyme (Custard Tart) with*
Pernod, topped with sea salt.

How I wish I could sample them all!

ABOUT THE AUTHOR

Isabella May lives in (mostly) sunny Andalusia, Spain with her husband, daughter and son, creatively inspired by the mountains and the sea. She grew up on Glastonbury's ley lines and loves to feature her quirky English hometown in her stories.

After a degree in Modern Languages and European Studies at UWE, Bristol (and a year working abroad in Bordeaux and Stuttgart), Isabella bagged herself an extremely jammy and fascinating job in children's publishing... selling foreign rights for novelty, board, pup-up, and non-fiction books all over the world; in every language from Icelandic to Korean, Bahasa Indonesian to Papiamento!

All of which has fuelled her curiosity and love of international food and travel – both feature extensively in her romantic comedies, along with a sprinkle of magic.

Isabella is also a Pranic Healer and a stillbirth mum.

THE FOODIE ROMANCE JOURNEYS

You can follow Isabella May's Foodie Romance Journey series at the following hang-outs:
www.isabellamayauthor.com
Twitter – @IsabellaMayBks
Instagram – @isabella_may_author
Facebook – facebook.com/IsabellaMayAuthor

Would you like Isabella's free novella, The Vanilla Pod Cafe, and would you like to be a part of her mailing list for news about her books?
Simply go to the link: https://bit.ly/30upqMi
You can unsubscribe at any time

Also published by Isabella May:
The Cocktail Bar
Oh! What a Pavlova
Costa del Churros
The Ice Cream Parlour
The Cake Fairies
The Chocolate Box
Bubblegum and Blazers
Twinkle, Twinkle, Little Bar

Coming soon:
The Wedding Cake
Christmas at the Keanu Kindness Cafe

Printed in Great Britain
by Amazon